absolute music

absolute music

A Novel

JONATHAN GELTNER

SL/\NT
BOOKS

ABSOLUTE MUSIC
A Novel

Slant Books
P.O. Box 60295
Seattle, WA 98160

www.slantbooks.com

HARDCOVER ISBN: 978-1-63982-109-9
PAPERBACK ISBN: 978-1-63982-108-2
EBOOK ISBN: 978-1-63982-110-5

Cataloguing-in-Publication data:

Names: Geltner, Jonathan.

Title: Absolute music: a novel / Jonathan Geltner.

Description: Seattle, WA: Slant Books, 2022.

Identifiers: ISBN 978-1-63982-109-9 (hardcover) | ISBN 978-1-63982-108-2 (paperback) | ISBN 978-1-63982-110-5 (ebook)

Subjects: LCSH: Fiction -- Literary. | Novelists -- Fiction. | Cincinnati (Ohio) -- Fiction. | Pittsburgh (Pa.)--Fiction.

Classification: PS3607.G45 2022 (paperback) | PS3607.G45 (ebook)

In gratitude for a childhood
immersed in the true fantasy
of the outdoor world
I dedicate this work of fiction
to my parents
David and Deborah

You can always come back but you can't come back all the way.

—Bob Dylan, "Mississippi"

A l'alta fantasia qui mancò possa....

—Dante, *Paradiso*

Contents

Felix Culpa

1

THE ENTIRE REGION OF CINCINNATI, OHIO, from downtown to the outermost exurbs and particularly in the moist clay of the many river and creek valleys, is home to a large and hardy population of native locust trees, both black locusts and honey locusts. The latter produce large, lightweight but very strong and sharp thorns, often formed in bristling clusters, which fall to the ground and are painful if stepped on barefoot or wielded as a weapon by a child in a game of fantasy. The thorns are strong enough to be used as nails. I have even seen the honey locust described in supposedly scientific field guides—so menacing are the thorns—as ominous, haunting, and terrible.

In the middle or latter part of spring the honey locust blooms in small white or pink and purple flowers, grouped like so many bouquets, and if you were to pluck such a sprig you would have a serviceable bouquet, for the blossoms are fragrant with a sweetness like honey. But the first part of the name comes from the pulp of the long pendulous legumes that the tree produces in autumn. The pulp is honey-sweet and may be eaten or used to ferment a kind of beer; it is also thought to possess medicinal benefit. This is what John the Baptist ate in the wilderness when his meat was locusts and honey—not insects, but the pods of the carob tree, which closely resembles the locust.

In the autumn the honey locust's legumes, papery and volute, drop; the small oval leaflets turn bright or sometimes golden yellow and detach individually from the compound stems early or midway through the season, though the trees are sensitive to the most minute local variations of light, temperature, and moisture, so that one tree may be still mostly green while another, not so much as a football field away, will have dropped all of its color. On the ground, the leaflets collect and, if it has been dry, as September and October often are, swirl in miniature cyclones. Answering the wind in this way, they make a softer sound than the larger leaves of the maples, mulberries, sweet gums, hackberries, sycamores, buckeyes, walnuts, and other hardwoods that blanket southwest Ohio, a kind of tinkling or tapping, rather than the rasping and rustling of the more massy desiccated foliage blown about on the ground or jostling in the crowns.

Since the day Hannah died, when I was fourteen years old, I have been fascinated by the crowns of honey locusts in winter, when they can be seen in their stark and eerie geometrical essence silhouetted against the sky. Winter is the best time to observe the bark of deciduous trees. That of the honey locust displays long, sidewinding ridges that grow more or less parallel to the direction of the trunk or branch. Alternatively, some might describe those ridges as the upcurled edges of long plates of a superficial bark secured firmly to a deeper layer, like a knight's steel armor, as though everywhere the trees grow were a field of tournament or battle. From a distance this feature of the locust also makes the trunk look like the spine of a wooded mountain range viewed from space—for instance the Blue Ridge, with the longitudinal plates of bark between the ridges like so many Shenandoah Valleys.

Or so it seems to me these days, when I pull up Google Maps during odd restless moments and scour the Ohio Valley and the Allegheny Plateau, all the places of our youth. Such a distraction would not have been possible when Hannah died—Google Maps had not been invented, for most people there was not yet an internet, and we could not easily have discovered what those mountains and highlands looked like from planetary orbit. But I did know even then, when I was fourteen, that honey locusts have a lithe and thewy appearance, and that there is something about the habit of the mature locust's crown, with its carefully proportioned pattern of delicate yet jagged and regularly undulating branches, which harmonizes with the skies of winter. This truth was revealed to me through that inflection point in the history of the world as I have known it: bare honey locusts against a low, gray sky forever remind me of the morning I learned that Hannah had died.

I was not by Hannah's side when she died. Her death came to me by report, from my father. She had invited me to the New Year's Eve party at her house the night before. It would have been predictable for me to be there: I was in love with Hannah. I think I had been in love with her since the day we first met, when we were seven years old. That child's love was still a living bond between us; we were always natural friends. But in the year or two before she died, my imagination of Hannah was complicated by adolescent desire, and I doubted she reciprocated that feeling. But I had to find out.

I knew that if ever there was going to be an opportunity for me to kiss her it would be at her New Year's Eve party, under the mistletoe that would still be hanging somewhere, left over from Christmas. Likely the mistletoe would be suspended over the front door, and it was not impossible that Hannah would answer the door herself, in which case I could kiss her immediately upon arriving. I had decided that that would be ideal, to do it right away as a kind of joke, and then again later, maybe at midnight if things had gone well—as an early birthday present, I could claim, for her birthday fell just a week later. I had been considering this strategy for weeks in the wild hope of being invited to her house for the party.

At last, I was invited. And yet the night Hannah died I was playing Dungeons & Dragons, and getting drunk (for perhaps the first time in my life), in a basement in suburban Cincinnati with my friends. I'm not sure that I've ever previously contemplated the mystery or the morality of that fact, but now that the memory recurs I find my absence from Hannah's party so strange that I don't know how to begin thinking about it.

Difficult though it may be to believe, I spoke the words of the preceding eight paragraphs, or the gist of those words, to my wife, Kew, on the evening of Friday the twentieth of October, 2017, as we stood in the shade of two large black locusts (or so I called them at the time) a block away from our house in Michigan, gazing up into the leaves lit by the setting sun, some still green and others fiery. Kew brushed the great mass of her straight bright rust-colored hair back over her shoulders, and it gleamed like amber as it caught the sun's last rays and hung down her back over her sky-blue dress all the way to her waist while she looked up into the trees while I spoke. There was not the faintest breeze to caress either leaves or hair. Finally Kew turned to face me with a sad and quizzical look, for I had derailed our conversation.

Just as I have always published under the name McPhail (not my surname but my middle name and my mother's maiden name)—and in fact those closest to me, since I was in my teens, have called me no other name but McPhail—so calling herself Kew is a simple affectation my wife has long adopted. Her initials (whether with her maiden name or my actual surname, which is Yiddish) are K.E.W., and when I first met her in the spring of 2004, shortly before we graduated together from the University of Cincinnati, she introduced herself to me as Kew—*like the English gardens* was the tag she always appended back then. To most people she met in that place it gave no clue as to how to spell her name but instead created an outlandish mystique.

But in my journals from those days I called her Autumn Leaf or Red Ale, since her hair is the color of both, indeed just the color of the heartening, rich ale you find historically in the British Isles. She is by preference and profession, as she would say, an Anglophile, but my wife is not at all English. Her heritage is mostly Irish on both sides, as manifest in her extraordinarily deep yet vibrant red hair, brilliant green eyes, and very fair skin—also, some might say, in a certain passionate and at times sentimental temperament. Kew denies this. . . usually. The Irish are poets and scholars, she says, and so she is herself.

Kew was born and raised in Portsmouth, Ohio, somewhat over one hundred miles upstream from Cincinnati, where the Scioto River flows into the Ohio, and for this reason she was able to say to me, standing down the street from our house in Michigan, that she remembered honey locusts and was I sure this was not one. I replied that I didn't think honey locusts grew in Michigan but perhaps black locusts did, and that there were no thorns. Kew nodded and said, "thorns fit to weave a crown for a king," and then she started us walking back toward our house. I trailed her by a few steps, still distracted and put out of sorts both by the story I had begun to tell and by the conversation I had interrupted in order to tell it.

Kew and I had been in odd moods all that week. The acute difficulty had begun at Mass the previous Sunday, the fifteenth of October, which, in the Roman Catholic Church (of which Kew and I were at that time strictly practicing members) is the Feast of Saint Teresa of Ávila. I had spent most of the liturgy holding our then-eight-month-old son, our first child, or changing him, or bouncing and swaying with him, or walking around the vast old church with him when he would not be quiet. He was a large and strong baby and desperately wanted to crawl, but was not quite doing it yet, and this made him restless.

When the sacrament was concluded and the congregation dismissed, we chatted over coffee with our fellow parishioners, many of whom were the parents of the children I was then tutoring in Latin, Greek, French, German, and English Literature through a Catholic homeschooling cooperative based in another parish, Saint Brendan's. One of these parents remarked to me that he was surprised to have learned recently that Saint Teresa, to whom he was specially devoted, was a Jew. I answered that she was not a Jew, only her paternal grandfather had been a *converso* and indeed he was almost killed for allegedly reverting to Judaism, but his son, Teresa's father, had been a successful merchant and bought his way into the lower aristocracy and a firm and respected position in Christian society. In any case, Teresa was not Jewish, I said, only the Nazis would have considered her Jewish, but even if she had been in a meaningful sense Jewish why should that have made her life or her contribution to Catholic Christian tradition any more or less remarkable?

The conversation did not move in a good direction from that point. The upshot was that my interlocutor did not consider himself anti-Semitic but that he had no qualms admitting, from *our* religious standpoint, to being anti-Judaizing. Surely I would agree with him, he said, since I myself had converted from Judaism (this was a common misconception among my fellow-parishioners), and why would I have done that if I did not prefer and assent to the Catholic Christian religion? All while I spoke with this man Kew blushed and glared at me (due to her complexion, the color of her hair and the brightness of her green eyes, her appearance is almost lurid and, I admit, appealing when she blushes and glares), but I was not sure what was embarrassing her.

Two days after that Mass, I had given to a student I was tutoring in French, the son of my anti-Judaizing fellow-parishioner, a copy of Arthur Rimbaud's *A Season in Hell*. And two days after that, I had instructed my literature students, among whom the same pupil numbered, to write an essay comparing Thoreau's experience atop Mount Katahdin in Maine to the Giving of the Law at Sinai, which I described to the students as the foundational story of Jewish peoplehood. The next day, that Friday the twentieth of October, I received a phone call from the headmaster of the homeschooling cooperative inquiring about my motivation for actions that were, he said, a departure from the curriculum and from my role as tutor. When I told Kew about this as we strolled home, I could see her go fiery as she'd done in the church, but she was silent.

I knew what she would say, though: You have no problems, you lead a blessed life, and what you call debility or unfair limitation is in fact grace. In those days, entering into the last fevered phase of the delusion that I had some sort of identity and personal destiny as a writer—which it is the purpose of this book to chronicle up to the moment of its strange evaporation—I was apt to feel resentful and sorry for myself at every turn. As we walked home, I thought only with dread and revulsion of Kew's ailing mother, who had come to live with us a month before, and I thought of *The Upper Country*, the soon-to-be overdue sequel to my novel *Repentance of the Gods* and in fact stalled out since our son had been born. What is more cliché than trouble with in-laws or a writer brooding over his book? But there was nothing I could do about it, and I resented even myself.

Earlier in the week I had told Kew that I didn't want to go that weekend to Chicago to visit old friends in celebration of my thirty-sixth birthday. Such excursions seemed more trouble than they were worth with a baby in tow. All I really wanted for my birthday was the briefest solitude in which to salvage my writing so that I might someday have a proper academic career like Kew's and would not have to spend my days scrambling for temporary appointments like I had in Chicago or doing things like tutoring at Saint Brendan's, a job I had only taken up to preserve my philological acumen.

To all this Kew said I was three or four kinds of ungrateful and that I envied her success: unlike me, she had finished her doctorate and obtained a good academic position, and now her keenly anticipated book, *Meditations for Margery Kempe*, was about to be published. Becoming a mother had in no way slowed her down. It rather seemed to have propelled her work, both scholarly and creative. Margery Kempe, the roving and vivacious fifteenth-century English mystic, began her book, the first autobiography in English, with the birth of her first child, and Kew had managed brilliantly and at the last minute to work into her manuscript the birth of our first child.

(But let me say here that that is only how *I* thought of our son. Kew thought of him as our third child. After a long gap in our acquaintance, we had married in the summer of 2014: Kew had a miscarriage less than a year later, and then a second early the following winter. It was these losses, in combination with her work on medieval English literature, which precipitated her reversion, passionate and intellectual, to her ancestral religion and her heartfelt request that I join her by converting at Easter 2016, in Ireland—a story to be told later in these pages.)

Nevertheless, Kew felt overwhelmed or under-esteemed in those days too, and more insecure than I could understand at the time. In the short walk back to our rented house, she told me that she could use solitude to work as well, and that she wanted to draw on my musical expertise for a major article she was writing on another medieval English mystic, Richard Rolle, and his *Melos Amoris* (Melody of Love). She added that I had become so churlish since her maternity leave had ended and she had gone back to teaching that she did not think of asking for my input, let alone for extra time to devote to her work.

When I answered by saying that she had enjoyed success, had at last found a good and secure job in which she would receive tenure almost right away (at the end of that academic year), and was no longer under pressure, she said it was not so, that unlike in my job—which she said I was privileged to hold and that for someone like me to devote himself to such a job was an act of deepest *charity*—her religious commitment was a liability in her work, offset for the moment (years would pass before Kew's words proved true—but not so many years) only by the fact that she was a woman.

Yet at the same time, there was nowhere Kew was perfectly at home. She felt that her intellectual and artistic career put her at odds with our friends in the Church. It transpired that the previous Sunday after Mass Kew had been upset not only by my awkward conversation about Teresa of Ávila's Jewish heritage, but also by the cool reception she had met with when talking about her forthcoming book.

I said, "The women you were talking to, your friends—"

"*Our* friends," Kew insisted.

"They've all got multiple children, and they've given up or scaled back careers to raise those kids, and they believe that's how things *ought* to go. Not you, you're sailing full speed ahead in your profession and wouldn't dream of doing otherwise. But more than that difference between us and them, is that we're not from here and they are. They don't fully trust us; we might uproot and disappear at any time. Aren't they right? We no sooner ensconce ourselves here in Michigan and start our family than we begin talking about where we'd rather be—return to Cincinnati, or what wouldn't you give to find a way back to England or Ireland? But we're here for a while, I think, *all* of us."

At this point we entered our house and were greeted by the rumbling and gurgling of Kew's mother snoring on the sofa and the static of the baby monitor.

"I understand," Kew whispered fiercely to me, "that you aren't terribly fond of having her live with us, that you think she's more of a burden than an aid—"

Indeed we did not dare to walk very far from our house, lest Kew's mother call for help with our son if he woke, for she could not lift him from his crib, so Kew and I would just go back and forth many times in the grid of nearby streets.

"—but maybe just maybe you could search your heart for some compassion?"

In truth, I was no longer thinking of Kew's mother and her failing physical health and crippling depression, which we hoped living with her first grandchild would ameliorate; nor was I thinking of my own parents now on the East Coast and in suddenly declining health, unable to visit us. I wasn't thinking of my students or of the disappointment my first novel had turned out to be, at least as a credential, and which my second, if I were honest with myself, would likely also prove if I ever got around to finishing it. I wasn't thinking of the ridiculous farce that had followed upon the spat about *anti-Judaizing*. The self-pity and anger were slipping away from me, chased off by Kew's whispered reprimand, sharp as a sword.

While Kew roused her mother I went into the basement where I did most of my work, and tried to think about the moment just passed under the locusts: the man and the woman under the boughs, the autumn air saturated with dust and uncanny heat and my mind without warning or apparent cause seized by the memory that despite every reason to be by her side I spent the night that my childhood love Hannah died far away from her, playing a game of fantasy and getting drunk.

Something about it felt less like recollection than prophecy, as though the event, or its absence from my life, would prove a key to the moral catastrophe soon to befall me. But like most recipients of prophecy, I was blind and deaf to the avertable doom.

2

OF THE FOUR FRIENDS with whom I was immersed in Dungeons & Dragons on the last night of 1995, I had known Gregory the longest, since the hour my family arrived in southwest Ohio, in the week between Christmas and New Year's Eve 1988 and only a few days before I met Hannah. At that time Gregory's family lived in the house diagonally back of ours, just down the hill. He would live there another seven years and become my constant companion, until in the autumn of 1995 his family abruptly moved to the house I would walk out of on New Year's Day 1996, the house with the row of honey locusts that I would go on to associate with Hannah's death. I wasn't happy about Gregory moving that autumn, and could see no reason for it other than what seemed to be random preference for one subdivision over another, one slope in our manifold topography rather than another. I was loath to spend the night in his new, unfamiliar house. On the other hand, there would be beer. We had procured twenty-four cans of Pabst Blue Ribbon, a sufficient quantity, given our inexperience, to ensure we all became drunk.

Hannah simply was not of this tribe. She was the daughter of my father's friend and senior colleague. We attended different schools and lived in different parts of the city. I had never been in Hannah's company when her other friends were around. We did not associate with each other except when our fathers got us together, which happened with some frequency because of how close the two men were, but the result was a pattern of meeting that was more like what many people enjoy with cousins.

Hannah's New Year's Eve party would be her own, full of her friends from the private school she attended. Her sister was going out and her parents entertaining their own guests. Hannah had invited me herself, *before* her parents invited my whole family over. My parents had already made plans for that evening with neighbors, but they would have taken me to Hannah's party had I wanted to go. The chance was clear and auspicious, an angel announcing providential windfall. Yet I renounced it, I refused the angel, and I was, I suppose, within my rights to do so. We are free to choose. Or so we want to believe.

If I did make a choice, it is hard to say whether it was for Gregory and Dungeons & Dragons or for getting drunk. Perhaps my friends and I sought the fantasy of alcohol for the same reason we sought the fantasy of Dungeons & Dragons: because we felt unfairly confined by our bodily existence. Hannah was not the type to see any appeal in drinking when she was fourteen—partly, I think, because she was too happily in her body and sensed no need for escape and transcendence.

Or maybe it comes down to the same thing: maybe she escaped in her own way. She was a dancer, a gymnast, an acrobat, a runner. She had a trampoline in her yard and could do somersaults and backflips in the air when she jumped on it. She could outrun me, with respect to both speed and distance, though I was by no means unathletic. I was a runner, too, and played soccer and football, and I liked to swim. But we would go together in summertime to the YMCA in the suburb where I lived, which had a huge outdoor pool, and Hannah would swim faster than me, and with better form.

In fact we both came up to our bodily limits. I was also a cellist and a pianist: constantly pushed to the edge of physical ability yet never good enough. It was in our encounter with such limits that our difference lay. For Hannah it was as if at each moment she could be nothing other than what she was and this pleased her, this constant succession of one actuality after another; whereas I chafed under potentiality, imagining freedom as a kind of infinitude or liberation from limits, so that I would not constantly be butting up against what I was not yet or was no more.

But I wondered if alcohol or fantasy had anything to do with my whereabouts on the last night of 1995. I wondered if there was really a decision. If I chose to summon the images, there, in that basement in Michigan, I could see Hannah jumping up and down, her emerald eyes flashing, her gaping smile, her slightly nasal, cackling laughter. It could all be right there if I wanted it. I could control the memories, recollect them. But when I was fourteen years old they were not memories, they were living images that occupied my mind and asserted themselves whenever they chose, dragging me into another world.

I write as though these images composed a real, autonomous being external to me, almost a real girl, for so it felt. Call her a fantasy. And what seemed to have been decisive that New Year's Eve was that in the last days of 1995 I was no longer in thrall to the fantasy. The images of Hannah—whether capricious or chaotic or cowed by my own fear of failure or obedient to some simple twist of fate—on the last night of 1995 those images of the fantasy Hannah abandoned me just at the moment when I was poised to draw nearest to the real, substantial, living Hannah.

The result was a conscious option for Dungeons & Dragons and puking up pilfered beer in the basement of my best friend's strange new home, and stumbling outside the next morning into bleary day, to be greeted by towering honey locusts against the indistinct gray sky and my father waiting in his car to drive me home. I stood transfixed by the sight of those trees—frozen with one hand on the passenger door—until my father honked the horn and I got in. His hands gripped the steering wheel with such force that his knuckles whitened. As we backed out of the driveway and he looked in the rearview mirror he said, "Hannah died last night."

One of the peculiarities of my upbringing was the fact that I knew the names of all the trees around me and had known them since I was barely seven years old. It was then, when my father was hired at the university by Hannah's father, that my family moved to Cincinnati from the East Coast, and my parents, perhaps to distract me from the disturbance of relocation or perhaps simply by virtue of being the kind of people they are—*tree people*, as Hannah called them—taught me the names of all the trees in our new neighborhood.

To me, the names of trees seemed to possess a kind of magic, as if they were ciphers or shibboleths that could, if only I were canny enough to wield them aright, decode or gain me entry to *the other world* that lay all around, the invisible, fantastical world where everything that was important—everything that was *real*—happened, or could happen, the world where, as a young boy clasping a fallen branch I might perform heroic feats of arms, and the world where, only slightly older, I might kiss the girl who could do handstands and somersaults in the air and who never seemed to take a false step.

For the sake of this faith in the other world, I despised the idea of coincidence—if that was all it was, *mere* coincidence. I had decided that if coincidence signified nothing, as many people seemed to believe, then it was illusion, a worthless idea unless there was a real, objective pattern in back of things, a *world behind the world*. It was clear to me that without that other world—the only world where I could meet Hannah as I was meant to meet her—there would be no point questing after anything, for there would be nothing anywhere to find, no girl, no eventual kiss, no way to transcend my limits or find peace within them.

So the names of the trees were much with me, part of the mysterious signature I could only begin to trace of an unseen hierarchy of meanings in or behind the world. And sitting in that basement in Michigan I could still see the honey locusts against the low gray sky and receding at the end of Gregory's driveway. I remembered what it felt like to know their name and say it to myself, unable to look away from them as my father said, "Hannah died last night."

My father spoke no more until we got home and the family sat around the kitchen table, the steam rising from my parents' coffee and tea and none of us touching the hot breakfast my mother had made. Nothing of what was said at that table remains with me now. I was gazing out the window at the trees in our yard, the hackberries, the sugar maple by the swing set and next to it the white ash—the white ashes had not yet been obliterated in southwest Ohio by blight, as they have been now all over the country—and the honey locusts overhanging the little creek, the magnolia by the driveway and the arborvitae in the corner where our yard adjoined what had been, until recently, Gregory's yard. In some depth of my mind I could almost feel a connection forming between the continuing pang of my friend's random departure from that home and its yard where we had played for seven years, and the shock of Hannah's death.

In my conscious mind, however, I was not in the world where my father was speaking, I was in the other world that has no name or too many names—the world I knew through, and with, and in the girl whose hair was all the colors honey can be. I was thinking it was wonderfully long and thick hair, coiled in some parts, wavy or curly or frizzy in others, and I knew what it smelled like, too—like honey— because of all the playing and tumbling around outside that Hannah and I had done together for seven years, but also from the times we lay side by side on our stomachs in her basement or in my living room, our shoulders an inch or two apart if they were not touching, more than likely watching one of the two movies with which Hannah was obsessed: *The Neverending Story* and *The Princess Bride*. I was like Dante in that I required two guides, one male and one female, in the other world, the fantasy that lies behind the so-called real world. The male guide was Gregory, and his counterpart, whom he never met (or so I thought then, sitting in that basement in Michigan), was Hannah.

3

I STILL KNOW GREGORY. I still know all those guys from the last night of 1995. We reunite once every summer, the five of us *sans* girlfriends, wives, or children, in the hills of southern Ohio. Though our lives have been interrupted by every manner of tumult and tragedy, since we began the tradition, we have never let anything cancel the summer reunion, not even a pandemic. At our reunion in the summer of 2017, just a few months before the events of this story began, we had played Dungeons & Dragons together for the first time since high school.

Gregory, who was by then a highly regarded teacher in the elite high school that Hannah had attended, had become interested in the game again—in fact had begun incorporating it into his teaching—and this time, when we all played together, he was the Dungeon Master (the DM, as we say), which is something like the writer or perhaps the narrator of the story that the players compose together. Instead of gaming in a basement, we sat around a large table of oak and iron on a covered outdoor deck, the slope of the hill falling away behind the head of the table, where Gregory sat, and huge tulip trees, straight as a ship's mast, towering over us in the evening light and then long into the night, shadowy presences rustling in the hot breeze. Instead of Pabst Blue Ribbon there was Short's and Bell's from Michigan and Mad Tree and Rhinegeist from Cincinnati. Always before I had been the DM. This time I was only a player, and I enjoyed the limitation, being just a character in someone else's story.

Afterwards, Gregory and I began corresponding regularly about the game and the challenges Gregory enjoys in using Dungeons & Dragons as a teaching device. He claimed to defer to my expertise as a fantasist, but I doubted I had been much help. Gregory has always been more than my equal as a navigator in the other world. When we were fourteen I thought of him as a guide, even if I was the narrator in our games then, and I still thought of him that way.

With surprise I realized that I had been jotting down these thoughts of Gregory and Hannah as abrupt, inelegant notes, rather than attending to what I'd descended to the basement to do. Perhaps at some level I already knew that the distraction of such memories had gripped me in its vise and would not release me for many seasons yet. But at the moment I brushed aside any such awareness and opened the file on my computer containing the first pages of my overdue book, *The Upper Country*: an old-fashioned novelistic description of the place where most of the action would occur, which melts into the first dramatic scene, in which the protagonist's twin sister dies very young.

It was no use; I couldn't concentrate on the screen. Instead I stared past its bright pale blur to the pile of books behind my computer: the *Don Quixote* I was using with the students I tutored at Saint Brendan's; Robert Byron's study of El Greco, *The Birth of Western Painting*; Eliyahu Ashtor's *The Jews of Moslem Spain* and Yitzhak Baer's *A History of the Jews of Christian Spain*; the collected works of John of the Cross, along with the philosopher Edith Stein's treatment of that work, *The Science of the Cross*, her final manuscript, still undergoing revision when the Nazis took her (she was a Jewish convert) from the convent in Echt in 1942 and martyred her in Auschwitz.

Such a list might give the impression of an intellectually ordered and focused life, or at least a coherent interest in Spanish history and literature, but the other books piled on my desk—the poetry of Kalidasa; a grammar of Old English; Rachel Carson's sea trilogy; Yukio Mishima's tetralogy of reincarnation, *The Sea of Fertility*; philosophical works like Franz Rosenzweig's *The Star of Redemption* and Catherine Pickstock's *Repetition and Identity*—indicated a rudderless and dilettantish mind blown from one footnote to another in a frantic search for it knew not what. I was trying to think about the passage on the screen without actually looking at it, and as I did so a feeling stole over me of horror and incredulity, beginning in my gut then heating my heart and making it race, and finally ascending into my brain and routing my thoughts.

That is when Kew came down into the basement. I expected her to want to talk some more, but she simply said, "If you really need the time alone, then I'll go to Chicago tomorrow with my mom instead. It's just a couple of nights anyway. I thought seeing our old friends would help with your writing, but now I'm thinking maybe they're not quite old enough friends. What was all that about under the locust trees?"

My eyes must have widened when she said this. I told her what I had just realized, that every book I had written or attempted to write (there were two failed novels before *Repentance of the Gods*), including now *The Upper Country*, took for a starting point a transfigured or sublimated version of Hannah's death. In each case I had rearranged the faces and given everyone other names. I had never given the true names and I had never told the true story.

"Is that what you were starting to do outside?" Kew asked.

"Perhaps," I said, "but I'm not sure I know the true story. How do you tell the story of someone who died a week short of her fourteenth birthday, twenty-two years ago?"

Kew said she didn't know, but she guessed that if Hannah and I had loved each other, even just as children, then maybe Hannah's story, some version of it, now was mine. "But," she said, "that doesn't mean it's the story you ought to tell."

4

THE NEXT DAY DAWNED CLEAR, promising the same dry unseasonable heat that had hung over Michigan for a month, extending summer far beyond its natural term. Feeling guilty that I would not be with them and regretting any time apart from our son, I had packed as much as I could for the excursion the night before—and it is amusing to me now to think how laborious I found that task when we had only one child. Our son by that time was sleeping quite well, still often waking in the small hours to nurse but then returning to sleep for two or three hours more, and Kew, who is not a morning person, would do the same.

I made a hearty breakfast for the household and played with my boy while Kew got her mother ready for the trip. They were off before ten o'clock, in time for our son to take his morning nap on the drive to Chicago. "I'll take him to the spot on the Lake where we married," Kew said, and she seemed to be in a more forgiving spirit, if still a touch melancholic. "Good luck," she called to me as she backed the car out of the driveway, and she blew me a kiss.

I went inside and washed up the breakfast dishes, then vacuumed the whole house. Feeling grimy after that chore, I took a shower and then went into the backyard and lit a cigarette. By then it was almost noon. The sense of omen and mystery that had overtaken me the previous evening under the locusts had not gone away—if anything, it had grown, and I found the emptiness and stillness of the house bizarre as well.

If I had really wanted to gain new purchase on *The Upper Country* I would not have looked at a single screen all weekend. I wouldn't even have opened a book. I would have shut my eyes to anything not right before me, present just there and then, and shut my ears too, not listening to music but simply letting whatever sound come to me in that little house in Michigan—the acorns still dropping by the bushel from the mighty oaks, the birds and woodland animals that thrived in our little suburb, the sounds of nearby construction work, delivery trucks, my neighbor taking his motorcycle out—whatever might arise I would let it arise.

Instead, I retreated into the cool dim basement and checked my email.

Among various items that clamored for attention, I opened only the email from my former student Annette. It was a short message asking if I would write her a letter of recommendation for graduate programs. She was writing to me from Atlanta, where she had gone to live near her parents after graduating from the University of Chicago the previous spring. Annette—whose name, I thought for the first time, staring at it on the screen, is the diminutive French form of the Hebraic name *Hannah*—had been my writing student during the 2015-16 academic year, the last year that Kew and I lived in Chicago and the only year as yet that I had taught full-time at the university level, thanks to the success of *Repentance of the Gods*. Annette had been a junior that year. She was the most precocious student I'd ever heard of, partly because of her unique background, which I'll dilate upon later when it will take on significance in these Suites. For now it suffices to say that Annette and I had cultivated a friendship and kept in touch after she was no longer my student.

In the summer of 2016, shortly before Kew and I moved to Michigan, we had Annette over for dinner. She and Kew had not gotten along spectacularly well. At the time I supposed this was because Kew was already a professional teacher. She finished her DPhil at Oxford in 2010, held her first position the next year teaching at Notre Dame, then spent three years teaching at the University of Chicago, followed by two years at Loyola University of Chicago. The timing was right for it, but Annette was never Kew's student, and so she could only take my word for the girl's brilliance, which Annette was too shy to demonstrate over a dinner at which Kew was not drinking because she was pregnant. But I was not much of a teacher at that time, and hardly thought of Annette as a student. Anyhow I was trying to treat her the way some of my younger professors had treated me and Kew when we were undergraduates. And I remember that Annette that evening tended to speak to me in her native French, a language which Kew can read but which she struggles with when spoken. Then Annette would blush and apologize, and on the whole it was a hot, stuffy evening and not great fun.

That was the last time I had seen my former student, but we continued to write to each other. Kew was unaware of how frequently and at what length I corresponded with Annette. There was nothing wrong with the situation, and yet I had the sudden intuition, sitting there in the basement and reading Annette's email, that it was not right either—and the feeling compounded the already weird mental fog I'd been drifting within since the previous evening when I recalled Hannah's death.

I continued to postpone my work by responding affirmatively to Annette's request, and then writing the letter of recommendation. By the time I was finished with the task, it was the middle of the afternoon. I brewed some coffee and went outside to smoke another cigarette—this was something I was only permitted to do when I was not around my son or Kew. The sun blazed midsummer heat, and it was as if my will melted in that wrong weather. When I went back inside, I decided that I would spend the rest of the day in the basement watching Hannah's two favorite films, neither of which I had seen in many years.

In *The Neverending Story*, the Nothing is the outward manifestation of a lethal illness that afflicts the Childlike Empress. We might call the illness *namelessness*, for The Childlike Empress has no name, only this title (she is indeed a child), and the lack is an existential crisis for Fantasia, the world over which she rules, as it is for the Childlike Empress herself. Until she is given a new name, she will continue to waste away, and the Nothing—realized in the film as a spectacular sky of billowing, whirling storm clouds of gray and purple and blood-red—will continue to roll through Fantasia, banishing into non-being its earth-like landscapes and otherworldly creatures, all appearance and all reality. Where once there was a mountain, there is no more mountain. Where there is a city of light and splendid palaces and spires, there will soon be nothing. And where there is a beloved young girl, there will soon be nothing, unless she, the Childlike Empress, can be given a new name—the only true, new name that she can have.

No one in Fantasia can discover and bestow the new name on the Empress, this cure can come only from a real human child: the boy Bastian, through whose experience we see Fantasia. Bastian is bullied by boys at his school. One day, arriving late to school and having stolen a book called *The Neverending Story* from a used bookstore, where he had gone in order to escape the bullies, Bastian hides out in the school's attic. He remains there into the night, reading with disbelief of his role in saving Fantasia, the necessity of his literally entering the fantasy world. What Bastian reads is the story of the quest, undertaken by a boy from Fantasia, Atreyu, to discover the Empress's new name.

As Atreyu ranges far and wide over Fantasia seeking a goal as unachievable as any Grail, the sky is the first omen of the death of fantasy in the Nothing. But it is also the realm of the film's affirmation and triumph. Fantasia is like Earth in all its beauty: full of mountains, deserts, forests, rivers, glaciers, oceans, animals, and clouds of less dread but no less beauty than those which herald the Nothing. The film reveals much of this world from the air, as Atreyu and eventually Bastian ride through every clime and zone on the back of Atreyu's friend, the flying luck dragon, as he is called, Falkor. A vision of the beauty and wonder of the Earth seems to make up much of the intention of *The Neverending Story*. Even the Swamp of Sadness, which induces suicidal despair in all who attempt to traverse it, has a dismal grandeur about it, most evident just after Atreyu's faithful companion, his horse Artax, succumbs to the malevolent charm and allows himself to be swallowed into the Swamp.

Rewatching *The Neverending Story*, I saw that there was more to the fantasy than a revelation of the beauty of the world. I could not have hit upon this insight when I lay on the floor with Hannah, precisely because she was still there in the surface-world, by my side. What I saw now was that the story is also about redemption or, to use the language of the Book of Revelation (whose narrative the film seems to retell after its own fashion), the passing of this world and its replacement by *a new heaven and a new earth*, in the course of which God *shall wipe away all tears*.

When, at the end, Bastian flies over Fantasia on the back of Falkor, he sees Atreyu astride Artax, restored from his death in the Swamp and galloping over the waving golden grass of the plains that are home to horse and rider, and that had, along with the rest of Fantasia, fallen prey to the Nothing. The death of Artax in the Swamp of Sadness was, when I watched it with Hannah, a scene of utmost distress for me. The fact that he was restored in the end was no consolation. But this is just what affected me watching the film in my basement in Michigan on an unseasonably warm autumn afternoon, this vision that the film presents of what Catholic theologians call the *felix culpa*, the fortunate fall: fortunate because what is restored in the end, the new heaven and earth, is greater even than what was first lost.

The simple, almost harsh trochaic Latin phrase *felix culpa* is attributed to the fourth century bishop of Milan, Saint Ambrose, but it was his pupil, Augustine of Hippo, who developed the idea when he wrote that God *melius enim iudicavit de malis benefacere quam mala nulla esse permittere*—judged it better to make good from evils than to permit no evil whatever to exist. So central is this idea to the Christian religion that the Easter Vigil liturgy of the Roman Catholic Church sings: *O felix culpa quae talem ac tantum meruit habere redemptorem*—O happy fall, which has merited for us so great a redeemer.

I sometimes wonder if a fantasist can tell any story but this one. Anyway, it is evident in *The Neverending Story*. Atreyu must go on his quest to find the cure for the Empress. It is in the nature of quests that they are hazardous and in parts—perhaps in the whole—futile. During one such leg of the quest, Artax dies. But the result of Atreyu's questing (in itself a failure) is that Bastian, who has been reading the quest, comes to understand and accept his own role in the fate of Fantasia; and at the last possible moment, after everything has been destroyed or consumed by the Nothing, he gives the Empress her new name—shouts it with all his might into the ordinary storm that is also, perhaps, the storm of the Nothing raging outside the windows of his school's attic—a name which may be the one that belonged to Bastian's deceased mother, whose name he has said was beautiful, though we cannot make out what he cries into the tempest.

And all is recreated, as if the suffering and failures of Atreyu's quest never were, and reader and writing, reality and fantasy, now dwell together. That union seems to nullify the very means by which it came into existence, yet it could not have been achieved otherwise than the story that involved such suffering, destruction, and death. Only that story could bring Bastian to Fantasia, or Fantasia to Earth, as happens when at the end Bastian, riding Falkor, chases the bullies through the streets and alleys of Vancouver, the same bullies who drove him into the bookstore whence he lifted *The Neverending Story* and without whose malicious agency, therefore, we may presume that none of what we have just watched would have occurred.

It all builds up an awesome idea, a fantastic idea, I thought, sitting in the increasing gloom of the basement in Michigan when the film came to an end. But is it true? Where is the girl, now, who first showed me this fantasy? In Revelation it says that only in the new heaven and earth, in the golden city of God, do we—or rather the elect, the chosen—learn our true names. Could I in some sense bring Hannah back by giving her a new name, her true name? Is this what Kew had meant the evening before? Is that what I had been trying to do for years without knowing it and without the slightest success?

5

I WAS BOTHERED BY the ending of *The Neverending Story*, when Bastian flies through Vancouver on the back of Falkor. This seemed like a gross aesthetic flaw, this conflation of two worlds. What are we supposed to imagine at the end of the film, that Bastian grew up and became famous as the only guy in Vancouver with a luck dragon for a friend, who, by the way, will chase you down an alley and make you climb for safety into a dumpster if you cross Bastian? I knew the film had been made from a book and I was sure the book could not have ended that way. So I soon found myself on the seemingly official website of Michael Ende, the author of *Die unendliche Geschichte* (*The Neverending Story*), who died in 1995.

There, I learned various interesting things about Michael Ende. First, that he loathed the adaptation of his novel. I also learned that Ende was a Christian. I discovered that he met his first wife, Ingeborg Hoffmann, on New Year's Eve 1952, precisely forty-three years before Hannah died. Ingeborg came up to Michael at a party and recited the first lines of a poem by Eduard Möricke, "To an Eolian Harp," and without missing a beat Ende recited the rest of the poem. Love, for them, was a coincidence that easy: a few lines of poetry and a New Year's Eve party. Finally, I learned that Michael Ende was, like me, fascinated by Japanese culture and literature.

This last fact prompted me to pull my copy of Matsuo Basho's *haibun* from the bookshelf next to my desk. I still wonder what (if anything) would have happened if I had picked any other volume, perhaps

The Tale of the Heike or *The Pillow Book*, as I might just as easily have done. What actually happened was that I flipped first to the maps of Basho's various wanderings. This led me to get on Google Maps and zoom in to the place on the coast of Japan where Basho reached the northernmost point of his famous journey into the deep north. I am at a loss to explain why I selected this particular journey, in a collection containing Basho's records of several journeys, or why I looked at the map at all, or why I selected the precise spot on the screen that I did, some little shrine on the water, where I thought the wandering poet was likely to have looked over Fuku Bay at Mount Chokai.

But select the spot I did, and I jotted down part of the GPS coordinates that Google provided: 39.201777 north latitude. I knew already that Cincinnati was approximately on the thirty-ninth parallel, so I slid along that line, as it were, and then zoomed in to the house where Hannah lived and died. I selected it on the map and wrote down the GPS coordinates that Google provided: 39.201743 north latitude. In the old degrees-minutes-seconds reckoning of latitude, that would be an identical marking down to the second of the degree. I then read what Basho had to say about the place where he turned and began the long journey home. Gazing on Chokai towering seven thousand feet above the sea, Basho compares the bay of Kisagata to Matsushima, where he just was, on the Pacific coast of Honshu. *Matsushima seems to laugh,* he says, *while Kisagata seems embittered. Grief piled upon loneliness: this place resembles a spirit in torment.*

You could call this mere coincidence. Or you could say that Basho was vouchsafed a kind of vision or fantasy, a glimpse of the world behind the world: one that I, too, discovered while standing on the same invisible but more than purely notional line three hundred years after the poet, staring at the façade of Hannah's house on the day of her funeral, blistering wind blowing fog and snow that seemed not so much to pile up as to blot out. This is how we become entangled with the world, with its echoes and superficies.

And then there are coincidences that do not surprise and fill you with wonder and an appreciation for the elegiac and fragile nature of beauty—instead, they are infuriating and banal, an insult to moments like Basho's in Kisagata, or the cancelation of them, an annulment of meaning like that represented by the Nothing in Fantasia. Consider that at the end of 1995, the *Billboard* Hot 100 placed Coolio's "Gangsta's Paradise" in the number one spot. I found out at Hannah's funeral, from one of her friends who had been at the party, that "Gangsta's Paradise" had been playing just before midnight, as MTV or maybe it was VH1 counted down the last hours of the year with the hits. The song begins:

> As I walk through the valley of the shadow of death,
> I take a look at my life and realize there's none left.

Minutes after these lyrics filled the basement, Hannah collapsed, a massive undetected aneurysm in her brain having ruptured. At the hospital she was pronounced dead on arrival.

I had to hear about the Coolio track immediately after discovering another fact that shocked me: the funeral was closed-casket. I had, in the two-and-a-half days since learning of her death, consoled myself with the thought that I would see Hannah a final time. In that interval I had been troubled because I could not recollect the last image of her—that is, the real, living, substantial Hannah—that I had seen. But her body had not been disfigured, I told myself, and so I would see her preserved, after a fashion, at the memorial service, and however horrid that might be, it would be my final image and I would know it was final.

It is difficult to say whether an open-casket funeral would actually have granted me the relief—or the surety, or whatever it was—that I hoped for. The point is moot, for among the things I had failed to hear when my father was talking over breakfast on the first morning of 1996 and I was looking out the window at trees, was the information, previously unknown to me, that Hannah and her family were in some nominal or partial—but now, apparently, influential—sense Jewish. This accounted for the relatively short interval between her death and her burial, as well as for the closed casket—as my father would explain to me in the bathroom at the funeral home, where he followed me upon seeing my distress. "But her family celebrates Christmas," I said to my father in the bathroom in the funeral home. Well, then again, so did we. It seemed that tragedy altered the nature of one's religious affiliation, and so I stood before a plain wooden box and failed to understand or believe that it concealed the beautiful girl.

I tried to think my way through this new revelation that Hannah had been in some way like me, since our fathers were both Jewish while our mothers were not, yet I had never known this about her, nor did I then grasp what (if anything) it meant other than that I was deprived of a final sight of her. On the drive home it would occur to me to ask my father if, were I to die, my casket would be closed as well, but he had no answer.

Standing there before her whom I could envision but could not see, I knew that she was the same, that if I could see her it would truly be Hannah that I saw, that all the atoms and molecules that had made her beautiful, made her who she was, were still there. Materially, chemically, she was still there. For some time after Hannah's soul had departed her body, that body was physically identical to the body of the living Hannah. A tiny change in its inner configuration and the soul, the principle of life, could no longer dwell with the body. Where, then, was it when I stood by her closed casket? Had it ceased to exist? Or did it hover nearby, an angelic presence waiting for me to do something? feel something? think something?

6

MY REFLECTION ON *The Neverending Story* was punctuated shortly after I finished rewatching the film by a call from my cousin Oriana. I normally avoided talking on the phone as much as possible, but Oriana I always answered. She had had a hard life in recent years. Oriana's half-brother Patrick died of an opioid overdose in the autumn of 2014, and Oriana's mother, my mother's younger sister Caitlin, died of complications resulting from alcoholism less than a year later. So I was in the habit of taking Oriana's calls, no matter what I might be doing.

On this occasion, she first wished me a happy birthday one day early. After that, another geographical coincidence asserted itself, for although Oriana lived at that time in Jacksonville, Florida, her chief purpose in calling me was to speak to me about our great aunt Gloria, who lived in Atlanta, not far from Annette. Gloria was like a grandmother to Oriana and me all while we grew up together, much of the time in the same house.

What Oriana now explained to me was that for several reasons, including my own mother's illness and Oriana's current marital difficulties, the line of succession, so to call it, was coming down to me. Gloria, then ninety-nine years old, was declining rapidly and in need of someone energetic, honest, and competent to settle her affairs and make arrangements for the end. Gloria's only child, a son who never recovered from the trauma he experienced in the Vietnam War, had taken his own life about twenty years before. He had a son, Ryan, a man a few years older than me, but this only grandchild of Gloria's was himself disturbed and estranged. He had been living in Hong Kong and other parts of the Far East since not long after his father died; now he had returned to America, but had just taken a very strict vow in a remote Buddhist monastery in California, and evidently it was not possible to contact him in any way for at least a year. So I would need to make a trip to Atlanta soon. Oriana had long ago been present for and presided over the demise of our grandparents. Now, she said, it was my turn, if I would accept the role and responsibility.

I accepted it, with some relief and eagerness at the chance to do (as I naively thought) some unmixed good. But it was funny that life had come to this, that here I was in my middle thirties but still so minor a man of letters and as of yet father to only one child (Oriana, who is a year and a half older than me, has two sons, then in preschool and second grade), so that it was not unreasonable that, given how decrepit or degenerate the rest of that side of my family was, the task of comforting and organizing a great aunt's passage to eternity should come down to me.

I told Oriana that I would take all necessary measures as soon as I was legally empowered to do so. Telling her this, I felt again the otherworldly sensation, which I had felt under the locusts with Kew, of past and future time settling about me. Latent in this conversation about my future visits to Atlanta—where Annette was living—was some portent that I did not, in that basement in Michigan, have the courage to face.

Perhaps that's why, when I had hung up with my cousin, I went into the backyard again, this time with a beer to accompany my cigarette. By then the air had cooled enough that it finally seemed a little like autumn. My patio and yard were covered with acorns. Twin oaks towered over our yard, as well as a white pine, a scotch pine, two firs, a spruce, and one tree that I could not identify even with the aid of my reference books, though I suspected it was some sort of plum from China. There were substantial yews and arborvitae, a magnolia, and a maple out front. The setting sun was burnishing the treetops, and in back of them to the north and east was, at last in that interminably sunny and hot autumn, a band of thick gray sky that had blown in, while shadows pooled on the ground, rising inch by inch. I saw in the boughs of the oaks that were in shadow that the season, despite the heat, had begun to paint them in patches, clumps of red and yellow amid glossy green. But all the trees that reached into that narrow interval of late light seemed heavy with a golden harvest, or like a city of gold coming down out of the sky, such as you read of the heavenly Jerusalem in Revelation. All too grand a fantasy, I thought. I had no heart anymore for writing my own, so I returned inside to watch Hannah's other favorite film.

Both *The Princess Bride* and *The Neverending Story* involve a storybook frame, in which a young boy discovers a fairy tale. Both films alternate between frame story and fairy tale, the primary and secondary worlds, though only in the adaptation of Ende's book are the two worlds conjoined by the end, and maybe that makes all the difference. The frame story in *The Princess Bride* shows a grandfather, played by Peter Falk (who will reappear in these Suites), reading a story called *The Princess Bride* to his grandson, who, like Bastian, is missing school—in this case because he is sick. Likely what drew Hannah to the films is that both involve adventure and questing, and the nature of the quest in both is the long-thwarted union of man and woman, or boy and girl: as Bastian must reach the Empress and give her a new name, so in *The Princess Bride* the farmhand-become-daring-adventurer Westley must retrieve his childhood love Buttercup from the grotesque Prince Humperdinck who intends to marry her.

Both films are comedic and romantic in the antique sense of the terms: episodic, wandering and digressive, and culminating in marriage or the reunion of the hero and heroine. For someone like Karen Blixen (also appearing later in these Suites and who, prizing joy, wrote under the name Isak Dinesen, for Isak means laughing), and perhaps for Hannah, that reunion simply *is* the essence of story. While *The Neverending Story* is cosmic in scope, proposing a marriage between reality and fantasy that works to the salvation of both, *The Princess Bride* works on a more earthly scale: in its own words it is about *true love*.

If I had been explaining it to my students at Saint Brendan's—as in fact I eventually would do, with mixed results—I would have said that the relation between *The Neverending Story* and *The Princess Bride* is like the one that holds between *Le Morte D'Arthur* and *Don Quixote*, between the genuine article and parody. I thought, sitting at my desk in the basement, that parody does not necessarily entail the repudiation or mockery of its source—it may elevate or transpose it into a different register. I would tell my students at Saint Brendan's that arriving at the end of *Don Quixote* one does not despise chivalric romance so much as mourn its passing, and upon watching *The Princess Bride* one does not disdain fairy tales or true love. Sometimes one comes away with intensified desire for the truth of the original form, a truth that is magnified and clarified through parody. But I knew, rewatching *The Princess Bride*, that twenty-two years before, the parody (not the joy) was lost on me and Hannah: we were not old enough for it.

So what did we get from the film? Perhaps a kind of elation. Hannah's two favorite films were endowed with metaphysical aura: spectacular in the cosmic Christian vision of *The Neverending Story*; something subtler, more inward, thrumming along the blood, in *The Princess Bride*, which was adapted from his own novel by William Goldman, who was Jewish. However it worked, *The Princess Bride* lifted our hearts, I remembered that much. But Hannah's favorite part of the film, and the part that confused me the most, was the darkest part, involved with the nature of the soul and its relation to the body—at least, that is what Westley's torture was about as far as Hannah was concerned.

At the lowest point of the drama, Westley is captured by Prince Humperdinck and turned over to the Prince's henchman, Count Rugen, a scholarly sadist who is writing *the definitive work on pain*. In his hidden, underground lair, the Count hooks Westley up to a large instrument simply called The Machine. The torture of the hero that ensues is rendered vividly. I found it compelling when I watched it with Hannah and felt something like the anxiety I experienced around the death of Artax in *The Neverending Story*.

Particularly the final session of Westley's torture struck me when rewatching the film in that basement, and reminded me of Hannah's insight, so much keener than my own. While the hero is bound to The Machine, which appears to operate simply by a series of glass suction cups, Prince Humperdinck bursts in and, despite Rugen's warning, runs The Machine for a few seconds at the maximum level—fifty— thereby subtracting, in a single burst of pain, fifty years from the young lover's life. Westley screams. The camera cuts to his comrade Inigo, who is looking for him in the Prince's castle; Inigo hears the cry and announces, *That is the sound of ultimate suffering.* How does Inigo know what he is hearing? He goes on to say, *My heart made that sound when Rugen slaughtered my father.*

Ultimate suffering, clearly, is not purely a thing of the body, yet The Machine is only a physical device. How, then, can it effect ulti- mate suffering? The answer must be that it does not, or that the body and whatever of us is not the body are perfectly, complementarily joined. Rewatching the film, I saw what I think Hannah understood all along, that Westley experiences ultimate suffering because of what the Prince says to him—that is, how he assaults the hero's soul—just before activating The Machine. The Prince has come from his captive Buttercup, who has stated her undying love for Westley despite what seems her now inevitable marriage to the Prince. Humperdinck, lean- ing over the badly reduced Westley, says, *You truly love each other, and so you might have been truly happy. Not one couple in a century has that chance, no matter what the storybooks say. So I think no man in a century will suffer as greatly as you will.*

Hannah and I grasped that *The Princess Bride* was about *true love.* But what does this mean? True, here, is often taken to mean faithful, as in the promise, *I will be true to you.* But it could just as well mean right or correct, corresponding to reality, as in a true statement. In that case, it becomes a question not of a quality of the love (fidelity), but of its very nature and that of the subjects it unites. So which love, or what kind of love, is true, or real?

When I would reenact *The Princess Bride* with Hannah, as she often wanted to do (somehow without the kissing parts), I was called upon to imitate the suffering Westley, and I did a fair job of it. But I always wanted to know how The Machine worked. All Hannah ever answered, as if it were obvious, was that The Machine *sucks out life and kills the soul.* Those were her very words. Rewatching the film, I paid close attention when Rugen explains to Westley how The Machine works. Rugen says The Machine sucks out life; he says nothing about the soul. Hannah could only have come by the idea through her awareness that *The Princess Bride* is the story of *true love*, which meant it must also be the story of *ultimate suffering*.

7

I SPENT SUNDAY THE twenty-second of October 2017 reading Alan Walker's three-volume biography of Franz Liszt, whose birthday it was, and listening to the composer's music. I've spent many birthdays listening to that music, since Liszt and I share a birthday 170 years apart. And I began re-reading Dante's *Commedia*, because the poem is supposed to take place when the poet was about the same age I was then. I also turned back to Dante because I knew that at two places in the poem—the middle of the *Purgatorio* and the end of the *Paradiso*—the poet used for what I believe was the first time in any European language the phrase *high fantasy*. It was Gregory who had first alerted me to this fact, many years before, when he christened the cabin where we meet every summer *Il Castello di Alta Fantasia*—The Castle of High Fantasy.

I knew that I had to get back to basics, to the origin of fantasy, if I was ever to rediscover *The Upper Country*. Kew would not be happy to hear this, that I spent the time she was gone, over my own birthday, watching movies, listening to music, and reading medieval poetry that had nothing evidently to do with my own writing, for the sake of which she had been willing to leave me alone over the weekend. I knew we would bicker about it. In those days it seemed we bickered about everything. We were new parents, with no support network, a hard and unnatural way to live. But as it happened, when my family returned the next evening, a remarkable event had occurred which canceled out my shortcoming: my son had begun to crawl. Just like that, Kew said, and her gaze glowed while she told me that she set him down by the lake on the very grass where we were married, and off the little boy went, as if he had been proficient at crawling for months. Indoors, as I soon saw, he was clumsy at first, often crashing his head into furniture and crying. But he was delighted in himself, and so we were delighted with him.

Over the next week the weather at last underwent a change as dramatic as my son's. The warm air blew away and the generally golden, dusty sky was replaced by a low, gray, moving sky sometimes blowing cold rain, which happens to be, when viewed above evergreens, particularly white pines, among my favorite skies, one that cannot be seen where I grew up due to the lack of evergreens, but which is a common sky in the country of the Great Lakes, what the colonial French called *le pays d'en haut*—the upper country. The next week, on a day when it was not raining, I bundled my son in the stroller as soon as I got home from Saint Brendan's and the sitter had left, and we walked to the small public library, where a pile of Michael Ende's books was awaiting me, culled from libraries all over the Upper Country.

This walk to the library my son and I took regularly, just as I did with my mother when I was a small boy, before I could read and even, she would tell me, before I can remember. My son enjoyed the walks, and he took them seriously, pronouncing as we went many arcane syllables in his idiolect and gesturing at the houses we passed, many of them a century old and designed with such detail (stained glass was my son's favorite when he could get up close enough), proportion, and individuality as cannot be found in their middle-class equivalents today. I was grateful that it seemed our walks would now happen in cooler weather under russet canopies. A few more hard freezes and most of the trees other than the oaks, which always go last, would drop their remaining leaves. Our route took us past the twin locusts where I had begun remembering Hannah to Kew, and true to the specie's individualism, I noticed that one of them had now dropped all its color while the other retained a host of golden leaflets.

It wasn't until the walk home that I realized it was Halloween. It was also the day when Kew taught her night class. Her mother had taken ill after the return from Chicago, which I felt guilty about, as it seemed the journey had been too taxing for her. She seemed only to have a cold, but she was fatigued and in poor spirits. She hardly ate the dinner I made, and I realized only as I was serving it that that was in part because she does not like seafood. Had she been feeling better, my mother-in-law is the type of person who would have insisted on sitting on our porch, despite the cold and rain, and giving out Halloween candy. Certainly Kew would have done this with our boy decked out in some costume, had she been home.

As things were, Kew's mother nibbled a little food and went up to her room for the rest of the evening. I hoped I would be both lucky and skilled in my execution of the bath and bedtime routine with our son, so that he would be down for the night by a little after seven, leaving me quiet hours in which to read, almost as if I were in the house alone. I was not going to allow trick-or-treating to interfere with that routine. To forfend the parade of children, I turned off as many lights as I could and then played for us over dinner Brahms's late composition for piano and voice *Vier ernste Gesänge* (*Four Serious Songs*), with Matthias Goerne singing to Christoph Eschenbach's accompaniment. My son, though he was still mainly milk-fed, betook himself with solemnity to his meal of pureed vegetables and cheerios and tiny pieces of cheese spread out on his tray for him to pick up one by one, carefully, sometimes missing his mouth, while the music played.

The *Four Serious Songs* are biblical settings. Brahms wrote this music when he knew that Clara Schumann was dying, when he had loved her for a very long time. The first three songs set two texts from Ecclesiastes and one from Sirach. They are bitter words, leveling man and beast, praising death over life, speaking of privation and futility.

But the fourth text is utterly different. In his first letter to the Corinthians, Paul speaks of love, or *charity* in the archaic English version, which I prefer because I can pretend the root is not Latin *carus*, which simply means dear, but the biblical Greek *chara*, meaning joy, and *charis*, meaning grace. These ideas too, and not only love, live for me in the word *charity*. And it means thanksgiving, as in the word *eucharist*, the central rite of the Christian religion: *Though I speak with the tongues of men and of angels, and have not charity, I am become as sounding brass or a tinkling cymbal. And though I have the gift of prophecy, and understand all mysteries and all knowledge; and though I have all faith,* *so that I could remove mountains, and have not charity, I am nothing....*

You often hear these verses at weddings, and the thirteenth verse as well, with which Brahms ends the song, *And now abideth faith, hope,* *charity, these three; but the greatest of these is charity.* But what you do not typically hear, in a nuptial context or elsewhere, is the verse that precedes this last, which makes sense of the *abiding* of this grateful and joyful love—for how should love abide if it were not in expectation of something?—and which Brahms includes in this last song he wrote for Clara Schumann, whom he would outlive by less than a year. *For now we see through a glass darkly, but then face to face: now I* *know in part; but then shall I know even as also I am known.* And the music plummets and rises, it runs in triplets and modulates to the distant key of F-sharp, and there is syncopation—which I always think of as a kind of expectation. You are waiting for the beat to fall and it does fall, just not quite in the place you expect. But that expectation, or hope—what is it if not for the restoration promised by the vision of *The Neverending Story?*

The first thing I did after putting my son to bed and bidding Kew's mother goodnight (Kew would later point out—correctly—that it must have been the music I played as much as the food I cooked or her sickness that sent my mother-in-law to bed early) was to open *Die unendliche Geschichte*, newly arrived via the library, in order to find out why Michael Ende was so disappointed by the film. I stayed up late into the night reading the book and came to understand why the author of *Die unendliche Geschichte* would have been mortified by the adaptation of his novel.

The film called *The Neverending Story* cuts out at least half of the novel called *Die unendliche Geschichte*, which would be more accurately translated as *The Infinite Story.* The film thus leads the viewer to believe that the supreme goal in the story is the regeneration of Fantasia, and that Bastian accomplishes this goal by giving the Childlike Empress a new name. This does happen in the book—at about the halfway mark. What then does *not* happen is Bastian's trite and absurd return to the real world on the back of Falkor. Instead, Bastian remains in Fantasia. Or rather, he meets the Empress in a kind of primordial void, because Fantasia has been obliterated by the Nothing.

Fantasia does not then reappear instantly *ex nihilo* exactly as it was, the way the movie implies. Instead, Bastian must participate in the creation of a *new heaven and new earth*. Now there is one more power and personality at work in Fantasia, that of Bastian the demiurge. His wishes will come true. He will wander the other world in an Adamic state, shaping it in part by naming what he discovers, and in part according to his wishes. Naming is free, but there is a cost to the potency of his desire: with each wish, he forgets more of the human world and what it was like to be Bastian in that world.

Naturally, two things happen. Bastian forgets who he is, and as he forgets, he destroys the new Fantasia almost as quickly as he creates it. Our hero means well. He tries to improve the lot of the Fantasticans, as they're called, while at the same time proving his own mettle in pursuit of a quite ordinary boyish vanity (he is an unpopular kid, bullied by the other schoolboys and, in the book, pudgy and unathletic, so in the recreated Fantasia he makes himself handsome and impossibly strong). But choice is not the rational intention we are so often told it is, and decision fatally lacks finality: we cannot know all the effects of our actions any more than we can divine their every cause or search the abyss out of which desire comes.

One thing leads to another and Bastian, simply in an effort to get to the Childlike Empress, because he feels things are going wrong and he longs for her, ends up marching at the head of an army and first besieging, then laying waste to the Empress's bright capital, the Ivory Tower. Of course, he does not find her there. He never finds her again, for she is no longer the object of his quest, his moral imperative. Now all he aspires to do is find a way back to the human world before, having lost his memory, he loses his mind entirely. It is a long road back, through a Fantasia that, if it has not been obliterated by the Nothing this time, has at any rate been upheaved and set to strife by Bastian's progress through it.

What the book does is to take account of the *culpa* portion of *felix culpa*—the fall or original and omnipresent fault. In the movie there is only the *felix*, the triumphant finality of the restoration of all things.

Bastian's restoration of Fantasia, however, is not final; in the book it is only the beginning of his spiritual awakening. For him to come to maturity of the heart, Fantasia must perish a second time, and not Fantasia only, but with it Bastian's memory and imagination. We recall that in the human world Bastian has lost his mother. In the wake of her passing, he has become alienated from his father. The two cannot grieve together, cannot come together to remember the woman they have lost. We may surmise that it is this loss (and the alienation it causes) which has hurled Bastian into fantasy, shown him the light of the world behind the world. But no one can remain in fantasy while still tethered to the human world. At most we try, here and there, to see by that other light, though it means we may look on a mountain rising over the sea and find only *grief piled upon loneliness.*

And how does Bastian finally make it back to his father, so that the two of them can recover their friendship? It is not by choice but by chance. There is hardly anything left of Bastian at this point, any faculty of his spirit, with which he might choose. Even when he was trying to use his power of wishing to find the way back to the human world, he corrupted himself with his own desire. No, he happens to see an image, a work of art like stained glass but made of ice, which he has patiently and blindly dug out of the depths of a peculiar mine in a forlorn wintry corner of Fantasia. The image reminds him of his father: you could say it recreates Bastian's mind, filling him with longing and compassion, though it is not an image of his father or of any person. This is all it takes, after the turmoil of story, and he is home. As if he saw the bare crown of a tree spread against the sky and it was enough to change one world into another.

The Genius of Renunciation

1

ONE GRAYLIT BLUSTERY AFTERNOON during the weeks following that
pivoting moment under the locusts, as I sat in the basement while our
son napped, I realized that it wasn't just Kew to whom I'd never before
mentioned Hannah—in fact, I'd hardly spoken of her to anyone since
the day she died. Even Severine, my first wife, whom I married only
five and a half years after Hannah died, might never have heard of
Hannah had not a chance encounter forced me to recount the story.

In the high spring of 2001, Severine and I were sitting in a café
at the top of Mount Adams in Cincinnati on a Friday afternoon, and
Hannah's mother, Marie, visibly and volubly intoxicated, walked in
with a woman her own age. Marie would have been in her middle or
late forties. Her appearance was still very much like Hannah's, a re-
semblance that had always intrigued me and which, in that moment,
I both cherished and abhorred.

I had not seen Marie at least since she and Hannah's father separated a year or so after Hannah died. Nor have I seen her since that
warm and breezy Friday afternoon in Mount Adams, cumulonimbus
clouds marching up the valley of the Ohio, and I have no idea of her
present condition or whereabouts. On that distant day I exchanged no
words with Marie. She and her colleague, dressed and made up in the
way that is specific to women engaged in the successful sale of costly
real estate (a success they seemed on that day to have been celebrat-
ing since lunchtime), sat at the bar across from me and at once we
recognized each other and froze.

Our respective companions and the woman behind the bar noticed our mutual recognition and our desire to abstain from greeting. Had there been a certain kind of novelist present, he might have been excused for deciding that the youth and the woman more than twice his age had enjoyed an erotic liaison. Severine, who was avidly reading the novels of D.H. Lawrence at that time, did entertain this notion until I was able to disabuse her of it afterwards in Eden Park.

To me, Marie looked the same as ever. To her, I must have seemed quite different from the last time she had seen me, which I thought might well have been at her daughter's funeral. That Friday I was wearing a jacket and tie, as I had at the funeral, but in the café, just as Marie and her companion were entering, I had loosened the tie, as though relieved to be free from a hard day of work. And I was fatigued. I had been to both ensemble practice and a master class, not to mention practicing on my own, between cello and piano about eight hours of playing and studying music: my limit, or beyond. But I was dressed up because I enjoyed looking good for Severine, as she enjoyed looking good for me, and I was going to take her out to dinner, and not just any dinner but one over which I hoped to have an important conversation.

It was a festive springtime for us. In a couple of weeks she would graduate high school and we would be married. In fact we would be married in the Immaculata, the church just down the road from where we sat sipping wine, elated that the proprietress had not thought to card us or evinced the slightest hesitation in serving us, had actually taken one look at us and immediately *offered* us wine. It was Severine who'd had the idea weeks before of coming to the café dressed professionally in the hopes that just this scenario would unfold. She'd had a feeling it was the kind of place where we could pull it off, and she was now proved right. There was the thrill of seeing whether our personae would convince. What we truly desired, though, was earnestness, to be taken seriously so that we might take ourselves seriously. Being served wine translated us into a serious young man and woman and enrolled us in what we thought of as the real world. By means of this wine we assumed our proper places and roles and were no longer, as we so often felt ourselves to be, fundamentally misplaced and, despite the seeming destiny of our incipient musical careers, directionless.

Though I had never spoken to Severine of Hannah, it had once or twice crossed my mind how unlike Hannah she was in a way which at the time seemed significant. Hannah was an autochthon, a scion of the minor aristocracy of Cincinnati. She was literally, as per her parents' involvement in real estate, of the landed gentry. Such people have a certain aura, something I was aware of when Hannah and I were children, long before I could articulate it. Hannah stood to inherit a kind of local status that almost no one in my family has enjoyed for generations, if ever, a position that comes not only from prosperity or a certain degree of education, but above all from being rooted in a place.

Severine, on the other hand, was an Appalachian émigré, as evinced by her essentially Celtic appearance (so I imagined it): black hair; blue eyes; very pale skin and a little freckled; high prominent cheekbones; and a thin mouth that could give her face a withering cruel expression of half-starved beauty that would not be out of place in a J.M. Synge play. Severine's parents were both from Pittsburgh or its coalmining hinterlands, and her family on both sides had been bound up in one way or another for generations with the mining of coal; even the great-grandmother on her mother's side after whom she was named came to America from the coal country of northern France.

Severine's parents divorced shortly after moving to Cincinnati, when Severine was very young, and both remarried. Her father married a woman from Louisville, the kind of woman who once looked me in the eye over the Easter ham I was devouring and told me that there were few more gratifying things in this life than watching a man with a good appetite eat food you had prepared for him. Severine's mother remarried a man I knew as Jack, who was from Cincinnati. Thus, by parent as by stepparent, Severine was thoroughly a creature of the Ohio Valley, yet no more native to Cincinnati than I was. But her stepfather Jack was from Mount Adams, which had still been, when he was born there in the early 1950s, an Irish- and German-Catholic working-class neighborhood. Jack grew up attending the Immaculata.

So the church in which I would marry Severine was the closest thing in her broken-and-rebuilt family to an ancestral chapel.

On that Friday afternoon in the spring of 2001, Severine and I headed in the direction of the Immaculata. We finished our wine and left shortly after Marie arrived. I made a point of walking past Marie as closely as I could on the way out, I don't know why unless it was to catch her fragrance, which was a sweetness very like honey mixed with something more jagged, almost like mint. Severine and I walked past the red brick neo-Romanesque pile of Holy Cross Monastery (now an event center), the green and gray undulations of the city spreading out behind and below, then turned toward my car, which was parked by the Immaculata. We walked in silence and deviated to pause at the top of the ninety-six stone steps that lead from Saint Gregory Street, a couple of tiers down the slope of Mount Adams, to the portico of the limestone church, quarried from the very hill upon which it sits. We leaned against the iron railing at the top of the steps, our backs to the Immaculata and our shoulders touching, and lit cigarettes.

Severine was well aware of the significance this spot bore for me: I had told her the story as soon as it became clear that, despite my reluctance to do so in a church, there was no chance of our marrying anywhere else in the city. I first knew these steps by way of Gregory. The very hour my family arrived at our new home in Cincinnati, Gregory and his mother Marybeth walked up the hill through the tall hedge of arborvitae that separated our yards and greeted me while I was kicking a soccer ball around our driveway. Gregory asked me, before saying anything else, "Are you Protestant or Catholic?"

He was at an age where such distinctions may become meaningful, and Christmas had just passed (it was *still* Christmas, I remember Marybeth telling us at some point that day or the next, the fourth or fifth day of it, and she sang "The Twelve Days of Christmas" to us in her clear contralto, the voice Gregory would inherit as a strong, sweet tenor). My answer, which may have come to mind because we had stopped over at my father's parents in Pittsburgh on our way to our new home, was truthful in a limited sense, but not accurate—I said that we were Jewish. This mystified Gregory, an exotic answer that he decided then and there (as he would tell me years later) made me a suitable companion in the world of fantasy.

Marybeth was the type to invite others to religious observances. This was a concept alien to my parents—indeed to them it was vulgar effrontery, for they eschewed all forms of religious tradition. They never accepted such an invitation. But I was intrigued, and I wanted a bond with my new friend and questing-mate. Several times in the following years I accompanied Gregory and his family when they prayed the steps, as the ritual is called.

At midnight on Good Friday, Catholic Cincinnatians slowly ascend the steps leading up to the Immaculata, a tradition that dates from before the Civil War. While they climb, they recite the rosary. On Good Friday 1989, I joined Gregory's family in praying the steps. That first encounter with the Immaculata was also the occasion of the first panoramic view of a city that I can recall, and it was a golden city draped like a fallen tapestry over the carved terrain and glinting in the currents of the great river, filling me with awe—a kind of terror.

All night, it felt, we had been climbing the stone steps, prayer muttering around me, Gregory's looming, strongly built mother occasionally looking down and smiling at us, and when I looked around, a floating sea of distinct points of light gradually revealing itself as we gained the summit of Mount Adams. Then, when we finally entered the church, I read for the first time what I knew to be a foreign language, for on the mural above the altar, in a banner beneath an image of Mary depicting her immaculate conception, are the words: *O Maria, ohne Sünde empfangen, bitte für die Bekehrung dieses Landes, Amerika*—O Mary, conceived without sin, pray for the conversion of this country, America.

The place remained with me, endowed with something of that first aura, so when I learned that the church played a role in Severine's life and that the priest who was to celebrate our wedding insisted on catechizing us at the Immaculata in the months beforehand, I knew a faint dread. But Severine undertook to make the best of the situation and introduce me to the neighborhood, which she loved for its altitude, and the shops full of clothes she could not buy, and the restaurants, and the young people out at night, and there was the Art

Museum and Krohn Conservatory, a splendid botanical garden just down the hill but still high above the river, in Eden Park. And she had more or less succeeded in winning me over, the wine in the café being her final triumph, to which the arrival of Marie had put an abrupt end. Leaning against the railing by the Immaculata and exhaling cigarette smoke Severine said, "Do you think we'll ever leave?"

2

THE YEAR OF REMARKABLE COINCIDENCE and failure that this book chronicles—beginning the autumn I turned thirty-six—was the last year that I still lived with the eternally frustrating conviction that some better life or version of myself lay *elsewhere* or in some *identity* which I had yet to fully adopt. Maybe another way of putting this would be to say that this was the last year during which I believed *happiness* was the point of life: a belief which made me and everyone around me very unhappy. And so it is not surprising that on that late autumn day when I sat in the basement of the house in Michigan where Kew and I lived with our firstborn son and Kew's ailing mother, I could still vividly hear, as if I were living it over, Severine's question: "Do you think we'll ever leave?" For this is the question of every soul in Hell or Purgatory, the question around which such a soul, like the pilgrim Dante, circles round and round.

I remembered the queasy moment of Severine's question many years before, the feeling of being trapped or sentenced. I could see in my mind how that afternoon the sky was moving in upon Cincinnati from the west with increasing insistence. At least, I thought I could remember the weather. While my son napped and I heard the faint static of the baby monitor, and the light played down through the thick well-windows onto the large-scale topographical maps of southwest Ohio affixed over my desk (as they had been in every place I had lived since moving away from Cincinnati, and as they still are), I closed my eyes against the light and the maps, and recollected the sky on that day when I last saw Marie and Severine asked if we would ever leave. Sitting in that subterranean gloom, I thought the weather came back to me—but could I really see it again, make it present again to myself?

The image, I soon realized, that came into my mind when I gave in to the spell of memory and at the same time tried to gain some control over it by making it present to me again, was no photographic recollection of a single real moment in Cincinnati in the spring of 2001. What I saw in my mind, to my surprise, was one of El Greco's paintings, a painting that, though it depicts a view of Toledo around the turn of the seventeenth century, somehow contained a truer image of Cincinnati than I had seen it on that afternoon. El Greco's is a city of gray and green, more green than gray, a city half-abandoned and desolate, perched at various levels on hillsides over a river, a city of spires and crenellations, at a distance from which we might hear muted sounds, and above it, dominating the town or perhaps (in a more musical sense) diminishing it, a sky of encroaching storm built of such proportion and radiance—but dark radiance, Milton's *darkness visible*, or *the nothing that is there*, as Stevens says—an overcast cracked and punctured in places, through which light streams down to the earth.

I don't know what Domenikos Theotokopoulos saw when he painted his famous *View of Toledo*, his adopted home, but I suspect that it was the world that lies behind the world, the world that Basho saw when he looked on Mount Chokai, and the world I saw on Good Friday 1989 from atop Mount Adams in Gregory's company and saw again in the same spot with Severine twelve years later. I wondered, sitting in that basement in Michigan, if I had ever seen any other world, whether it was not the world *before* the world, and only that world, which people called real, that I would rather see. I could conjure Marie at the wine bar, the sensation of Severine's shoulder leaning against mine on the railing by the Immaculata, the weather rolling in—those were real, but the mind will not stop at them. The mind wants to know the truth that lies behind and beneath, and the secret cause that was before its time, and it wants these things even if they are nothing.

In the spring of 2001, Severine practically crackled, like the electric air before that storm, with desire to flee, and I knew even as it happened that Marie's apparition could only add to that feeling. It was all we talked of in those days leading up to the wedding, this trap we seemed to have fallen into or whether, after all, we had made the right decision. I had stayed in the city for Severine, applying only to the College Conservatory of Music, and now she, by accepting admission to CCM as well, was going to stay for me. We could have gone elsewhere, and we both imagined elsewhere a better world. But how could I leave Severine for a year while she finished high school? And what if I had gone somewhere she could not follow? It had not been a risk I was willing to take. And in fact the Conservatory was a good place to study music composition; it was, considering the uncanny talent with which Severine was endowed, a less prestigious place for her to study violin, though still quite good, especially if Severine wanted to build her career locally. But she did not, and neither did I.

And yet, our ability to imagine ourselves living elsewhere was in inverse proportion to our desire to live elsewhere. It is a bizarre season indeed, when desire can run so high but the power to envision ebb so low. The reverse—for fantasy to roam unbounded but hope and yearning lie low—might have been healthy, perhaps it would have meant an openness on our part, as a couple, to potential, but an openness tempered by contentment in the present, the actual. And love is not love that knows other than the present. But present life was blocked for us in that high spring, and the mere fact that this dark electric creature would be my wife in a matter of days was as far from my comprehension as the infernal twinkling world I had glimpsed from those steps on Good Friday 1989. Now the city was gloomier as the clouds, billowing, darkening, tumbling, and expanding with each passing second, moved over it.

I told Severine I didn't think we'd be stuck there forever, and she said, "Let's go to the park before it storms and you can tell me what the fuck that was all about in there."

We walked down to the Mirror Lake in Eden Park and circled the water and I told Severine about Hannah. This was not what I had been planning on telling her in the park and discussing with her over dinner. The plan had been to tell her that I had made a decision: No more music. I wanted to write, I would tell her, but not music. You must know this. You yourself, I would tell her, asked me a year ago if I was making the right decision in going to the Conservatory. I had dodged the question then by saying all I knew for sure was that I wanted to marry her, and that was good enough.

And it had been good enough, a decision. Now it was time for another decision, a cutting off, as I could tell her—having studied Latin on my own all year—that the root of the word meant. To cut off one potential world and open another. She would be surprised to learn I had been studying Latin and had taken an entrance examination so that I could begin the next year in the advanced intensive Latin course, and had already filed the paperwork transferring me, as of the next autumn, from the Conservatory to the Classics and Romance Languages Departments, as if I'd never lost any time learning to compose music that could speak to no one. Literature and languages would give me a better language for life, for our lives together, I would tell her, and in a few years we might go anywhere.

But that conversation had to be postponed, because first I had to explain about Hannah, who died nine months before I first met Severine. Around Mirror Lake we walked, and when I had finished remembering Hannah to Severine, she said, "I'm sorry, that's horrible, but I don't understand how you never talked about her before. Like, maybe one of the first stories you would have told me about yourself, instead of right before we get married, and now only because we saw her mother in a café? Oh my God, this is like that story!"—Severine had just read Joyce's "The Dead" for her advanced placement senior English course.

When Hannah died, I told her, she didn't just die. It was like she vanished from existence, even from past existence. We never talked about her in my family, we didn't talk about her when her family would still visit with us, although that pretty much stopped happening anyway, and certainly her mother never came over anymore. But almost a year after Hannah died, I told Severine, her father came over to our house one evening. It was just before Christmas, and Will, Hannah's father, had a Christmas gift for our family with him. (He told us, though, that he would no longer observe the holiday and had returned to the observance of his parents' religion.) Will had taken the corks of wine bottles—there must have been a hundred of them—and assembled them into a hexagon, then bound them with copper wire to make a mat or hotpad, or simply a piece of art that one might display on a coffee table, because it was quite intriguing in its color if you turned it over so that the wine-stained sides of the corks faced upward. These were not cheap bottles, Will said, they were a good fifty dollars apiece, and Marie had drunk at least one of them per night every night after Hannah died, until he made her stop, and that's when they began to split up. But after that evening, none of us ever remembered Hannah to each other. We let her go.

We were quiet for a while, Severine and I, while we made our way upstream, the direction of our parents' homes and the direction— many curves of the river above that suburb—of Severine's origin in Pittsburgh. I don't know why I've always thought of her as having floated down the Ohio. Perhaps it's because Pittsburgh, where my father was born, has played such a large role in my life. And the trajectory of Severine's life has turned out to be both riverine and oceanic: she floated down the Ohio from Pittsburgh, stopped for a time in Cincinnati, then kept on going. She followed the river to the sea, living in New Orleans for a time, then would go to medical school through the US Navy and serve in various places on the other side of the Pacific, including Japan, before settling in Hawaii and remarrying there about a year after Kew and I married. How amazing, I thought there in the basement, that she once wondered if we would ever leave Cincinnati.

We went past the Krohn Conservatory, glimpsing its botanical wonders—more lush even than Cincinnati's rank springtime greenery—through the glass walls, and Severine asked if I had spoken of Hannah with Father Nagel, the priest who would celebrate our marriage and who had long before brought Severine and her mother into the Catholic Church. I had not. "He's a good man," Severine said, "but he comes from another world." It was evidently not the world in which it was possible to speak of Hannah. It never occurred to me to speak with Father Nagel. It was as if—I told Severine as occasional fat drops of rain began to plummet all around us and one hit her nose, exploding and making her laugh—I had vowed, without knowing it, never to speak of Hannah again after she died. "In that case," Severine said, "I'm sorry for making you break your vow."

We arrived at the northeastern terminus of Eden Park, an overlook that contains, next to two irregular pools known (ridiculously, for they are in fact very small) as the Twin Lakes, a bronze sculpture, situated on a marble block, of Romulus and Remus suckling at the so-called Capitoline Wolf. The statue was given to the city in 1931, but the date *ANNO X* is carved on the base, indicating the tenth year of Mussolini's new fascist era. We're going to get wet, I told Severine as we sat on the bench by the wolf. She shrugged and leaned into me affectionately. The drops were smacking on the sculpture with greater frequency. A train howled as it moved alongside the river, on the Kentucky shore. Cars drove past on the nearby road. There was no one else at the overlook where we sat by the fratricidal father of the western world. I picked this moment: "Sevie," I said, "I'm leaving CCM. I've been accepted in the Classics Department. They've given me a full ride, and I aced the Latin exam so I'll have a stipend on top of that."

The result of my announcement departed considerably from previous fantasy. Severine leapt to her feet while I remained seated on the bench. I looked up at her, at the gray above her where lightning flashed. After standing there frozen for a moment, she cried out, "You can't be serious! You can't do that!"

"But it's my decision to make," I insisted.

"No, it's not," she said. "You were meant to make music."

I asked her how she knew and she said the same way she knew we were meant to be married. "It's not two separate things," she said, "you and the music, that you can put together or take apart."

For as long as I've known her, Severine has exhibited this tendency to make complex philosophical arguments in single unpremeditated sentences. Normally in delivering such utterances she would bring to a grinding halt weeks or months of secret cogitation on my part, and such was the effect on this afternoon. She gave a disgusted but bizarrely sing-song grunt and turned away towards the river and crossed her arms, already perhaps considering the dramatic response to my decision, with which she would shock me a short while later.

I wanted so much to be able to tell her how I had felt earlier that day in ensemble practice—how I had felt so many times for a year or more, even when playing with her—that this music that people call a *conversation* had come, in its wordlessness, to feel like a *prison* to me. I would never be able to say what I had to say, what my life depended on my saying—I thought in such terms back then, and still did, even as I sat in the basement in Michigan—through music, not through what I could play and not through what I could compose. But I could not say a thing more to Severine in that moment. Instead, I sat staring at Romulus and Remus, at one of the most incomprehensible stories I know.

3

IN THE DAYS WHEN HOMER'S STORIES, already old, first took the shape we know, on the other side of the Mediterranean another story was beginning.

Numitor was king in Alba Longa. But he was deposed by Amulius. Numitor's daughter, Rhea Silvia, a priestess of the goddess Vesta (and as such vowed to celibacy), was seduced or raped by Mars, and the fruit of that illicit union were the twins Romulus and Remus. Amulius, the usurper, was perturbed by the appearance of heirs to his still living rival's line, and he had a servant take the twins away from the city and slaughter them—it would have brought down divine wrath to do it in the city itself. But at the last moment this servant was overcome with pity or cowardice (or sheer laziness, according to Livy), and so instead of murdering the infants outright, he abandoned them in a basket on the Tiber.

The river deposited them gently on the shore, in the shadow of the Seven Hills that would one day cradle the Eternal City, and they were suckled by a she-wolf. (The wolf never had any name but *Lupa*, which means a female wolf, and was slang in antiquity for a prostitute: the Romans, like the Hebrews of the same period and the Christians who would inherit the sensibilities of both peoples, understood their relationship to the divine as primordially involved with adultery.) When Romulus and Remus outgrew the care of the wolf, they were raised to manhood by a shepherd. Thereupon the twins became involved in a struggle to reinstate their grandfather Numitor on the throne in Alba Longa.

It was only in the course of that struggle that the twins learned of their ancestry. Upon its successful conclusion, the royal youths set out to found their own city, and they happened to choose for its location the Seven Hills where the wolf first discovered them. Discord ensued, however, for the men could not agree on which of the Seven Hills to build their city. They resorted to augury to make the decision, but the augury was ambiguous and they fell to argument, then to outright combat in the course of which Romulus murdered his brother. (Again, and passing over the baby-in-a-basket motif, we see a parallel with the stories of the Hebrews, for in them civilization begins with Cain's murder of his brother Abel and his subsequent accursed wandering: it is Cain who founds the first cities.)

A sculpture of the wolf was known to have existed anciently in Rome. The one situated in Eden Park, where I told Severine that I had decided to renounce music, is a replica of one that dates to the eleventh or early twelfth century. She is beautiful and haunting, this *Lupa*, neither meager nor voluptuous. Her head is turned to the side and her jaws parted slightly. She is tired, but also joyous and eager: the same expression that every new mother I've seen has worn. In the story she is able to nurse the infants because she had recently lost cubs of her own, and I think there is sadness in this wolf's eyes along with the surprise of finding herself a mother after all.

But why should the Sons of Italy, in conjunction with Mussolini himself, have gifted Cincinnati this sculpture?

European settlement of southwest Ohio began in the late 1780s and soon centered on the large semicircular basin to be found at the confluence of the Ohio River and Mill Creek, coming from the north and, opposite Mill Creek, the Licking River coming from the south. The first name for the city was *Losantiville*, a portmanteau meaning city-opposite-the-mouth-of-the-Licking-River: the *L* for Licking, *os* meaning mouth in Latin, *anti* opposite in Greek, and *ville* the French for city. But a number of the first European settlers were veteran officers of the Revolutionary War and soon decided to rename the place after the Society of the Cincinnati, of which they were members. They had taken the name for their society from an archaic Roman figure almost as legendary as Romulus and Remus: one Lucius Quinctius Cincinnatus (*Cincinnati* is the plural of his cognomen, which means curly-haired and is thus perceptibly related, in the Indo-European root, to our word *kink*, as for example *a kink in the river*, for among the early Romans a *c* always sounded like a *k*). The veterans put themselves under the aegis of the legendary Roman because his story is one of humility, renunciation, and careful labor upon the earth—themes as central to the early Roman mythology as to Jefferson's ideal of an agrarian republic.

But shadowing Cincinnatus's story of humility, renunciation, and the strength of self-restraint is another tale—one of violence, scandal, fear, and failure. Lucius's son Caeso committed an act of insurrection, which, though it failed, involved murder, earning him a death sentence. Lucius expended the bulk of his old Etruscan wealth in buying his son's life, though Caeso still had to go into exile in neighboring Etruria. Lucius retreated to the modest remainder of his estate, on the hills opposite Rome (perhaps roughly where the Vatican is today).

Soon after this disgrace, however, the senators came to Cincinnatus on his farm, bearing his old senatorial toga and begging for his aid in defending the city against the invading Volsci. This was only two generations or so after the last of the Roman kings was overthrown, an event Lucius Quinctius would have remembered from his boyhood. The republican order that had replaced the monarchy was still nascent and now in danger of premature death. The senators made Lucius *dictator*, a position of supreme and emergency authority, and in that capacity he defeated Rome's enemies.

Rather than remain in power, as he easily could have done, once the threat had passed Lucius Quinctius surrendered the *fasces*, the rods bundled about an axe, which symbolized absolute power. He returned to his farm. This story repeated itself two decades later, and despite his by then very advanced age Lucius again saved Rome and a second time gave up the *fasces* the moment he was able to do so. At Sawyer Point, on the river in downtown Cincinnati and almost visible from the Immaculata atop Mount Adams, there is a large bronze statue of Cincinnatus, one hand on the plow at his side, the other arm extended, holding the *fasces*, remanding power to the senate and people of Rome.

So why should Cincinnati keep, in an out-of-the-way corner of one of her hilltop parks, the sculpture of the fictional Capitoline Wolf, especially considering that it was a gift from Mussolini, whose fascism stood in starkest contrast to the values epitomized by Lucius Quinctius Cincinnatus? The city where Hannah was born and died was named for a man, not for another place, but in taking its name from Lucius Quinctius, Cincinnati became associated with his city, particularly as it was asserted that Cincinnati was built, like Rome, on seven hills. Over time, the idea of a City of Seven Hills—despite its association with the beast in Revelation—took on an auspicious aura, though no Cincinnatian could tell you why it matters that a city should claim to be built on seven hills (as many cities do, including Athens, Jerusalem, Moscow, and dozens of others), just as no two Cincinnatians will give you seven identical names for the foundational hills. This is because the city was not founded on seven hills, but in the central basin, between Mill Creek and the Ohio. She was, to begin with, not a city set upon a hill but a river city, cradled by the hills into which she would later leap. It is the river that imparted to Cincinnati, as Harry Graff wrote in the 1943 WPA Guide to Cincinnati, *a lustiness which still lingers.*

There is no understanding the person I was in that springtime, and the person Severine was, without understanding the place where we lived and loved each other. I knew it intuitively then and have always believed it since: we are creatures of place. Severine and I may not have been born in Cincinnati, like Hannah and Gregory, but we were nonetheless an expression of the City of Seven Hills. Somehow our hometown's namesake is part of us and our story and all the mythical association he brings with him; but also the very shape of the place is involved with us, or we are involved in it.

The hills of Cincinnati are actually punctuated and carven tablelands. It is called dendritic terrain, after the Greek word for *tree*, and indeed the gouges made by the water running to the Ohio make a pattern like the branching of a tree. If I had to name seven distinct cradle hills surrounding the wide and often miasmic Mill Creek valley where it flows into the Ohio—haven of pork-packers and iron foundries, soap- and bourbon-makers, rail yards and interstate highway—I would say that from the west arcing around north and back down on the east they are: Mount Echo, Price Hill, Fairmount, Fairview, Bellevue, Mount Auburn, Mount Adams. That's four *mounts*, two *views*, and a *hill*.

Throughout the rest of the city's fifty-two neighborhoods and uncounted suburbs, there are at least a dozen more places that include *hill* or some version of *mount* in their name. One always has a sense of being either up or down and even the topland is not flat. Of those seven cradle hills, five are crowned with large parks. The hills make a ring of colorful palisades. From the center of the city look to any horizon, including mirroring formations in Kentucky, and you see green in summertime or purple-shadowy or golden-gleaming brown and gray bare deciduous trees in winter. The hills are spotted with houses and girdled with streets that run at steep angles. There are also public stairways; once there were funicular inclines, vineyards upon the cradle-hills, and long cellars tunneled into them for the purpose of lagering beer.

The uneven landscape of Cincinnati divides the neighborhoods and suburbs sharply from each other, giving the city a parochial and cliquish character, and the hills cut her off from the rest of the state of Ohio. Cincinnatians are not really Ohioans—they belong to the river and the hills that define their lives. A strongly felt disparity divides east and west in the City of Seven Hills, one side or the other of Mill Creek. But these halves are themselves composed of isolated pockets. It is ultimately topography that brings some Cincinnatians close and alienates others from their kindred spirits if they happen to live a hill or a valley too far. And yet the city's compartmentalized nature also makes it a palimpsest or manifold, endowing it with mystery and amplitude, as if it were somehow larger than it is.

Seven bridges connect the center of the Seven Hills to Kentucky. In the early stage of the city's growth, an arm of the Miami and Erie Canal flowed through the center of Cincinnati under what is now Central Parkway. This route divides downtown from Over-the-Rhine, and it was the canal that gave *Rhine* to the name of that neighborhood.

The German immigrants who settled on the north side of the canal in the early and middle-nineteenth century hailed from the Rhineland, and they were predominantly Catholic.

After I moved away from the city in 2005, Over-the-Rhine (or OTR) gentrified at a meteoric rate. By the time of my thirty-sixth birthday, OTR's blocks upon blocks of Italianate architecture and its people of every age and color mixing together would come to seem the heart of the City of Seven Hills. So much entertainment and culture had moved to OTR by then that other neighborhoods (like Mount Adams that Severine had loved) now felt obsolescent. But in the spring of 2001, Severine could still be in love with the idea of drinking wine in Mount Adams. And at that time all anyone talked about in connection with OTR was the rioting that had occurred there six weeks before, when Cincinnati police officer Stephen Roach, a white man, shot and killed an unarmed nineteen-year-old Black man named Timothy Thomas.

4

I HAVE NOT FORGOTTEN my young self and Severine sitting in Eden Park. The storm broke over the Seven Hills while Severine and I walked back to my car. At times I thought she might be crying, but I couldn't tell in the rain. We got in the car drenched, and I started to drive down and out of Mount Adams. When we came to the Art Museum, she told me to pull into the almost deserted parking lot. The museum had closed an hour before. When I parked the car Severine said, "I want you here, right now."

We got out of the car and into the back seat. It took her some doing to remove her jeans because they were soaking and clung to her. The rain on the hood of the car and the windows was deafening while we made love. When we had finished and I was driving down the hill again, Severine said, "If you're quitting then I quit too, I never wanted to play, not like I have been, competing, always competing—you wanted that for me."

I couldn't believe what I had heard. Once again I had no words, and she seemed to expect none. Nor would Severine have anything more to say on the topic until she was getting out of my car to return to her mother's house. "You're really quitting music?" she asked, and I said I was. Then her voice went very quiet and delicate as she asked, "But we'll still play together at the wedding reception...."

"Of course. Sevie, this is an exciting change, not a bad one. It's how we're going to get out of here someday."

She tossed her hair back and recovered some strength in her voice as she said, while rolling up her window, "It's just us two. Before somehow there were three of us—you and me and the music. Now there's just us two. It's going to get lonely."

I have never understood Severine's intuition and prescience, and when I recalled these words in my basement in Michigan on that autumn day in 2017, I felt again the same unease I had felt sixteen years before. Perhaps there was something about the shadowy gloaming light of that afternoon that was analogous to the storm light of the spring day in 2001, for at some point I lost control over the memory and it sprawled into another. I remembered another afternoon of sex in my car in the Art Museum parking lot and another stormy sky altogether.

Almost exactly one year previously, in the early spring of 2000, Severine and I had skipped school together for a whole day, a last-minute decision made at Severine's urging, and spent hours wandering our city that we did not know we loved. On that day we left the Art Museum when it closed and waited in the parking lot for the other cars to go, before having sex for the first time with each other. I was not a virgin, nor was Severine, but I was nervous in a way I have only been, apart from that afternoon, when playing music. For I knew that the act would seal our fate together; and indeed, not many days thereafter we became engaged.

The other stormy dark light I recalled from that day in the spring of 2000 was that of an El Greco painting I had just been looking at in the Art Museum called *Christ in Agony on the Cross*. In the later stage of his career, from which this painting comes, Domenikos Theotokopoulos took to inserting fantastical depictions of his adopted city in many of his paintings, as if he could not imagine those religious scenes occurring anywhere other than in the city that had come to live in his mind.

In this painting, the Crucified One dominates the canvas, but he is not what transfixed me. At the foot of the cross, instead of a kneeling Mary and John or the soldier who would pierce Christ's side with a lance and let loose twin streams of blood and water, we see only dusty, pale human bones, including a skull. Paler than the bones,

Christ looks skyward. In the middle distance, of the same size as the human remains, a knight and his retainer (like Don Quixote and Sancho Panza) make their way toward Toledo, which lies, in the distorted perspective of the painting (as if you were face-down at the foot of the cross, peering over a ridge at the city), entirely under Christ's feet. The sky that rises over Toledo and provides the background to the Man of Sorrows is similar to the sky in the *View of Toledo* in that it is gashed and torn—rent like the Temple veil, perhaps—but it is pitch black, in accordance with the scriptural narrative that tells of the sun blotted out at the moment of Christ's death, though it was the middle of the afternoon, a Friday. Yet those gashes remain, a blear light shines through so that the overcast almost looks like receding snow-clad mountain peaks, illuminated by flashes of lightning like those that would flicker around Severine and me in Eden Park on another Friday, a year after I first saw this painting, when I told Severine I was giving up music.

5

THAT NOVEMBER WAS COLD in Michigan, as if to make up for the scald of September and the lingering heat of October. But at the end of the month, about a week after the train of thoughts recorded in the foregoing movements of this Suite had occurred to me, there came a day when warm air blew in from the southwest and the skies, which had been wet and concrete for four weeks, for a few hours became pale autumnal prairie.

The fluke day affected me. As I was driving home from Saint Brendan's I was listening to Alisa Weilerstein, whom I would call the greatest cellist of her generation—which is to say my generation, since she is just a few months younger than me. I was listening to her recording of Elgar's Cello Concerto, a work I have known by heart since I was a boy. This particular recording was historic because Daniel Barenboim conducted Weilerstein. Barenboim had not conducted the Elgar Concerto since his wife Jacqueline Du Pré, possibly the greatest cellist of her generation, was the soloist, in the 1960s. Du Pré suffered from multiple sclerosis and had to stop playing when she was not yet thirty. She died at the age of forty-two and was buried in the Hoop Lane Jewish cemetery in Golder's Green, London, for she had converted upon marrying Barenboim. Her short career was legendary, and her most famous piece was the Elgar Concerto that I was now listening to Weilerstein play.

The music had almost concluded when I was stopped by traffic next to the parking lot of an abandoned storefront. A decaying phone booth, once cerulean blue but now rusting gray, stood in one corner of the lot. Around this booth half a dozen teenagers were gathered. They were taking pictures of the phone booth with their cell phones, smirking and sneering, and one girl seemed to point at the booth and guffaw in mockery through the veil of her coiled honey-brown hair blown across her face. For an instant she seemed frozen like that, as if I had taken a picture of her. Then she moved and the traffic moved and I looked away.

When I returned home I dismissed the babysitter, who had just put my son down for his afternoon nap; my mother-in-law was already napping. The prospect of an hour's rest invited me. I ought to have slept right away, but driven by Weilerstein's playing, I first went into the basement and removed my cello from the closet where it had remained untouched since we had rented that house in Michigan. The instrument had been broken for a decade. The bridge snapped one sweltering summer in Chicago, where I never had air-conditioning. I didn't replace it, so the sound post promptly collapsed.

The cello was made in Germany. It is the second cello I have owned. The highest quality student instrument one might play, it cost my family close to ten thousand dollars in the late 1990s; professional cellos can easily cost five times as much. My parents were beginning to think about how they could someday afford such an instrument for me when I left the Conservatory. The bow is the only one I have ever owned and it is of high quality: a thin wand of wood and horsehair once worth a thousand dollars or more, it had been neglected so long amidst violent oscillations of temperature and humidity that I was not sure what would happen were I to have it re-haired and tightened. Possibly it would be as playable as ever. But the cello, I thought, might have become warped and lost its worth, an obscene waste. Yet I could not part from it.

I sat on the futon and laid the cello across my knees. It was partly illuminated by the light that shot through the glass block well windows and streaked across the gray carpeted floor and up the opposite wall by my desk in a prismatic splay that kaleidescoped back and forth as the wind played in the wilted hydrangea outside, dancing its shadow around the interior of the basement. Someone standing in front of me, in the place of the bookshelves containing literature from East Asia and reference works on Welsh, Irish, Old English, French, Greek, German, Latin, Hebrew, and Sanskrit, might have thought that the cello and I made a bizarre *Pietà*.

I had not opened the case and touched the fashioned wood since before we moved from Chicago. Now I ran my hand along the instrument's top, from the scroll down the fingerboard to the empty space where the bridge should have been. I touched the curve of its flank. A film of dust was visible on the surface, and I smelled the ghost of rosin, the extracted essence of the very pines that I so admire under a low, gray, moving sky in the Upper Country. It was better, I thought, that the instrument was ruined, for if I had been able to play it, whatever sounds I produced would be more than I could withstand. But it was good to hold the wooden form, its smoothness and proportion and airy weight, and smell again the old scent. I remembered the cello's voice, silken in the lower registers and not too bright in the upper; in color it is like caramel and maple syrup.

As I rose to put the cello away in the closet, words came into my mind: *So let us rest, sweet love, in hope of this, / And cease till then our timely joys to sing, / The woods no more us answer, nor our echo ring.* These verses come near the end of Edmund Spenser's *Epithalamion*. In the closet, forming the base on which my cello had been resting, was a stack of notebooks and unbound printed paper that constituted the only tangible remains of my abandoned dissertation on the sixteenth-century poet Edmund Spenser.

The *epithalamion* is an ancient Greek form that was recited in celebration of a wedding. Spenser wrote his *Epithalamion* for his own wedding, a gift to his bride, Elizabeth Boyle. It is perhaps the most numerically perfect poem in the language. And number was once the lifeblood of meaning and beauty: for it was the domain where mundane and transcendent, created and creator, met one another and married.

The poem tracks a day, and so it contains twenty-four stanzas, one for each hour. But in fact it indexes and recapitulates all earthly time. As the scholar A. Kent Hieatt observed long ago, there are 365 long lines and sixty-eight short lines in the poem, which latter figure is the sum of the weeks, months and seasons. Spenser married Elizabeth

on the eleventh of June 1594. The Julian calendar by then had fallen
ten days behind, so the eleventh of June was the summer solstice.
Almanacs would have told Spenser that on that day, in southern Ireland where he married Elizabeth, there were sixteen and one-quarter
hours of daylight. Accordingly, one quarter of the way into the seventeenth stanza, the phrase *Now night is come* appears. The poem can
thus be located precisely with respect to latitude and ecliptic, making
the poet's gift to his bride a day and a place, their wedding at Kilcolman Castle preserved in poetic and astronomical precision, *for short
time an endless monument*, he concludes, setting the day in a place of
cosmic significance.

Time, in its ordinary running, was finally, despite the true joys it
brings, a ruinous evil to Spenser's Neoplatonic way of thinking: time
was a prison, or contamination, from which we must be rescued or
redeemed. When he writes *timely joys* he means the joys of mundane
time, at best pale shadows of the eternal counterparts to which they
point—if we are wise enough to understand the meaning and if they
arise at the right time and place, among the right persons. In number we can grasp this. Mundane, fallen time, through cycle and ratio,
must be linked to the transcendent, stable time of the foretold new
heaven and earth that are forever arriving yet already begun in the
heart—or in memory with its revisionary power. The hope of which
the poet speaks in the lines I remembered as I put away my cello is of
delivery into that other world—the same hope expressed in the vision
of *The Neverending Story*, the vision of time and world redeemed. As
in the film, so in Spenser's poem it is the union of male and female
that sits mysteriously in the center of the perfected cosmos and its
life-giving time.

I once made a point of standing, on the summer solstice, in
the center of the feeble overgrown ruin of Kilcolman Castle, where
Spenser married Elizabeth. The ruin sits in a farmer's field on the
fringe of a marshy seasonal pond. Nothing announces the site, for
the Irish do not remember Spenser fondly. He was a champion of the
English imperial venture and a servant of the oppressive colonial re-
gime in Ireland. Kilcolman Castle, Spenser's last home, was destroyed
in 1598, burned out by a revolt, and the poet died shortly thereafter in

London, where he had gone to bring report of the turmoil in Ireland. It is probable that he lost a young child in the attack and that this loss contributed to his sudden illness and death at the age of forty-six or forty-seven. Elizabeth was his second wife, his first having died of natural causes.

I was with my second wife when we went to Kilcolman. In fact it was the summer of 2014 and Kew and I had just married. We spent the whole summer in Ireland, mainly at a small cottage in West Clare belonging to Kew's extended family. But we also roamed around a lot, and Kilcolman, off the road from Limerick to Cork, was our southernmost jaunt.

Kew was dubious. It is not a spectacular or restful or resonant place. I stood there and I was nothing but a trespasser in some farmer's field, ankles spattered with muck beneath a heavy, warm, damp North Atlantic sky and the Ballyhoura Mountains low and dark on the horizon. I felt nothing, but I thought of what Spenser often brings to my mind, how he made a choice at some point when he was still young—at least it looks like a decision—to make his poetic career away from the growing cultural center in London. He sought to transfigure the landscape in Ireland where he had ended up, to make of the provinces and frontiers of Tudor civilization a great myth and to discover in his far-flung outpost a center and symbol of all creation and gateway to the world behind the world, which Spenser called Faërie. We easily judge Spenser as the witting instrument of a harsh overlordship, and the judgment is not false. But neither is it complete, and if you read his poetry you know he loved his place, whatever version of it he could see.

Severine and I married on Saturday, the sixteenth of June 2001. The sixteenth of June is known as Bloomsday, after the day in 1904 when Joyce's *Ulysses* is supposed to have taken place in Dublin. Joyce picked that day because it was, in his true life, the date of his first romantic excursion and sexual encounter with his future wife, Nora Barnacle. Severine and I were conscious of this coincidence when we married—in fact, as the reader may recall from the episode in Mount Adams, we both placed high value on the writing of James Joyce and were in the habit of looking for the truth of his stories reflected in the world we knew.

We filed for divorce on Tuesday, the twelfth of November 2002. Taking that date for the end, it is possible to say that we were married for 513 days. The area code for southwest Ohio is 513, and I always thought of the place whenever I saw this configuration of digits, on a clock for instance, or when I called anyone who had a Cincinnati number, including Gregory—or, more rarely, Severine, who somehow managed to keep the same cell phone number for decades after we divorced.

It is hard to say what any of this means, and most people would say it means nothing. Spenser was among one of the last generations of the Christian civilization of Europe that looked for meaning in number and heard the music of reality in the patterns of nature. And in fact it was my own catastrophic lapse from such a conception, it seemed to me as I replaced my cello in its obscure den on that mild November day in Michigan, that led me to abandon my dissertation and the profession to which I'd pledged myself since leaving music behind, a work that had seemed suddenly as stifling as music had seemed not ten years before. I had, for once, become absolute in this world and knew neither the light nor the music of the world behind the world. For once? I should say, *finally*. For was it not what I had always wanted, I who was so much haunted by fantasy? Yet when it was so, when I felt myself at last free to live in this world and in no other—thus a monarch of a worthless realm (like every solitary, buffered self, in my own conception relative to nothing and no one)—then I could do nothing but withdraw, renounce, betray.

6

I HAVE SAID THAT SEVERINE was from Pittsburgh: this fact has always remained with me. My father was from Pittsburgh. There is one more new character to introduce now, my friend Joel Stein, and he also is from Pittsburgh. In renouncing music I betrayed Severine, for as she knew without thinking about it, knew in her being but as I was only to learn too late and too abstractly, our very bond was that music. In renouncing scholarship it is even less clear to me what I gave up, but it is surely my father—a scholar, a scientist—and my friend Joel Stein, who first encouraged me on the path of higher learning, whose legacies I betrayed. And so, while Cincinnati is the city I have lost, it is Pittsburgh I associate with these twin renunciations and—if such they are—failures. The stories of Joel and of Severine are intertwined with each other even as they are with Pittsburgh, a fact which will become clearer in the next Suite.

I met Joel in the cavernous study area of the Cathedral of Learning, the towering centerpiece of the University of Pittsburgh. My father grew up in the Squirrel Hill neighborhood of Pittsburgh, not far from that university, and his parents lived there almost to the end of their lives. We visited my grandparents frequently when I was young. When I was a teenager in the 1990s, I began to roam about the city freely, and I would often spend the whole afternoon into the evening reading or writing (pretending to be a college student, I suppose, for the same reason Severine and I would drink underage atop Mount Adams) in the Cathedral of Learning. One such evening, when I was fifteen years old, I was sitting in the Cathedral jotting something down, and in front of me on the little table were two books: a music theory textbook and Schopenhauer's philosophical masterpiece *The World as Will and Representation,* which in some ways hinges on his theory of absolute music. A young man, a Pitt student of course, came over to me and said, "What the hell, if you're reading Schopenhauer how have we not met?"

This was Joel Stein, five years older than me, earnest but loquacious and amiable. Joel was a short and round-faced man who resembled the filmmaker Kevin Smith. Actually, it would be more accurate to say that Joel resembled the character Silent Bob, portrayed by Kevin Smith. Joel in those days wore a long black coat and a backwards baseball hat and he smoked heavily. He grew his black hair long and wore a beard, which was less common at that time. Joel was aware that his appearance was a cliché, as he put it, and that he looked like Silent Bob. But Joel thought everything around the end of the millennium had become a cliché, and he found a kind of liberation in this state of affairs. If everything is a cliché, he would say, then nothing is; or he would say that if there's no chance of anyone appearing *authentic* then one may play one's true role unselfconsciously. He would often say Zen-like stuff, such as: *When you eat, eat; when you fuck, fuck; when you shit, shit.*

Joel was from an academic and secular Jewish family in suburban Minneapolis. He had come to study philosophy at the University of Pittsburgh. Joel also harbored literary ambitions in those days. Despite my being younger than Joel, we became fast friends from that very hour and would spend as much time as possible together whenever I came to Pittsburgh. We lingered in cafes and bars (easy to get into underage back then and in that city), went to open mic poetry readings or occasionally more respectable literary events, and to music shows. But mostly we hung out over coffee, often into the small hours, and talked.

It was in no such circumstances that Joel appeared to me in the dream I will narrate. Since the day at the end of November when I had unearthed my dissertation, uneasy, unlooked-for memories of Joel had occurred to me. Already by the time I had begun that dissertation, Joel and I had ceased to be friends. But as I say, I always thought of him in connection with any part of my career that had been academic and scholarly, because he more than anyone had encouraged me in that direction. Even my dream of Joel would prove weirdly erudite.

Things were not going well for me at Saint Brendan's. More accurately, the parents of my students—some of them our fellow parishioners—looked askance at me since I had assigned the essay on Thoreau and the Giving of the Law at Sinai. This was another thing that weighed on me as 2017 came to an end. Shortly before Christmas I fell ill with the flu. On Christmas Eve I was still exhausted, so only Kew went to Midnight Mass. My absence, I feared, would only compound our fellow-parishioners' suspicions of me as an insincere convert. While Kew was there, I dreamed the following dream, startling awake when she returned home.

7

THERE ARE NO MORE STORIES, MCPHAIL.

Joel Stein spoke this sentence on a bluff of the Loop Head peninsula in County Clare in the West of Ireland. I knew this place well. Some of Kew's distant relations owned a small, very old cottage in Loop Head and we had on several occasions passed a lengthy sojourn there. Now Joel and I were walking southwest out of Kilkee on the cliff road that traces the sea. The sun was westering and the air was full of diaphanous, auspicious vapors.

I know it to be a real light, no mere somniofacture. I've seen that light in that place, and it's not like any other light. Various factors combine to create the effect of this glowing, irradiated air. There is the ocean—on our right as we walked—and the land on the left. The presence of the ocean means there's always moving moisture in the air. The land is the famous Irish verdure with almost no trees, a shadeless green (but sometimes shadowy beneath running clouds) that affects the colors of the sky. And there's the angle of the sunlight to consider, as per latitude and season, which is to say in this instance not the summer solstice, as when I visited the ruins of Spenser's Kilcolman Castle with Kew, but an afternoon around Eastertime, and just better than fifty degrees north. There's no describing the particular luminosity, a diffuse and palpable translucence that is yet not overcast but a sort of clarity.

And there was Joel walking beside me, looking much as when I had last seen him, more than a dozen years before, save that his beard was far more massive and wild and his hair was even longer and more tangled, so he looked like a Nazirite, an ancient Hebrew ascetic. Immaterial darkness shrouded Joel; it was no match for the glowing, encompassing day, but worrying all the same. He walked on my right, between me and the Atlantic, and when he spoke it was as if the sea wind whipped his words upon my ears with strange intensity.

Joel was dressed in a beautiful *kashaya*, the robe of a Buddhist monk, colored in a pattern of flecks and fragments of golden and purple hues, like I had seen some years before in an exhibit of such Japanese robes at the Art Institute of Chicago. The garment was both bright and dim, the gold and the purple mixed together, insistently present yet disappearing, cloaking him.

For a great master like Dōgen, eight hundred years ago, the kashaya was a symbol of high importance: though a thing made of discarded cloth (the fouler the better), it is also assurance of the face-to-face teaching (like the Christian idea of apostolic succession or like the Hasidic masters holding court), essential to the authentic transmission of the dharma. The kashaya was passed from one master to the next, and by no means was just anyone worthy of such a robe. *A kashaya is neither made nor not made, neither abiding nor not abiding. It is the ultimate realm of Buddha.* So Dōgen writes in the thirteenth century. *Those who have no wholesome past actions,* he goes on, *cannot see, wear, receive, and understand a kashaya even if they live for one, two, or innumerable lifetimes. Those who cannot receive one because of their hindrances should repent.*

As for me, in the dream I appeared to be wearing the costume of this Zen-Joel's Western counterpart: the rough brown homespun of an Irish ascetic from the early Christian era, before the Roman Church extended its sway over the island, when not bishops and priests but abbots and abbesses and wandering, wonder-working saints and poets and scholars were the men and women of renown and high station.

As if they were the iconographic totems of a saint, Joel carried a book in one hand, from which he would eventually read, and a pack of cigarettes in the other. I carried a book, from which I would read in turn, and a flask: the very flask that Severine's father gave me on my eighteenth birthday to take hunting with him; its steel is embossed with an image of a mallard taking flight amidst reeds and cattails. As Joel and I walked, I sipped from this flask and found that it contained lukewarm water that tasted of rich earth, like a river carrying silt from some unspoiled country nowhere to be found anymore on this Earth. Joel was not mocking as he repeated his mantra—*There are no more stories, McPhail*—and he shook his head as he looked at the ground and I looked at him and at the rolling breakers and spindrift and heard the booming of the tide behind and below him.

We spoke no other words at first as we walked out the long arm of land, the thrust of County Clare into the North Atlantic. Mostly level and rolling with a few conical prominences, Loop Head is bounded by the open sea on the northwest and the Shannon estuary on the south. The land slopes down towards the Shannon estuary and there the shoreline is gentler, but on the northern coast where Joel and I were walking there is a sheer and ragged drop of about two hundred feet to the ever-heaving Atlantic.

The violence of water over long time appears to have cloven tall chunks of rocky earth away from the mainland, with which the tops of these islands (if you want to call them that) remain level, at a distance of anywhere from a few feet—daring you to leap the gap—to over a thousand. The sea has eroded looser material to leave these weird islands, like columns of a primordial giants' temple, looking as if they broke away drastically when in fact they have only been severed gradually and are still connected just below the surf, as can be seen at low tide. The subaqueous relation between these islands and the main bulk of Ireland is like the bonds that persist between disunited friends. We paused for a while across the chasm separating the cliff road from a large, severed prominence called Bishop's Island and stood looking at the grassy top of the isolated rock abounding in gulls and thrust hundreds of feet over the churning surf.

The story—which only the oldest farmers still remember—is that two monks came to that country in the sixth century seeking escape from the trials with which the social order burdens the soul. And yet this extreme edge of the known world was not remote enough, so they prayed God to further separate them. The Almighty obliged and broke the land away. You can see stone ruins on the edge, a little cell and an oratory where one of them is supposed to be buried. The other recluse, I suppose, became food for the gulls or the fish when his soul departed his body. However averse to the ways of the world these two men were, they were at least not averse to each other; they were at least friends.

A few minutes' walk farther down the high coast, Joel paused us again, this time turning his gaze inland at Tobar Caoidhe, the holy well dedicated to Saint Caoidhe—Kee, as it's poorly anglicized. The name intrigues me for its indeterminate verbal root, which may have to do with blindness, lamentation, or even paths, so I have joked to Kew that Kee is the patron saint of those who go lamenting down the pathways of the blind, or the blind who walk in the ways of lamentation, or those who lament their blindness as they struggle to follow the Way.

All over the countryside of Ireland are to be found in abundance two kinds of ruin: holy wells (*toibreacha*) and what are known variously as ring forts or fairy forts: in Irish they are called *rathanna*, which means the circular embankments themselves, or *liosanna*, which denotes the enclosed spaces. And so these are, enclosures of earthen mounds or hedges in ring-shape, sometimes quite large and set within each other concentrically. They are usually left untended, whatever grows on them uncut, for to meddle here is to invite otherworldly interference. They are artifacts of human culture, not that of Faerie, built and occupied from the Bronze Age through the early Medieval period. But it is as if the assumption came naturally and worked itself out in folk idea, that when humankind no longer cares for these earthen ramparts they should become the province of the world behind the world, its strongholds and gateways. Kee's Well is in the middle of a fairy fort. Usually these wells are thought to cure some ailment, and at Kee's Well the water is supposed to help the eyes.

Around and around the inside of the ring of hedge Joel and I walked, seeing over the hedge the cattle in the pastureland and the larks overhead, or the jagged shore of Clare tilting away and crashing into the sea. The raised earth of the fairy forts reminds me of the sinuous mounds built by Native Americans in the valleys of the Ohio that so fascinated me as a boy. Always an uncanny feeling would come over me by those worn, green edifices, and I felt the same thing now at Kee's Well.

Eventually Joel put his hand on my elbow and guided us away from the ring to the little structure, like a miniature chapel, that housed the well in the center. The structure is simple, whitewashed, a small cross on top. You can hardly go inside, the floor being mostly the open face of the well. The interior walls bear a crucifix draped by a rosary, icons, a few votive candles, and other paraphernalia, all left there over many years but none of it of recent devotion, and I don't know when the last Pattern Day would have been celebrated at Kee's Well. In the strange imposition of English upon Ireland, *pátrún* (as in a *patron* saint) morphed into *pattern*, as if the Communion of Saints—in this case, Ireland's local, legendary saints with one foot in Faerie—were coordinates on a vast holy map of the island.

Joel caused us to kneel before the well, and spoke again about story, something about one true story that makes valid all storytelling. And he was saying something about marriage, the marriage of complementary spirits: Spirit of God and spirit of place; the holy person and the holy place. The word of God, he may have said, is a true window on the world, yet fragile. Oh, how it is threatened, a marriage dying away, a passion spent, love misconstrued.... Something like that, and Joel was warning me that if the marriage of the Spirit of God and the Spirit of Place were broken, then language itself would be broken and there could be no more story.

I was mystified and annoyed by this and made to rise from the well, but Joel bade me first drench my eyes in the water, and I did. As I washed my eyes, I began to weep, because I could make no prayer and felt no faith. And then: *Whatsoever faith shall safeguard this Earth and all her times and weathers, that shall endure,* Joel said as he stood and I stood next to him, *and whatsoever faith shall waste this Earth, even that shall be swept from off the face of this Earth; nor shall the Earth remember that falseness any more than the Maker of the Earth and all her times and weathers remembers the sin of the repentant man.*

Then I followed Joel away from Kee's Well and out of the fairy fort, and we walked on down the coast. There were other fairy forts on higher ground inland and everywhere the scent of dung and turf fires in the air. Always we could hear the sound of the sea, cold and beating on a broken shore. When at last we came to the end of Loop Head, Joel pointed over the water to a distant mountain peak glaring over the waters and said, *When there are no more stories, it is time to float.* And with that we stepped off the cliff and walked across the air over the mouth of the Shannon and Tralee Bay, and soon found ourselves at Slea Head on the coast of Corca Dhuibhne, standing where the skirts of Cnoc Bréannain come down to the sea.

The mountain is, like the holy well, named for a saint, Brendan, who in legend sailed from that place and discovered America in the sixth century after having sighted it from the top of the mountain. The peak stands more than three thousand feet over the Atlantic. Joel and I ascended in silence up what I know to be one of the southern slopes, though if one were in fact to walk over the water toward the mountain, one would climb the saint's mountain from the north. But I knew this was an ascent from the south, for it was the way I have walked up the mountain in my real life here in the world before the world, a path that goes between fourteen simple wooden crosses painted white, representing the Stations of the Cross.

The summit attained and the glowing atmosphere having thinned over the West of Ireland so that all was in cold, subdued clarity, we could see Slea Head in its topographical drama below us, and Loop Head to the north, and even the slim silhouette of Aran far to the north in Galway Bay. We sat on the brink of a sheer drop of many hundreds of feet, looking at a still, small lake below, a lake of shadow it seemed.

I opened the book I had been carrying and discovered it was the *Periphyseon* (*Treatise on Nature*) of the ninth century Irish scholar known today as John Scotus Eriugena—John the Celt from Ireland, more of a description than a name. Now I spoke to Joel of the *quinque modi interpretationis*, the five modes of speaking of reality—or as they're also known, the five modes of being and non-being. There is nothing, for Eriugena, that cannot be said *not to be*. Even God is *nihil per excellentiam* and *nihil per infinitatem*—nothing by virtue of excellence and nothing by virtue of infinity. According to another mode, that which is actual has being but to that which is potential we attribute non-being.

The souls of the unborn we state in the mode of non-being, though this does not mean they are not real, that they are not or never were *really there*. What is non-being in one mode is being in another. The non-being of pure potential still exists, Eriugena says, *in secretissimis naturae sinibus*—in the most secret sinews of nature.

In response to all this, which I had been speaking in Eriugena's Latin, Joel with ceremonious gesture withdrew a cigarette and lit it by means of a match he caused to light itself. He dragged on the cigarette and then exhaled the fume for what seemed a freakish while, and then opened his book and read in the manner of a monk chanting a mantra or a psalm. His words were a passage from Henry David Thoreau's account of his descent of Mount Katahdin in Maine: the very passage I had assigned to my students at Saint Brendan's two months before, asking them to compare it with the Giving of the Law at Sinai. Here is Thoreau's account of his epiphany atop the mountain in the New World:

> I stand in awe of my body, this matter to which I am bound has become so strange to me. I fear not spirits, ghosts, of which I am one—*that* my body might [fear]—but I fear bodies, I tremble to meet them. What is this Titan that has possession of me? Talk of mysteries!—Think of our life in nature—daily to be shown matter, to come in contact with it—rocks, trees, wind on our cheeks! the *solid* earth! the *actual* world! the *common sense! Contact! Contact!* Who are we? *where* are we?

When Joel finished reciting these sentences, the sky in which we perched was replaced by a dense, swift influx of white cloud off the Atlantic, obfuscating like the gunpowder smoke of a battlefield, or as if the sky emerged from Joel's cigarette smoke. This new sky was terribly cold and wet and came upon us with palpable fury. We huddled in the lee of the cross at the summit, shivering inside the cloud, in its very heart. My arm went around Joel's shoulders, over the rough kashaya both present and disappearing, golden and purple, but then Joel was gone. For a moment I couldn't see my hand in front of my face. When the air cleared somewhat, I knew I was alone, and I began to stumble down the mountain, my lungs burning as if the cloud really had been smoke, and my face wet with tears, regaining one station after another on the Way of the Cross.

Rosenzweig in Pittsburgh

1

As if the dream cured me, my health improved rapidly from Christmas Day onwards. My spirits too. This may have been because other than the fluke day at the end of November, when I unearthed my abandoned dissertation, it was a long cold winter that settled over Michigan. I welcomed such a reminder that the Earth could still keep her customary seasons. Now I think that in no other time could I have conceived the work, soon to take priority, of what would eventually become the first version of these Suites—a book behind the book, as my friend Gregory would call it. A number of things had to happen first, though: the discovery of two objects, a disaster, and the revelation of two pieces of news.

No doubt subtly guided by the dream of Joel Stein in Ireland, I recalled that on the day when I looked at my forsaken work on Spenser and the *musica universalis*, my glance had happened to fall on the two objects just mentioned, neither of which I had known I still possessed. One of these was a stack of small music composition notebooks tied up by a single fraying bootstrap. The unmarked paper was yellowing, but the books were made of good thick sheets firmly bound, and I decided I would compose in them the first draft of this work, charting my remembrance of Hannah to Kew under the locusts and all the thoughts of my life shaped by Hannah's absence that arose of their own accord from that moment. When I told Kew of my intention to set down prose in old music composition notebooks, she laughed curtly and said it would be a truly American book, then, if it could pull itself up by its own bootstraps.

Perhaps my wife's response is why I hesitated to begin composing the early version of this writing. Or perhaps I was waiting for some shift to occur during the long winter doldrums of the Upper Country, some gathering of momentum and inevitability that was invisible to the superficial glance, yet undeniable, like water flowing beneath the frozen surface of a river or like our little son growing—striving very hard to walk by his first birthday in February, a goal he achieved with great success. In fact, there was plenty afoot, but it was the transition from one thing to another, the space between one of the boy's steps and another, and the moments between the moments, that seemed impossible to catch and comprehend.

This feeling of striving for comprehension, along with the dream of Joel, led me to take up some more philosophical reading again. On Christmas evening, after we had gotten our overexcited little son to bed (this was his first Christmas), I began to read through the works of the now forgotten German Jewish philosopher Max Picard. Kew had given me several of these books for Christmas. Picard lived much of his life in a Swiss valley near the Italian border, which is how he escaped being martyred by Nazis. After the Third Reich fell, Picard remained in his mountain province, preferring the place to anything more cosmopolitan, and was eventually received into the Catholic Church.

What caught me in Picard's writing was not his ideas so much as the poetic way he expressed them, so that I was able to imagine that Picard had, like Spenser, heard the *musica universalis*, and that when he looked at a tree spread out against the sky he saw more than the tree and the sky. On Christmas night, I read in his 1934 book *The Flight from God* a rapturous description of the words *Himmel* (sky or heaven) and *Baum* (tree). He gives these German words as examples of the soul of a word, as he puts it, perfectly filling out its body. He wonders if French *ciel* (which has the same double meaning as *Himmel*) and *arbre* are similar darlings of the language, as he says, and concludes that they are not. Each tongue picks its own perfections, he thinks, or like grace itself, he says, the grace of a language chooses its own resting place.

According to Picard's way of thinking, all *true* utterances, regardless of the particular language, arise from *silence*. For Picard, silence is not absence of sound or speech but something originary and real in itself, the ground and guarantee of speech, always present in speech. It wasn't until about a month after I began reading Picard, on one of the many mornings in that long cold winter when I was shoveling our driveway and sidewalk while the rest of my household slept, that I thought I understood what Picard meant. I heard the sound of my shovel scrape against the concrete, and the silence between the thrusts of the shovel. The sound was endowed with shape, it possessed contour, crescendo and sudden cessation, and there was a contour to the silence that intervened. I understood that the silence between the thrusts of my shovel was a single silence, and the sound of my shoveling was a single sound, and each implied the other, present always.

When I understood this I thought that I should write in such a way that each word comes not only from other words but also from silence. I have never written such words, I thought, standing with the shovel on my driveway in the morning redness of Michigan. But perhaps I should remember Elijah hunted in the wilderness, I thought, where he saw a storm and an earthquake and a fire, but the LORD was in none of these things, only in *kol d'mamah dakah*, the voice that is there and not there, the thin silent voice. I have been afraid to begin any kind of writing from that silence, I thought standing in my driveway, because I have been afraid that it would lead back into silence at the end.

Later that same day, while my son napped, I listened to music that, as I now thought of it in the wake of reading Picard, had been composed from silence: the Andante mistico, as the composer titled it, from Ernest Bloch's first piano quintet, from 1923, which he composed while living in Cleveland, Ohio. Bloch was a Swiss Jewish composer (the geographical and ethnic coincidence with Max Picard no doubt led me to pick out Bloch's music) who lived in America during two separate periods of his life, which fact, in the second instance, was responsible for his surviving the Nazi conquest of Europe.

Bloch spent most of the last two decades of his life on the Oregon coast composing and collecting agates from the beach, which he would polish. But the first piano quintet comes from a rather different coast and from the period of Bloch's earlier American sojourn, when for a time he was the first director of the now prestigious Cleveland Institute of Music. I've heard various accounts of the scenery or cultural spirit one is meant to imagine for the *Andante mistico*, from a nebulous essence of Judaism to visions of orgiastic yet lethargic South Seas isles (this latter supposedly closer to the composer's own yearnings as he worked on the music), but to me it has always been wintry music befitting its composition by the shores of Lake Erie.

The piano begins with the andante rhythm on a single note, the feeling of walking at a good clip with the occasional stumble or skip ahead out of eagerness, or belatedness, or flight. Over this the strings settle and build like the saturated strata of the atmosphere over the solid earth in the mythical time of creation. The music builds in longing and expectation to a first, descending climax, epic and tragic. There follows a long development of icy and crystallizing sound, now less airy, more like layer upon layer of snow falling, colder and heavier by the minute, and blowing harder and harder over the long water of Lake Erie, piling up against the buildings of the dark Rust Belt city, blocking out the lights, stretching into the countryside and covering it, peaceful accumulation but with power that grows to another climax, this time agonized and panicked, like a lover who knows this will be the final tryst.

And yet, this is only the middle of the movement. Another six or seven minutes remain, a long, hesitant, once more expectant and yearning leave-taking, something you feel is only accomplished with difficulty; tonal calm, perhaps resignation, emerges about two minutes from the end—but then the strings tremble again, still anxious, not quite ready to fall silent. At last the tapping rhythm, the essential andante, returns in the piano, but it comes and goes, less strident and sure than in the beginning, until finally it is the piano that climbs out of the musical weather, the wake of this changeful winter storm, in a soft minor scale, whether resigned or as a beleaguered triumph I have never been sure.

This, I decided, was how I must compose these Suites, each word coming not from some other word but from silence, the way each note of Bloch's music came from silence.

2

In the heart of winter, the dead season between Christmas and Lent, and just a few days after I listened to Ernest Bloch's first Piano Quintet, I delivered an unusual lecture to my students at Saint Brendan's. I was supposed to be talking about Augustine of Hippo's idea of evil as *privatio boni*—the privation or lack of good, since, as Augustine saw it, evil could be no real, substantial thing in itself, or else God would have to be said to have created evil. Instead, evil had to be an imperfection or a falling away, the mistaking of a lesser good for a greater or opting for the right thing at the wrong time, something like that.

I found myself standing before a group of a dozen seventeen-year-old Catholics and producing totally unpremeditated sentences that at first more or less had to do not with *privatio boni* but with the idea of the *coincidentia oppositorum* as it is found—so I asserted, at any rate—in various forms of Vedanta, in both Tantric and Zen Buddhism, in Taoism, in Kabbalah, in Neoplatonism (I am not sure what I meant by the term in this instance, but in light of the Irish ancestry of many of my students and thinking of the patron saint of the church where we were gathered, I mentioned the early medieval Irish philosopher Scotus Eriugena, who had been lingering in my mind since my dream of Joel in Ireland), and the coincidence or sameness of opposites is, I declared, the very life blood of German Idealism, where it becomes dialectic. To illustrate what the idea entails, I then summarized for my students Isak Dinesen's story "Babette's Feast," and quoted from the speech that General Löwenhielm gives at the eponymous feast, when he is old and in the presence, for the first time in many years, of the sisters whose love, long before, he had won but had been unable to keep, bound as the women were by the strict rules of their father's religious community:

> We tremble before making our choice in life, and after having made it again tremble in fear of having chosen wrong. But the moment comes when our eyes are opened, and we see and realize that grace is infinite. Grace demands nothing from us but that we shall await it with confidence and acknowledge it in gratitude. Grace makes no conditions and singles out none of us in particular.... See! that which we have chosen is given us, and that which we have refused is, also and at the same time, granted us. And look: Everything we have chosen has been granted to us. Aye, that which we have rejected is poured upon us abundantly. For mercy and truth have met together, and righteousness and bliss have kissed one another!

I have known these words by heart, I told my students, since New Year's Day 2003, when I was living by myself for the first time—having separated from my first wife only a month before—in a studio apartment perched on a hillside in Cincinnati. It was a gray day and damp, so that the cold seeped into my bones. I told my students that I had driven back to my apartment that morning from a friend's house (in fact it was Gregory's parents' house with the honey locusts by the driveway). I was sick with a hangover and with despair, I said, the sickness unto death. I don't know what could have happened that day, perhaps even the worst, but at a certain moment I came in from my little balcony, where I had been chain smoking, and read several stories by Isak Dinesen, including "Babette's Feast," which was contained in one of the volumes of Dinesen's work that my friend Joel Stein had recently given me.

It may not be an exaggeration, I told my students, if I said that her story (and by extension, Joel) saved my life: My apartment was on the fifth floor, and a fall from the balcony to the parking lot below would have been fatal. It is at any rate the story that led me to understand what the *coincidence of opposites* means, its bittersweet joy. And I unfolded for my students the etymology of this word *grace*—in the biblical Greek it is *charis*, which I have mentioned in this writing as rooted in joy, something directed outwardly upon the world from which it is inseparable, in thanksgiving.

But all this about the coincidence of opposites and dialectic can seem, I said to my students, like what Kierkegaard called the System, a too neat and too complete assumption of the human mind's commensurability with the divine mind or transcendent reality, an unwarranted triumph of rationality, a hubristic claim to wisdom. This would be a mistake, I told them, but it would be a valid mistake, for what we crave is that something should break in and disrupt what we think we know and think we are and demand of us what Kierkegaard called the leap into faith. Perhaps we wish to be able to name God, I told them, but not to define him. Isn't it intolerable, I asked them, that any story should end exactly the way it begins, or that the equation should come in the end to zero? There must be the new thing, for our nature—all of nature—demands it. We can endure neither a straight line nor a perfect circle, but only the spiral, which says, like the musical scale, *the same again but different*. The most important thing, I told them, is that you imitate God in this way: that you too should feel at some time that you are infinite and the world infinite around you, forever beyond you yet in your power.

In order to do this, I told them, you have to stop thinking, as most people do without knowing it, in terms of the actual, the potential, the impossible, the unthinkable. All these categories you must collapse and start again—not from nothing, but from the art of those who have gone before you and who have felt the germinal unity, the meaningful coincidence, of that which is and that which is not, and have put that feeling into whatever language and forms speak to you. So read and listen freely, look fearlessly. You cannot allow anyone to tell you that a voice is false because the philosophical convictions or moral habits (let alone the accidental traits to which we give the fallacious name *identity*) of the one it belonged to are now deemed incorrect or somehow intrinsically wrong. Virtue, I told my students, is, as you know from Shakespeare, subject to *the interpretation of the time*.

I told them, by way of example, that D.H. Lawrence did not always have the best ideas, and yet by reading Lawrence, and perhaps only by reading him, my first wife, who married me when she was scarcely older than you, I told my students, had been able to discover something that the rabbis also taught, looking to the jealous love of the Lord God for Israel, or that Catholic tradition, I said, understands in the union of Christ with his Bride, the Church: that the Shekhinah, the wandering feminine presence of God, dwells especially with the husband and the wife. The man and the woman in the garden: that is what lies at the beginning of beginnings. You will make many such vital discoveries, I told them, which may lead to action bold as love, decisive as marriage—*if* you fear no evil, for evil, as we see Augustine taught, is nothing, a kind of unreality that is nonetheless part of reality, there yet not there—a kind of idolatry, the simulacrum of essence.

Two days after I delivered this unusual lecture to my students at Saint Brendan's, word of what I had said (a very complete account, it seemed, evincing far better note-taking skills than I was accustomed to expect from my students) got to the headmaster, including the previously undisclosed information that I had been married once before. He drew me aside after my last class of the afternoon and informed me that I would not be invited to teach at Saint Brendan's again after the present term ended in the spring.

"The wide range of your learning and tastes," the headmaster said, "is compromised by a tendency to err equally widely from any firm foundation in faith. Often with converts," he said, "there is the problem of overzealous or narrow belief. With you it's different. You seem to think of yourself," he said, "as an artist primarily, which seems to mean to you a skeptic and at the same time a daydreamer, in any case not as the teacher of young men and women whose parents wish only to ground them in the basic truths and conditions of human life which the world about them is intent as it has never been before on concealing or distorting.

"Belief does not seem to be for you what it is for most people. You give the impression that your deepest belief is that nothing is as it appears, and that while one idea might be likened to another, nothing is ever proven or refuted. You are detached rather than committed— even when you speak of commitments such as marriage! Well, at the end of the day it's hard to know where you stand, because of your poetic way of thinking and putting things. But truth for you seems to be provisional; you know that a Catholic Christian believes that Truth is *incarnate*.

"We are thrown into this life of contingency, yes, but also of eternal truth, and if we do not misuse or overuse our faculties of mind, we are able to find our way. Creatures of the between, perhaps you would say, like your philosopher...."

"William Desmond," I supplied, "a Catholic."

"Yes," said the headmaster, "if he's a *practicing* Catholic, and that is just my point: practice is more important than profession of belief. We're not just floating along. Even granting a certain validity to your position, or refusal of a position, this doesn't change our circumstances.

"If the world," he said, "were what it was when I was young, or even what it was when you were young, perhaps your style of teaching would be productive, even inspiring; but the world is not the world of your youth, let alone of mine, and your style of teaching leads only to the students' confusion and their parents' dismay. There has been now one too many tangents, one too many writers we are not paying you to teach, and what I can only describe as too personal a connection with some of the students."

3

THIS WAS THE DISASTER I mentioned. You might think it more absurdity than disaster. Consider that I was informed so far in advance of my actual discharge from the homeschooling cooperative. I did not mind the early warning of my dismissal, though, and I suppose the headmaster knew and respected me well enough to know that I would not. For that matter I respected him. Probably I agreed with everything he had said to me. And yet I felt life was moving as it must, and this derailment too was part of it.

But when I got home that evening Kew was there and she immediately said she had something to tell me. I said I had something to tell her too, and regretted it right away, for I could see the fires die down in her eyes and her shoulders slumped: she perceived that my news was not good. We argued over who should go first. I could see that what Kew had to say was joyful. I eventually persuaded her to let me go first, and I told her I had more or less lost my job simply because I had been absent-minded and digressive. I trailed off and looked out the window into the cold evening.

Kew said, "You're an idiot. But at least you're still attractive, which explains why my news is that I'm pregnant—must have been our little New Year's Eve celebration."

For a while we simply embraced in silence. What else is there to do in the face of the awesomeness and the ridiculousness of human generation? It takes almost nothing—a passing enthusiasm—to bring new life into the world. And it takes courage, fullness of the heart: almost everything. But of course Kew was not going to let me off so easy.

"Let's see," she said, "you were abundantly over-qualified for a job which almost no one else wants—in fact, a job for which almost no one else would be even *minimally* qualified. It would normally take two or even three people to tutor in as many subjects as you offered. Must have required real effort to get fired from a position like that."

"Yes," I said. "Consider it an early birthday present. I spared neither pain nor expense."

She laughed, a little ruefully, and said, "At least you'll be able to find something else easily enough—if you bother looking."

She knew that I did not intend to bother. Not right away. I could do nothing else until I could write fantasy again. But what must I do before I could write fantasy again?

Kew didn't know any better than I did, but now she was in a hurry for me to figure it out so that I could make something good come of writing fantasy. It might seem that my employment mattered little, because Kew was the one with the stable income (she was to receive tenure that spring) and, most important, a job that provided good health insurance. But standing in the kitchen and listening to the sounds of our son playing while Kew prepared food for him, and staring at the notebooks and texts I had brought back from Saint Brendan's (various grammars I glance at for inspiration in lecturing, along with Kew's *Meditations for Margery Kempe*)—I knew how things really stood and I wished we were more dependent on my job: not so that its loss would mean something, but because Kew and I had never meant to be living the way we were, with her as the breadwinner.

I realize this will strike some readers as strange and disturbing, as if Kew and I were archaic figures plucked from some colorful lapsed age and deposited unregenerate in the wholesome radiation therapy-light of the present. I don't think so; I think we are as modern as anyone. But we wanted children. *As many as God will give us*—that is how she put it, seeking somehow to atone or make up for the miscarriages and to live by the idea that marriage should be *open to life*, as Catholics say. For if it is not, Kew thought, then sex is robbed of risk and poetry. She had no intention of giving up her intellectual and artistic existence and ceasing to write and publish, but she preferred not to be away from the home while our children were young. And she preferred to be around family and old friends. (By calling all this *preference*, I reveal just how modern Kew and I were; she would not deny it.)

This model of life would work out fine, Kew thought, if I would just support us by my writing, or perhaps some job my writing could win for me. So I had better figure out how to be a fantasist again, how to recapture that feeling—or whatever the hell it was—that I knew as a kid, when reading fantasy was like encountering *revelation*. For us, this was a problem of place, a problem of home. But suppose there is no home. Suppose we are always floating, like Joel said in the dream. *When there are no more stories it's time to float.*

"It's simple," she said on the evening of her birthday, a week after our son's birthday, with winter giving no sign of lifting but the thought of springtime already burgeoning: "I want to live somewhere and raise our family somewhere where I feel at home, and I don't feel at home here. It's fine to live in a provincial place if you're from that province or marry into it, but if you're not then it's awkward—like you're always complaining about our friends at church. I just want us to promise to each other that we'll make our goal moving to *somewhere home*—Cincinnati, or maybe by my cousins in Ireland."

All this, presumably, with Kew's mother—magically rehabilitated?—in tow. The unlikely prospect of expatriation aside, she was the only family of Kew's there was much chance we would live near. Her father had long been remarried to an insufferable woman and set up another family, with whom we had nothing to do, in the ugliest region of California; and her brother eked out a destitute and slovenly life in the drug-ravaged, economically eviscerated province where he and Kew had been born: we certainly would not relocate to Portsmouth even if I could make millions in royalties and movie rights from as yet totally unimagined and probably unimaginable books.

Talk about fantasy. Even as a birthday wish, *somewhere home* seemed to me sheer fantasy, to use the term in a purely pejorative way. But what I told Kew was that I agreed, and that we could think of this concerted action as a vast military campaign. "We shall give it," I said, "the code name Operation Overneath." Kew smiled. I chose *overneath* because it is heard in various parts of the Ohio Valley. I believe the word comes from the construction of bi-level bridges over the Ohio River. If one travels on such a bridge, one may be going both *over* the river and *beneath* the other stream of traffic. It may have some more bizarre origin that only a true philologist could elucidate. But also it seemed to me that *overneath* encapsulated much of what I had been trying to tell my students about *coincidentia oppositorum* and *privatio boni* on that wintry day in that church in Michigan dedicated to the saint who, if only in legend (and is anything truer than what happens in legend?), was first among the people of his faith to discover these shores of the world where somehow or other Kew and I had to make a home.

4

I HAVE SO FAR SPOKEN of one of the items I discovered by my cello, and the disaster, and one of the pieces of news. Now I must explain the other item and the other piece of news.

If I were ever to write a true sequel to *Repentance of the Gods* and create a lucrative mythopoeia, it seemed there was no way to that fantasy but through this deflected story of Hannah, this different music I felt compelled to make. I did not begin writing—or composing, as I thought of it—until it finally felt like springtime, and then it was the following movement of this Suite that I first composed.

And it took more than the weather. I went into the basement crawlspace on a day in late April, a day which should have been early spring but had relapsed to winter, shortly after an ice-storm in which we lost power for two days and many of the neighborhood trees suffered serious damage. There I retrieved the other item mentioned at the beginning of this Suite that I had noticed under my cello on the warm day at the end of November. This was (to my knowledge) the only surviving manuscript of an unpublished novel my former friend Joel Stein wrote and gave to me in March of 2003.

To this day I cannot explain why I waited so long after the fluke warm day in late autumn to read Joel's book. Even when at last the cold spell at the end of that following April mysteriously impelled me to do so, I sought to delay the experience—the memory—a moment longer, and perhaps I would never have read the novel if that very attempt to procrastinate had not fructified so unexpectedly.

This brings me to the second piece of news. In my email—just as happened with Annette's message the previous October—a message had arrived to distract. The email in question was from Severine, and she was writing to tell me that she was pregnant. The timing was less than a month behind Kew's pregnancy, it seemed. The news surprised me, for Severine appeared content to begin her family in Hawaii, far from any of her relations or indeed anyone she grew up with or knew in her youth.

Now, at the time I opened this email, I was thinking that however it would end up, Severine was not likely to read the piece of writing that I now knew would take shape in the music composition note-books. Severine, who was once a great reader and who loved the prose of James Joyce and D.H. Lawrence when she was eighteen, no longer read much. Not only did she desire to never live again in any place where she would hear the word *overneath*, but she would prefer not to read a book in which that sort of word appeared. Severine preferred bodily exercise for recreation, and on the rare occasions when she read literature she would only read a work that she could be sure was what she would call fiction. The more purely fictional or even fantastical a piece of writing, the more likely it would be to distract Severine from the rigors of her chosen profession. In fact, by this time she read almost exclusively (when she read at all) the kind of genre fantasy that Kew was certain I could find financial success writing. Severine did not seek edification from her reading, nor a return to a world she once knew, but escape only. But for some reason she didn't say, Severine hoped, while she was pregnant, to resurrect her reading life and make it again something you and your ilk, she wrote to me, would find respectable.

So I realized Severine could end up reading these Suites after all, and this, along with unearthing Joel's manuscript, is what finally allowed me to begin composing them. For I remembered something Severine said to Joel in a diner called Ritter's in Pittsburgh in September of 2002, at about two o'clock in the morning. What Joel and Severine said was something that seemed relevant to the questions that had preoccupied me all winter in Michigan and may have had some bearing on the valence of a word like *overneath* and the *coincidentia oppositorum*.

Joel had asked Severine and me whether we thought that only what is is, or whether what is not also somehow is. Severine had answered that she didn't know, but she thought that whatever has been, is always. Shortly after that September, once we had filed for divorce and I had moved out of the apartment we shared and into the efficiency where I would soon fall into despair and read "Babette's Feast," Severine began signing her emails to me with the valediction *Always*. This has been her style of valediction ever since, and it is how she signed the email in which she announced that she was pregnant and was looking for recommendations to get her reading again.

When I had remembered these things about Severine, I also remembered something I said to her long ago in a café in Cincinnati, across from the Conservatory, a café called Baba Budan's, which no longer exists. I said, "You know that someday I'll write all this." Severine said that when I did finally sit down to write it I should begin the story, as she called it, in a café. "People think about important things in cafes," she said, perhaps thinking of the café in a neighborhood called Mount Lookout where I had taken Severine on the morning of the day, not long before, when I proposed marriage to her.

When Severine and I exchanged these words in Baba Budan's, our mutual understanding of the term *café* did not include places like the one in Mount Adams where I had seen Hannah's mother on a day in the spring of 2001, or any such place as goes by the name of café now. We understood by the term a place like the one where we were (or where I would hang out with Joel Stein), a dingy and poorly maintained place where one was apt to encounter curious people and to have unexpected conversations at odd hours, because no one yet owned portable electronic devices with screens to beguile them and conceal from them the human faces they might otherwise meet. And when I had remembered these words Severine and I exchanged, I decided that of all the cafés I have known, it was a certain café (which no longer exists) in Pittsburgh that I would single out to bestow with a special grace in these Suites.

5

THERE IS A LONG HALLWAY in a house. The walls of the house are brick, outside and in, and the hallway is dark. Yes, very dark, because the bricks are not the cream of Milwaukee brick or the crimson of Cincinnati brick or even the ruddy brick of Chicago. The house is in Pittsburgh and the bricks are dark as dried blood. The ceiling is low and the walls are close in the part of the hallway where I have just entered it, toward the back of the house, where the hallway terminates (or originates) at the entrance to the master bedroom and, at a slightly higher level accessed by three stairs leading to a very short passage, two other bedrooms and a bathroom. I have come out of one of these bedrooms.

In about the middle of its course the hallway down which I walk becomes wider and the ceiling higher, no longer perpetually darkened but illuminated on this day by a low gray sky that refracts a chilly light through the house's rectangular clerestory windows. At this juncture in the hallway where one passes from dark to light (or from light to dark) there is a vestibule off to one side, which gives onto a bathroom and a fourth bedroom. The house belongs to my father's parents. The bedroom just mentioned was used for some time by my father's paternal grandfather Meir, until he died in 1981 (a month before I was born), and then by my father's maternal grandmother Rokhl, until she died in 1991. (In fact she died on Christmas night, having lived just long enough to see the collapse of the Soviet Union: one of the last events she witnessed in this life, on a tv in that bedroom, was

Mikhail Gorbachev's resignation and the lowering of the Soviet flag from the Kremlin for the last time. According to my father she then spoke something in Yiddish he couldn't quite understand, and died.) But the time I am writing about is the noon hour of Thanksgiving in the year 2000, and the fourth bedroom is occupied by Severine.

I am walking down the hallway having put aside my studies. A textbook on Baroque music lies open, and next to it a composition notebook (the same kind in which I first drafted these Suites), on which I have been sketching music for keyboard that I would not myself be able to play very well. What is evident to me now is that the music I was in the midst of setting down could easily have been made into a duet for violin and cello. But at the time of which I am writing my mind was capable only of abstraction and I could not imagine real players making real music from the notes that I wrote down, and so I was unable to compose music for Severine and me to play together nor indeed for anyone to play.

At the moment I am writing of, I am driven by hunger to go to the kitchen, where my father's sister and my mother are preparing the large meal. I have decided to purloin several small pastries commonly available in Pittsburgh and known as *thumbprints* for the indentation made by the thumb in the small round dough and filled with frosting. The hallway is carpeted, so I make no noise as I go. But the hallway is not silent.

Shortly after I begin walking down the hallway, my progress is arrested by the sight of my grandparents in the vestibule adjoining Severine's room. They are very still, hunched and tilting forward so that my grandfather Isaac can press his right ear and my grandmother Miriam her left ear to the door behind which Severine is playing her violin. I am able to make out that Severine is playing the Sarabande from Bach's first Partita for Solo Violin. My grandparents are eighty-five years old at this time and hard of hearing, yet it seems to me that this is not the only reason they have drawn as close as they can get to Severine's music without disturbing her. (She is in her senior year of high school, preparing—despite her stated intention to remain by me in Cincinnati—for auditions at several conservatories and therefore nervous. She will gain admittance anywhere she applies, but neither

her teacher nor I can convince her of this and she is always anxious and insists on practicing even throughout most of Thanksgiving Day.) My grandparents have never before heard Severine play. They met her for the first time the previous night, when we arrived from Cincinnati. I say nothing as I walk past them.

As I go by, a remarkable event occurs in my mind. It is as if, hearing her music, I am able for one or two seconds to see Severine. Not only do I see her through the door and the dark brick wall, as it were, but at the same time, or right afterwards, I see her from outside the house. One wall of the bedroom where Severine is staying communicates with a small greenhouse, which can also be entered from the yard. The greenhouse contains various cultivars of geranium, which my grandmother has kept there since her mother Rokhl spent her final years in the bedroom that Severine is now using. As I am passing my grandparents listening to Severine—as I move from the dark and narrow part of the hallway into the broad and luminous part—I seem to see Severine from outside the house, as though I were looking in through the greenhouse full of red geraniums. I see Severine wearing a carnelian sweater and playing her fox red violin.

This warm image has the feel of reality or truth, something that I see with my bodily eyes. It has that feeling when it appears to me in the hallway of my grandparents' house, as I recall it in a basement in Michigan in the spring of 2018, and even now as I write. At the time when I am walking down the hallway of my grandparents' house in Pittsburgh to fetch some thumbprints on Thanksgiving in the year 2000, I have never seen Severine practicing music in the geranium room, as we called it, either from outside the house or from within.

Of the uncounted memories, the horde of images of the past that seem to make up the bedrock of my mind, only this one seems to consist of both real and unreal elements. Or, to put it another way, the image is composed of two perspectives—perhaps something like contrapuntal music. A perspective implies one who perceives. So these two perspectives, if they are both mine, must be mutually exclusive, for I cannot be in two places at once. One of these perspectives was real, the perspective from where I actually stood; the other is merely realistic, in the sense that if I had walked outside to see Severine playing the Sarabande from the first Partita that Bach wrote for solo violin, what I would have seen would have accorded with the image that presented itself to my mind.

But surely this is not taking the matter far enough. In fact *both* images, both perspectives were purely potential—or you could say fantasy. I did not in fact see Severine at all. If the door had been open and my grandparents not in the way, or if I had X-ray vision and could look through a brick wall, then the image of Severine as seen from the hallway would also have been realistic. I am now in the situation of calling two totally fantastical or potential scenarios realistic. What kind of sense can this make?

I have come to see this compound image, this two-part fantasy, as a glimpse of the *unreality* that exists at the heart of reality: the world behind the world. And it is important that one part of the image was the perspective that would have been mine in the world of actuality had not the wall or my grandparents intervened. I have come to think that fantastical images of this kind—rooted in and departing from a real position—compose the bedrock of my mind.

If Joel were to read this piece of writing, he might invoke the categories of *actuality* and *potentiality*. He would describe this pair as one of the polarities of being: everything that can be said to exist falls under one of these categories, potentiality or actuality. Potentiality is not non-being, since non-being is not a category. Fiction, Joel would likely say, enjoys the kind of being called potentiality, and he would add that traditionally potentiality has been understood as the inferior of the two kinds of being. Perhaps he would add that on Thanksgiving Day in Pittsburgh, in the year 2000, I beheld a vision of Severine transfigured into fiction—indeed, a doubled vision. Nor could it have been otherwise: the world of actuality is the world of the singular; the world of potentiality is the world of the many, the infinitely receding horizon.

When I wrote the phrase *bedrock of my mind,* I made use of a metaphor so common as almost to have become what is known as a dead metaphor. However, I used this particular expression in a personal or, you could say, a living way. For a long time I've thought of my mind as a landscape. Contrary to the headmaster's complaint, and no matter where I really am in the wide world, some part of me stands in a very certain place: a place of four seasons, where hardwood trees flourish upon limestone and clay in a terrain described by the incontrovertible logic of water running in ever greater courses to one almighty river. Since I was a child I have wondered that the waters of this place, which is the place of my mind as well as the place where I was raised in the wide world, can flow only ever with one tendency, whereas a human person has the potential to go against the intention of the waters. As a child, I wondered only at the flow of waters in the wide world. But in the springtime of 2018, sitting in a basement in Michigan and surrounded by large-scale topographical maps of the terrain in the wide world where I was raised, I wondered at the mind's capacity to go against the tendency of its own waters.

The bedrock of the middle and upper parts of the Ohio Valley consists in many places of limestone or other rock that contain many fossils. As a boy I spent a lot of time wandering our local creeks with Gregory and examining the fossils exposed there in the beds. We collected the more elaborate and arcane specimens that caught our eye, if we could carry away the rocks that housed them. Sometimes we would chip away at a piece of limestone rubble that was too large for us to carry, so that we could take the part containing the fossil home. And sometimes this effort ended in our destroying the fossil.

I would notice, when we visited my father's parents in Pittsburgh, the many strata of such rock visible in the cutaways made by the interstate. I came to think of the ground I habitually stood and walked and ran upon as containing innumerable images, frozen memories in the mind of the Earth of her ancient days. This conception of the Earth as a bedrock of memory persisted and grew until now it figured my own mind. When I read in *Die unendliche Geschichte* of Bastian *unearthing* the frail and glassy image that would allow him to return to the world of what was, for him, actuality (as Joel Stein would explain it)—the world of Bastian's father, and his dead mother—I was unnerved in the way that Bastian was unnerved—perhaps horrified—while reading a book that seemed to have been written about him.

When I think of how, on a certain cold and gray day in Pittsburgh at the turn of the century I saw Severine practicing and at the same time I did not see her, and when I think of how writers of various kinds have struggled to understand and say something about what is not, or what is not there, or what is no longer, I also think of a poem by Friedrich Hölderlin that I read closely on the occasion of my last visit to Pittsburgh before I remembered Hannah under the locusts and began composing these Suites, in November of 2015—almost exactly fifteen years after Severine played Bach's first Partita for Solo Violin in my grandparents' house and my grandparents leaned into the door to listen and closed their eyes and trembled with great age and also with a feeling that I cannot name and perhaps do not know.

The occasion of this last trip to Pittsburgh was the wedding of one of Kew's friends from college. I had not at that time been to the city for over ten years. Kew had suffered her first miscarriage six months previously. To cope with this lingering sorrow, I had decided to translate some poetry, and Hölderlin was my choice. During the time Kew drove on the way to Pittsburgh from Chicago, I read Hölderlin's poem "Heidelberg" aloud (Kew understands spoken German much better than spoken French). I had been struggling to translate this poem to my satisfaction. I explained the problem to Kew, and she guessed that while I grasped the emotion that the poet had embodied in the poem and recognized it as one that I too had felt, the emotion had become dead to me, she said, a sort of fossilized artifact.

The difficulty persisted until the day after the wedding, when we were at our leisure to roam Pittsburgh for a time before heading back to Chicago. I had decided to show Kew a few of the sights that had once been dear and familiar to me. For breakfast I took Kew to a café called Beehive on Carson Street, the main drag in a neighborhood called the South Side Flats. This was one of two cafes in Pittsburgh where, between the mid-1990s and 2004, I habitually loitered and drank coffee and smoked and talked with my friend Joel Stein—the other being Ritter's on Baum Boulevard, already mentioned. Kew and I had had a wet and unusually warm journey to Pittsburgh, but the murk blew away during the wedding and was replaced by cooler, dry air and stark sunlight that pierced the city down to the last turning oak leaf and blown detritus.

When we had finished breakfast in one of the cozy alcoves girded by bay windows and protruding into Carson Street from the Beehive (the very table where Severine had once told Joel Stein: "You'll never be a writer: you like the idea of writing more than writing"), I walked us out over the nearby Tenth Street Bridge. On the other side, the right bank of the Monongahela, Duquesne University sits up on the hill, but I just wanted the perspective from the middle of the bridge, one of the most glorious superfluvial views in the city. And there in the crystalline day, poised over the water that would reach the City of Seven Hills after flowing four hundred-fifty curving miles, I understood Hölderlin's poem as another instance of the kind of beguiling fantasy I had had in my grandparents' home on Thanksgiving Day in 2000, or for that matter the vertiginous fantasy of Cincinnati that I saw from the steps below the Immaculata with Gregory on Good Friday 1989. In particular, I understood the third verse of the German poem, for I could now see why the poet had chosen the word *schien* (past tense of *scheinen*), that the pathos of the poem which had previously been dead to me was ensconced in this one common word.

The poet is speaking, in the third stanza, of a time he walked over a bridge in Heidelberg, which city he has called *ländlichschönste* of all the cities known to him—*fullest with a country beauty*, as I would go on to translate it. In the third stanza the poet says he was transfixed on the bridge, as if by gods. Hölderlin is always talking about the gods. They are, for him, the sense of the realness of reality, guarantors of the depths and richness of being, which is something from which he most often feels himself exiled. This is a difficult idea, but even more difficult for me was the second part of the third stanza.

> *Und herein in die Berge*
> *Mir die reizende Ferne schien.*

What makes the sense so hard to grasp, I realized standing on the Tenth Street Bridge, is that *scheinen* means both to shine and to appear or to seem. The word is, in fact, very like the Greek root of *fantasy*, with its paradoxical double sense of radiance and illusion. What the poet says in these lines could be described as a fusion of immanence and transcendence. Something from afar comes innermost to the poet, and he, in turn, is carried, without leaving the spot, beyond his ken.

Right here, to me—so it seemed—
into the hills the distance shone.

We were looking downstream. The spires of downtown loomed ahead and to our right. To our left the golden dome of Saint John the Baptist Ukrainian Catholic Church glared from the level of Carson Street, the South Side Slopes rising behind it. I picked out for Kew, from the palimpsest of spans and pylons, the Liberty Bridge, the Panhandle Bridge, the Smithfield Street Bridge and, farthest among those we could see, the Fort Pitt Bridge. I explained what I had realized to Kew and she said, "I don't think we ever get free of it, that double fantasy."

6

KEW MAY HAVE BEEN RIGHT—for herself and for me. But some people, at any rate, do get free of fantasy (perhaps only to trade it for another), and here follows the story of one of them.

My former friend Joel Stein, in the days when he still hoped to become a published novelist, was of the opinion that the opening sentence of a novel was of utmost importance. When in the early spring of 2018 I re-read the only surviving manuscript of Joel's novel, I met again the opening sentence as one rediscovers the long-lost photo of a first love, remembering the high esteem in which I once held it and indeed all the skill Joel displayed in the only novel he wrote. Here is the opening sentence of Joel's novel, which he titled *Into Life*:

> *I could light a cigarette with a match in a hurricane.*

This is a sentence that I heard Joel utter on several occasions, most memorably while he lit a cigarette with a match on a cool blustery Friday evening of light rain in September of the year 2000, outside a bar on the edge of East Liberty called Kelly's, which is another of the places in Pittsburgh where I spent a lot of time with Joel. With me and Joel, on this first occasion when I heard him claim that he could light a cigarette with a match in a hurricane, was a woman named Alison, who, like Joel, lived in East Liberty, which at that time was not a trendy or safe neighborhood. I was a month shy of my nineteenth birthday, Joel was about to turn twenty-four, Alison was twenty-seven. Joel had recently finished a Master of Arts in philosophy at Pitt, where he had met Alison through her younger sister, one of his colleagues in the graduate program.

Joel was in love with Alison, but in September of 2000 he had not yet admitted it to anyone, including himself. He was at a loss what to do with his life—his Master of Arts was in fact an unfinished PhD; what he really wanted to do was to make it as a writer. He was working in an underpaid capacity for an insurance company, and Alison worked in the meat department of a Giant Eagle. Severine, to whom I had just become engaged, was not present, as the high school year had already begun, but my first year at the conservatory would not begin for another week.

Joel's novel is about suicide. As a student of philosophy, Joel had been devoted to more existentialist and poetic modes of thought, including the work of Camus, philosophy that could express itself best through other genres, like fiction. Like Camus, he took the question of suicide seriously. Was life worth living? Joel was not entirely convinced that it was, though you might not suspect this since he was, as I wrote in the previous Suite, a gregarious and pleasant guy.

What is *really* there? This was Joel's favorite koan, and to any answer or none his response would be to poke you in the chest and say nothing, or else to grab your hand and shake it wildly with both of his and shout, "Nice to meet you! Nice to meet you!" Joel loved to go on like this to me and Alison—and Severine when she could come with me to Pittsburgh. Perhaps, contradicting his own existentialist aspirations, he spoke more than he wrote and lived and that was his problem. Then again, if his speech was living, perhaps Joel lived too much to devote himself to writing as much as the art required. Severine turned out to be right when she said that he wouldn't amount to a writer. Severine often turns out to be right when she makes her oracular and aphoristic pronouncements, though it's not clear that the reason she supplied for Joel's renunciation of literary ambition—infatuation with idea over the real thing, with talking rather than doing—was the correct one. In any case, Joel did write the one novel, and he wrote it to discover if life as it really was, and not as some story about itself, was worth living.

The narrator of Joel's novel, who bears the same name as Joel, begins his story having decided that he will kill himself, but he does not have the courage to do so. He therefore places himself in dangerous situations, hoping that he will be killed. The novel opens in the liquor store where the narrator works. The store is robbed by an armed man, whom the narrator antagonizes in the hope that the robber will shoot him. Unfortunately, the narrator's caustic wit and preternatural psychological insight instead reduce the robber to a state of horror, despair, and regret, and the man leaves without even robbing the store, only to be promptly arrested and brutalized by the police. Other incidents of mixed blessing and catastrophe like this unfold, and the narrator seems to be miraculously unlucky in his attempts to get himself killed.

Instead, he falls in love with a woman named Alison, who is a few years older than him. Alison works in the meat department of a Giant Eagle and feels she has somehow failed at life. She is convinced she has psychological problems and she undergoes therapy (in those days a rarer thing), but she is full of zest for life all the same. The contrast between Alison and the narrator, who appears to be quite terrifyingly sane but has lost the will to live, is obvious. Alison is fond of the narrator, but any possible romance with him is forestalled when she meets and becomes enamored of his younger friend, a passionate but also excessively intellectual classical musician to whom Joel gave the name McPhail—which is, as I've said, not only my mother's maiden name, my middle name and the name I publish under, but also the name by which I've been known by my close friends, including Joel, since I was thirteen.

Gradually the tenor of Joel's novel shifts. The tragicomic beginning in which the narrator is trying to get himself killed by various ridiculous means gives way to a story of failed love between the characters. The young friend, McPhail, has a young wife, Christine, who is also a classical musician. When these two younger friends enter the story (they are about eighteen or nineteen and the narrator is twenty-three), they appear to be happy together. But McPhail soon quits music to fashion himself into a writer. His wife is outraged by this decision, instinctively recognizing in it not some utilitarian choice or act of self-fulfillment, but denial of, and willful deafness to, the profoundest bond she had shared with McPhail. And yet her reaction is to quit music as well; however, unlike McPhail, she is aimless without the music.

It is through watching this young couple over the course of two years that the narrator learns to feel something strongly again. He wishes happiness for his friend McPhail and is disturbed first by his friend's renunciation of music and the damage this causes his relationship with Christine. Gradually, new pathos emerges as McPhail and Alison are more irresistibly drawn to each other. The narrator's feelings grow stronger and more conflicted, as he seeks to safeguard his friend's happiness and marriage, but also begins at the same time to resent that his younger friend, who already seems to have a full love life, is obtruding between the narrator and his desire, namely Alison. He is confused by the fact that Alison, nine years older than McPhail, would be so attracted to the younger man.

At last there is a second shift in Joel's novel. McPhail and Christine's marriage collapses shortly after an incident late one night when Christine discovers McPhail and Alison having sex after everyone else in the narrator's apartment—there had been a party for the narrator's birthday—has fallen asleep. This infidelity is not presented as the immediate cause of the breakup of the marriage, but it seems to mark its doom and to provide a technical excuse for its ending. McPhail and Christine dissolve their vows two months later, on a cold blowing rainy day in November. Outside the courthouse where they file for divorce, the narrator meets them and repeats his opening line about being able to light a cigarette in a hurricane with a match.

The narrator is at this point in a much darker place than where he began his story. He has watched his young friend ruin his marriage, and concomitantly the narrator has failed in his own romantic venture. The world is now for him a flat and barren place, and he has arrived at the point where he might finally take his own life directly. But Christine appears to be almost relieved by how things have worked out, for she senses that some illusion has been dispelled. On the steps of the courthouse where the narrator has lit his cigarette against all meteorological odds, she suggests that the three of them go to a used bookstore before their usual destination, the Beehive Café on Carson Street.

In the used bookstore, the narrator of Joel's novel finds a work of philosophy he had never heard of, *The Star of Redemption* by Franz Rosenzweig. The owner of the bookstore sees the narrator thumbing through this book and comes over to the narrator. The owner starts up a conversation, in the course of which he tells the story of how he went from being a die-hard atheist foiled in love to reverting to his Orthodox Jewish heritage, marrying, and having children while opening the kind of bookstore where he might be able to sell the masterwork of the great Jewish philosopher Franz Rosenzweig to *the right man*, as he says. It becomes apparent to the owner that the narrator is the right man when the narrator shares a version of his own story.

Joel returns to his flat in East Liberty and draws a bath. He sets a razor on one side of the tub and *The Star of Redemption* on the other, and lights what he thinks will be his last cigarette. (This choreography seemed melodramatic to me, I must admit, when I re-read the manuscript in the basement in Michigan; I much preferred the scene in the bookstore, where Joel thinks, *Why shouldn't a dying Jew spend fifty bucks on a book?*) He then picks up the book and begins reading. After a few minutes, without pausing from his reading, he tosses the cigarette in the bath and gets out and dresses. He reads all through the night and through the next day until he has finished *The Star of Redemption* in the same bar in East Liberty where he has written most of the novel. Needless to say, Rosenzweig's *new thinking*, as the philosopher called it, convinces the narrator that life is worth living.

In order to live, however, he decides he must give up his former passions, must renounce his love for Alison and his desire to make great literary art. For this narrator-Joel has come to agree with what Rosenzweig says about art, and he realizes that if the book he has been writing and we have been reading is his idea of art then he is not an artist, for art, he now perceives, must be neither the representation nor the pretense of actuality. He resolves instead on repentance and the rediscovery of his Jewish heritage—*that*, he declares is actual, *that* is really there—as Rosenzweig did. He will become just in the eyes of G-d and return to his family in his native Minneapolis. He will find *the right woman,* as he says, *and plant a garden, as it was in the beginning that we tell stories about because we do not remember.* These are the last words of Joel's unpublished manuscript.

Joel was in no particular hurry to give me his manuscript. I just happened to be in Pittsburgh right after he finished it. I had gone there then, in March of 2003 (five months after my divorce with Severine), to visit my grandfather Isaac for his eighty-eighth birthday. I thought it would be the last time I would see him alive, and so it proved to be.

In Pittsburgh I met my father coming from the East Coast, where my parents had recently returned, leaving me to my studies and my divorce in Cincinnati. I did not meet my father at the house of blood-red brick where Severine played the Sarabande from Bach's first Partita for Solo Violin. For the last year of their lives my father's parents lived in a so-called assisted living home, Schenley Gardens, perched halfway up the eastern face of the long hill in the center of Pittsburgh that is like the broad spine of the triangular zone between the Allegheny and Monongahela Rivers where they flow together to make the Ohio. From my grandfather's room we could look out over Baum Boulevard running east through the lower and relatively flat land that contains Bloomfield and Shadyside, out to East Liberty, where I first heard Joel Stein claim that he could light a cigarette in a hurricane with a match, and where I first met Alison.

My father's parents never knew that Severine and I divorced. As I have already reported, Severine and I filed for divorce on the twelfth of November 2002. A month later Miriam, my father's mother, died. She was eighty-seven years old, but her death was unexpected and sudden, because she had seemed in excellent health for her age and everyone thought she might see a hundred. I had not told her about the decision to divorce. Severine and I had last visited my grandparents in September of that year, and while blood may have boiled in the night in East Liberty at Joel Stein's birthday party, by day in Schenley Gardens Severine and I were as we had always been together. Contrapuntal. It was not a show, not mere appearance or pretense. We were together and we were not together; people saw in us what they wanted or expected to see. But time was moving differently, attenuated and compactified, as the physicists say of higher dimensions, there were

not days and nights like there are for me now, but seasons in an hour
and lifetimes in a drink, and things could happen precipitously.

My grandfather also did not know I had divorced. He suffered
from Alzheimer's and dementia in the last years of his life. Once his
wife Miriam was gone, he could not long endure. That following
March, when my father and I visited him, my grandfather Isaac began
starving himself. In the high room in Schenley Gardens, looking over
the city still barely brushed with pale green, toward Kelly's where I
would meet Alison and Joel later that night, I sat by my grandfather's
side. He looked into my eyes and it was like a newborn baby's gaze,
as if he saw and he did not see. Then this old man, who had retreated
into near-total silence in these last days, began repeating urgently to
his son, the only person left whom he recognized: "Who is this man
by my side? Who is this man by my side? Who is this man by my side?"

When I had recalled, in the basement in Michigan, these words
by my grandfather, which were the last words I would ever hear him
speak, I remembered that I had in my possession a patchy memoir
of his time in France in the Second World War, and I dug around in
our unpacked boxes of junk until I found it. The memoir contains
interesting episodes. At one point he describes almost being killed by
a sniper high up in Chartres Cathedral, and how long it took to *remove*
the man, as he puts it. There's a strangely poignant passage about a
nurse in Paris that he slept with one night, possibly the first time in his
life he used a condom. Amusing and interesting as much of it is, as I
was reading it none of my grandfather's memoir gleamed with meaningfulness, none of it seemed to *exist* in the philosophical sense that
Joel Stein would have recognized, the etymological sense of *to stand
out* from the background radiation of reality, of nothingness—except
one passage at the end. The story caught my attention because it suggested to me why on Thanksgiving Day 2000 my grandfather, at least,
might have been so captivated by Severine's playing a form of music
originally intended for stately dancing.

My grandfather described a stretch of the winter of 1944-1945,
which he spent in Brittany. He was entranced by the weather, an otherworldly misty brightness day after day, and by a young woman named
Joséphine, daughter of the local tavern-keeper. By my grandfather's

description of Joséphine, she was like Severine in appearance, that dark kind of Celt rather than the flaming-hair kind that Kew is. The Nazis had taken Joséphine's husband two years before, and she did not know if he was still alive. Her mother, the tavern-keeper, saw her daughter grow sadder each day and thought some civilized male company would improve her spirits. The GIs wouldn't do, so she asked my grandfather, an officer, to befriend Joséphine.

This is the episode where my grandfather's memoir breaks off. I don't know if he spent more than one afternoon with Joséphine. On the day he records, the Jewish-American captain and the young Breton woman go for a walk by the ragged seashore as the bright mist that fascinated my grandfather blows in from the sea. There is something of a language barrier between them, but also natural friendship and camaraderie. She invites him into her home, and this is how my grandfather ends his account of his time in Europe as a soldier:

> There was bread, cheese, liver pâté, ersatz coffee. We hardly spoke while we ate, but she seemed happy, almost elated. Joséphine said I was the first American she had seen that she wanted to be friendly with. I blushed and looked away, and that's when I noticed an old phonograph in the room and asked her if it worked. You had to crank it, she said. She had only a few old records, the Bach Partitas for violin, of all things. So after lunch we carried the dishes into the kitchen and moved the coffee table aside, I cranked the phonograph and we danced!

7

PITTSBURGH, LAYER UPON LAYER and fold within fold, must be one of the most confusing cities in the country to drive. The City of Three Rivers is far worse in this respect even than the City of Seven Hills. On that clear autumn day in 2015, I decided, while standing on the 10th Street Bridge, that on our way out of town I wanted to give Kew a tour of the parts of the city that had once been most dear to me: and I required no map, no navigational aid or forethought, as if I had been planning our devious route all along.

When I was a boy, my father gave me large-scale maps of Pittsburgh: the same kind of USGS topographical maps of Allegheny County as I had of southwestern Ohio and northern Kentucky tacked up all around my desk in the basement in Michigan. I pored over those maps of Pittsburgh as I did over the maps of Cincinnati and memorized them: not just the names of the roads and the places they ran between, but also the unique way they wind over the undulating land, so that I could know where I was by dint of the curve of pavement and vista. As soon as I was old enough to drive, my parents would turn me loose, on our visits to Pittsburgh, in my grandparents' archaic Cadillac if I wanted to use it, and in a mood compounded of melancholy and lonely excitement I would drive around the city for the sheer pleasure of knowing—I could almost say caressing—its spatial mystery and complexity.

I have never understood or been at ease in windswept Cartesian places, and like I say, my inescapable mental landscape is a dendritic terrain of limestone. By the time I had begun composing these Suites I had come to think my heart was wholly committed to the grade of the earth or concrete over which I moved, mixed up with the vibrations and viscosity of the air I breathed. By that springtime, when I had re-read Joel's manuscript and revisited my memories of my father's ancestral city, I could not, despite the metaphysical commitments Kew and I espoused, get beyond that earthy sense, unless it was to memory and in that way to the world behind the world—but that world seemed to be made of the same stuff as the one where you taste the bitter cigarette and see light glance on flowing water or in grief-widened eyes.

The last stop Kew and I made on that autumn day in 2015, before driving back to Chicago, was a place in the northern suburbs called Adath Jeshurun. This is the cemetery where my paternal grandparents and two of my great-grandparents are interred. While we drove through Pittsburgh and its environs, I saw the oaks coming to the climax of their autumn beauty, copper and a cold hard red. But there are also many evergreens in Pittsburgh. When we came to Adath Jeshurun in an out-of-the-way corner of the northern suburbs, we parked in the small gravel lot and looked around to woods on two sides of the cemetery, colored in places by the dark blue-green of firs and pines and somber groves of hemlock, and elsewhere by a dull oaken flame. Though it had been more than a decade since I had visited the graves of my family, I remembered precisely where they were in the lower and older part of the cemetery.

As I led us there, Kew asked what the name of the place meant, and I told her it was something like *congregation of the righteous*, which is another biblical name for Israel, the Jewish people. It was an Orthodox congregation that established the cemetery, but the synagogue is no longer in existence. (The synagogue, when it did exist, was less than a mile from Kelly's bar in East Liberty, where I met Alison and Joel Stein uttered the first line of his novel, and Kew and I drove by the building on our way out of town: we saw that it had become a church; but today, I believe, it is abandoned.) Adath Jeshurun was the first Jewish cemetery Kew had visited. She remarked on the uniformity and neatness of the graves, the similar sizes of the headstones amid their beds of gravel. I told her this was typical, at least now and in this country as far as I had seen.

"But I don't really know anything about this place," I said. "I mean this is something that is in me, that is somehow supposed to make me who I am, but I don't know it, it's not real for me. My grandparents renounced their heritage as Jews. Anyway, it wasn't a meaningful part of their lives as far as I could see, and it wasn't for my father either. I think Isaac and Miriam were glad to lose themselves in postwar middle-class American culture; I think it was a kind of deliverance for them."

My father was never bothered by the renunciation of his heritage, and maybe that's how it had to be for his generation. Now you get people who will tell you that the lure of American prosperity and assimilation did what the Shoah and pogroms and millennia of Christian anti-Judaizing and its later racialized form, anti-Semitism, could never do; you get people like my former friend Joel Stein, I thought, who had to write a novel to find out if life is worth living, and the novel taught him that life is worth living and novels are not worth writing unless, as Franz Rosenzweig says of all true poetry, they *disclose the way into life*. That is what I was thinking about, looking at the graves of my ancestors, that Joel Stein had to go back to Minneapolis and forget about Alison and his friend who had betrayed him, and seek after his Jewish origin and strive to make himself just in the eyes of God.

"But you do know about this," Kew said.

"Yes," I said, "I know a little *about* it, but that's not the same as just knowing it."

"I think you *know* it," she said. "What does the Hebrew say?"

"Those are their Jewish names—their true names. My grandfather is Isaac son of Meir. And there next to him is Meir, son of Samuel, whose remains are in the Ukraine, though he would have known it as Galicia."

When I said this, I thought of something the Jewish writer Joseph Roth said in one of the many books he wrote before drinking himself to death (luckily perhaps) in Paris in the months before the Second World War began. Roth was born, like my father's forebears, in a province, Galicia, which no longer exists. He was talking, in this book that I remembered, about the Jews of Eastern Europe:

> For Jews, their names have no value because they are not their names. Jews have no names. They have compulsory aliases. Their true name is the one by which they are summoned to the Torah on the Sabbath and on holy days.... Their family names are pseudonyms foisted upon them.

And what did Franz Rosenzweig have to say about the proper name? Rosenzweig came from a family of assimilated German Jews. He very nearly converted to Christianity, but at the last minute, in the wake of revelation he experienced during a Yom Kippur service, he changed his mind and devoted the remainder of his life (which a rare and painful disease ended just short of his forty-fourth birthday) to recovering and deepening his Jewish heritage and faith—though he came to see this task as impossible, or infinite (*unendliche* you could say), in part because he would never, he felt, sufficiently internalize Hebrew, the sacred language.

Not long after that epiphany Rosenzweig fell in love with Margrit Huessy, the wife of a good friend, Eugen Rosenstock, a Jew who *did* convert to Christianity. Rosenstock, it seems, more or less condoned his wife's relations with his friend, though the woman Rosenzweig would eventually marry, Edith, did not. Over the course of about five years, Franz Rosenzweig wrote over a thousand letters to Margrit—he even wrote them during his own honeymoon—and from these letters, only made available to the public shortly before I revisited all these memories of Pittsburgh, we know that his love for her was the other major driving force, besides the return to his Jewish heritage, behind the supremely charged and lyrical and convoluted *Star of Redemption*. When my former friend Joel Stein read Rosenzweig's book, he knew about Rosenzweig's conversion experience from talking to the owner of the bookstore, who would appear in Joel's novel. But Joel didn't know about Rosenzweig's romance with Margrit. Yet that passion is woven into every sentence of the *Star* and without it maybe the book would not have gone on to save at least one human life—a fictional human life, perhaps.

So, what did the narrator of Joel Stein's novel read about his name—which was the same as Joel's—in *The Star of Redemption,* in the hours when he was deciding not to kill himself? He would have read that the proper name is what makes the world a true world, not a creation only but something revealed and redeemed. For the name is revelation. The bookshelf behind my desk in the basement in Michigan contained many works of Jewish and Christian philosophy and theology, and in the center of the middle shelf was my English-language copy of *The Star of Redemption,* translated by William Hallo: a dark blue cover with white lettering published by the University of Notre Dame Press in 1985. Joel Stein gave me this book in the spring of 2004, at our last encounter, which will figure again at the end of these Suites. One muggy evening in the spring of 2018, as I wrote the first draft of this Suite, I removed the book from the shelf and found the passage, near the middle of the book, that had come to my mind in the Jewish cemetery outside Pittsburgh a few years before:

> The name is the midpoint in space, the beginning in time. These two, at least, have to be named, even if the rest of the world still lies in the darkness of anonymity. There must be a where in the world, a still visible spot whence revelation radiates, and a when, a yet echoing moment, where revelation first opened its mouth ... at one time, both must have been founded at a single blow. The ground of revelation is midpoint and beginning in one; it is the revelation of the divine name. The constituted congregation and the composed word live their lives from the revealed name of God up to the present day, up to the present moment, and into the personal experience. For name is in truth word and fire, and not sound and fury as unbelief would have it again and again in obstinate vacuity. It is incumbent to name the name and to acknowledge: I believe it.

However that is, we did not end our time at Adath Jeshurun in dry speculation, but in a more tangible manner. Kew saw the little pebbles on the shoulders of many of the headstones and she asked me about those too.

"Well, it's a dark and superstitious matter," I said, "but solid, too, and sacred. In the Bible, you'll remember, the altar of God is stone. Stone endures, like the soul. The souls of the dead are thought to remain in the grave. And you don't want them coming out, even if they're good. The stones are meant to keep them there. That's one way of thinking about it, or so I've been told. But the stone marks your visit, too. And the stone is a prayer that God will count this soul and keep it with him."

Kew saw that there were no stones on my grandparents' graves. They all would have fallen off long ago in the wind and rain and snow. She asked if she could pick some up from the beds of gravel belonging to the headstones. I told her I wasn't sure if that was how you do it, and not wanting to risk offending souls she could not see, Kew trekked off to the edge of the woods to look for *the right stones,* as she put it. I stood there by my grandparents Isaac and Miriam and my great-grandparents Meir and Rokhl, and looked across the street to the mid-twentieth century suburban house with its American flag waving desultorily in the thin cool light. Kew was gone awhile and when she came back she was carrying more stones than I expected her to have. I counted them and said, "Are these twelve stones for the twelve tribes of Israel?"

"Three for each of your family's graves: from you, from me, and from the one we lost."

Dust and Ashes

1

IN THE SUMMER OF 2018, the time at last came for me to travel to Atlanta, bid earthly farewell to my great aunt Gloria and see that she was buried with the proper rites. In this case, that meant the older usage of the Episcopal Church, for Gloria to her dying day was a theologically rigorous and, as they say, *high church* member of the Anglican Communion. I went by myself, as I had done on a visit in February. But that had been a brief and busy visit entirely occupied with legal and logistical matters. Now I ended up staying two weeks in Atlanta.

Kew was by the beginning of July about six months pregnant. She has always endured the American summer bravely, but it taxes her (this may go a ways toward explaining her love of the British Isles and desire to live there again), and she regards the worst misery to be summertime travel while pregnant. Consideration of her health while pregnant, of which she was very sensitive since the miscarriages, contributed to her decision to stay home that summer.

When I drove to Atlanta on the last day of June, I had the notion that the change of place, despite its somber cause, would improve my state of mind, which had grown stranger and bitterer and more pent up since I had begun drafting these Suites in the old music composition notebooks. In fact, I can't say even now what was the matter or what I thought was the matter. I suppose I was feeling older than I ought to have felt in my thirty-seventh year. Life was not flowing and opening out, it was calcifying and closing in. And I must have told myself that for the sake of encountering some revivifying youthful energy

I was also looking forward to seeing Annette. It was good timing, for it turned out she would soon be moving to Pittsburgh to begin the very doctoral program in philosophy that Joel Stein had quit eighteen years previously, as I had written just before going to Atlanta in the initial draft of the previous Suite.

Apart from my great aunt Gloria in her last moments and my cousin Oriana (now divorced a second time) and her boys, who would come up for the funeral, Annette was the sole person I was looking forward to seeing in Atlanta. The rest of my mother's extended family are dysfunctional, degenerate, crude, scheming, litigious, callow, avaricious people, with whom my cousin and I have as little to do as possible. My mother was too unwell to travel, though she would have valued a last moment with Gloria and a visit with Oriana. My deviation from regular life in Atlanta, however, would prove anything but rejuvenating. And the reward afterwards of three days of role-playing with my friends at *Il Castello di Alta Fantasia* (as the reader will recall my friend Gregory named the cabin where we met) would also be extraordinary.

2

GLORIA DIED IN HER HOME under hospice care about a week after I arrived and a month shy of her one-hundredth birthday. She had had professional part-time in-home assistance for three years before I had set up the full-time and hospice care the winter before she died. Until she was in her ninetieth year she had been able to live independently, and in fact had insisted vehemently on doing so; after that time she was able for five or six years to continue living in her home with the informal assistance—the charity—of her church community. But it was the hospice people who made sure I was by her side at the moment of her passing. I almost didn't make it in time, but at the last she lingered. She would not go even after I had arrived, though her senses and her major organs were failing or failed.

Then one evening the hospice nurse, a woman who seemed younger than me, took me aside after sundown while the sky still glowed lavender and said, "Sometimes they do like this, they don't want to go, but if you tell them it's alright they can go now, they'll be on their way. If you're ready, you tell her."

So that's what I did, I took Gloria's right hand in both my own and I didn't say goodbye or any sort of prayer or pious thing, I just said, "It's okay, Gram, you can go now, we'll be alright here, I promise."

There was no sign that she had heard me or felt my hand, but Gloria Grace Scarborough's heart then stopped beating and the nurse recorded the time of death.

I went out onto the patio of Gloria's home, the same home she had lived in for more than half her life, and smoked a cigarette. There is nothing tragic about a woman who has lived for a century finally closing her eyes on this world. Gloria said to me when I arrived that she felt like she had outlived her earthly life by many years. And I was confident that I had fulfilled my role to the best of my abilities: I had seen to it that she had received as much medical care and living assistance in her final years and months as would make her comfortable; I was in the process of ensuring that what was left of her estate would be disbursed according to her wishes (the proceeds from her house were to go to a charitable destination, and a tract of land outside the city was to be donated to the Audubon Society); and in those last days I spent with her, when she could hardly speak and could no longer eat, I played her favorite music (Mozart's piano music) and upon her request I read to her from the King James Version of the New Testament, and I recited Psalms for her, sometimes in Hebrew, a language she had studied on her own during the last thirty years of her life and even at the end of her decline knew better than I did. So why did I feel so rotten out on that patio, smoking and pacing?

What gnawed at me, I thought as soon as I reentered the house and beheld the hospice people tending to their equipment and to my great aunt's body, was the apprehension that the world from which my aunt came was vanished utterly and that all the tradition and ceremony to which she cleaved, which had given her mind clarity and her life shape and dignity to the last, was no more than shadow-play, an etiolated cultural memory that had seemed real and vital just minutes before but was now, immediately upon the death of Gloria's body, easily dispatched to the margins of reality by the medical-industrial-bureaucratic apparatus we employ to conceal or trivialize that death and make it as comfortable as possible for the dying and for the living.

This is what has become most real for us, I thought, this antiseptic procedure and regalia, this polite little pageant showing under the signs of compassionate palliative and hygienic care a secret blight of revulsion, horror, and incomprehension of our universal and insurmountable human condition. What I wished for was symbolic ritual of overpowering truth and authority *right then and there*, some immediate and binding protocol that would not cancel the grotesquery of our condition but show it to be natural or, as in more fantastical or faithful moods I believed it was, an accident clinging by ill chance (or by some fortunate fall) to our essential selves.

As things stood, Gloria would, about a week later, receive more piety and decorum than most who die in this time, but there was first the awkward interval. I would be sleeping alone in Gloria's house that night: her body was to be removed right away. This did not seem proper, I felt that I ought to remain awake the entire night by her side, chant some prayer, perform some sacred *askesis*, sacrifice, or ablution. As none of this was an option, I called Annette and met her at a bar. It was the first alcohol I had drunk in months, and I became so drunk that my former student had to haul me from the taxi to Gloria's front door in the small hours, fish the keys out of my pocket and see to it that I entered the house. I fell asleep in the foyer and woke a few hours later to Kew calling me. My brain felt like it was melting and ready to ooze out my ears.

3

MY GREAT AUNT WAS INTERRED on a sweltering afternoon. I stood on a hillside in Crest Lawn Memorial Park, sweating through my dark suit, and looked at the amorphous sweep of Atlanta spreading away below us. All around me were gravestones marked with *McPhail* and *Mortmain*, *Lafferty*, and *Scarborough*, my mother's people, Irish and English. And here I must report that, despite their varied handicaps of character, my mother's relations had come in large numbers from the Carolinas and Florida, Houston and the sprawling suburbs of Atlanta, as well as rural New York and Massachusetts, to pay their respects to our last matriarch.

Gloria's grandson Ryan, however, was not present. No one had been able to contact him at the Buddhist monastery in California. But even some of the family of Gloria's husband, who divorced her many decades before so that he could start another family with a younger woman, had come to see her laid to rest. And of course Oriana came up from Jacksonville with her two sons Michael and Henry, who were eight and five at that time. We are very close, Oriana and I, for we grew up in the same house until Oriana was nearly nine and I was seven: that is when my family moved to Ohio and Oriana went to live with her mother, stepfather, and half-brothers. Now she stood by my side and held my hand, while her other arm rested on Michael's shoulders, and he held his younger brother's hand.

As they began to fill the grave, after those of us closest to Gloria had each cast into it a spadeful of dirt, Oriana leaned her head against

my shoulder. I was thinking of that dirt, and thinking of some lines
from the funeral service in the church that had jumped out to me:

> *The first man is of the earth, earthy: the second man is the Lord*
> *from heaven.*

These words come from the same source that I referenced in the first
Suite of this writing in connection with Brahms's music, Paul's First
Epistle to the Corinthians. When I heard the line, I thought of the
Greek that is here translated as *earthy*: it is the word *khoïkos*, which
is the adjectival form of the word that, in the Greek translation of
the Hebrew Scriptures made by Hellenized Jews before the time of
Christ, translated the Hebrew word *aphar* in the second chapter of
Genesis, where it is written that God fashions Adam from the *dust*
(*aphar*) of the ground (*ha-adamah*). But that earthiness that is the
stuff of life, *aphar*, comes from the same root that gives the word *epher*, the ashes that in the biblical mind are sign of mourning, disgust,
humiliation, and shame, as when a penitent man or indeed a whole
city covers itself in sackcloth and ashes. In the eighteenth chapter of
Genesis, Abraham uses both terms, calling himself dust and ashes, as
a rhetorical gesture of self-abasement in bargaining with the LORD to
spare Sodom and Gomorrah. It is also a reminder to God of the lowly
matter from which he made Abraham (like all human beings), and
the argument runs that if Abraham is so made and feels such mercy
toward the sinful cities, then surely God is more merciful still.

But it is hard for me to *hear* the difference between the very
matter of the human—into which God breathes life—with its cutting,
inescapable moral sense, and the stuff that signifies human abjec-
tion and moral failure. And when I heard the King James English I
thought that if there are two modes of human being, the first man and
the second man, surely there are then two worlds or two modes of life,
reality and fantasy. From the biblical point of view there could be no
question that it is this life down here in the muck and mire of space
and time, the life of *aphar* as of *epher*, that is the fantasy, though it is
also, as Scotus Eriugena and many other metaphysicians have taught,
theophany: not the show of what is false or fleeting only, but also at

the same time and through the same things the showing forth of what is divine or eternal.

Those two words, fantasy and theophany, manifest the same Greek root verb, *phaino*, which means to show or appear. If Kew had been present and able to intrude into this train of thought as I stood sweating by my great aunt's grave, she would have reminded me of the medieval English mystic Julian of Norwich, who called her visions of salvation and the perfection of creation *shewings* (also sometimes *revelations*, and the etymology shows us that it could with more justice have been rendered *fantasies*), and Kew might have said that it's showing all the way down, that what shows or seems *is* true being, the same over which the Spirit of God hovered and into which he condescended to be born, and so there might not be two worlds after all even if, as she said on the Tenth Street bridge in Pittsburgh, we seem to live inextricably in a doubled, fantastical world.

Such was my musing when Annette arrived at the end of the interment. I had invited her, but she had not been able to attend the services earlier because she was at her job, in a Starbucks. As she approached us her expression was apologetic, for she had gotten lost on the way, and then, as she got closer, puzzled. The reason for this was easy to guess. Oriana and I do not appear to be related by blood. Oriana's father is Bengali. She never knew him when she was young and she doesn't know him now (he is the fourth father to be mentioned in this writing, after Kew's father, Gloria's husband, and the father of Gloria's grandson Ryan, who left his first family to form another), but Oriana favors him in appearance; whereas her mother, my aunt Caitlin who died in 2015, had very pale skin, bright coppery wavy hair not unlike Kew's, and small silvery blue eyes that glinted like ice crystals—the opposite to Oriana's dark bronze skin, large and deep dark eyes that do not glint and flash in showy display like her mother's but draw you in with secrecy and wisdom, and her hair is thick and straight and almost black.

Before I could introduce my cousin to my former student, the Episcopal priest who had presided over the funeral, a poised and austere woman in her sixties with long flowing gray hair that lofted in the breeze in a way that I found beautiful and thought somehow fit her office, or rather improved her office and made it more like that of a druid than staid and shopworn Western priestcraft—she came over to us, and the brief conversation clarified matters for Annette. The priest was a close friend of Gloria and her longtime pastor; I had met her on several occasions over recent years, and of course I had consulted with her about Gloria's final arrangements. She thanked me and Oriana for the care we had taken of our great aunt from afar, and she thanked me in particular for planning out the memorial service and the old-fashioned wake held the night before. She also mentioned my scholarship, as she put it, how it had pleased Gloria to be able to speak with me about biblical philology, something she had told me more than once before.

I was able to answer, as I had on those previous occasions, that I took pride in being related to a woman of such independent spirit and keen intellect, who had taught herself so much, and into a very advanced age. In fact, my admiration for her was vast. Gloria had obtained a university education at a time when that was rare for women, and then had gone to graduate school—even rarer—and had a successful career as an environmental engineer and urban planner, not to mention a canny investor in real estate on the side (perhaps you could say that Gloria was to some extent of the *landed gentry*, or she won her way into that estate, to employ a term from earlier in this writing that I used to describe Hannah's family)—all in order to support herself and her son after a divorce that, like her education and professional success and personal intellectual interests, was something that simply wasn't done in her time and place. In her century of life my great aunt Gloria Grace Scarborough wasted no time and minced no words, something I was not sure I could say for myself. When the priest praised Oriana and me for our dutifulness, I was at a loss, as was my cousin: for we thought in outmoded terms of duty, obligation, virtue, and objective morality, something I had come to call simply the Code.

This has not always been my term for the basic moral, emotional, and aesthetic orientation I share with my cousin and with Kew and the friends I was to meet at *Il Castello di Alta Fantasia*—Gregory, Zach, Mark, and Geoff—who were the first to hit upon this means of stating it. When we first became conscious of our morality and discussed it, my friend Zach said it was simply *good torah*. That word means guide or teaching, and so Mark, with his interest in the *Sanjiao* of Chinese civilization (*three teachings*: Buddhism, Confucianism, Taoism), suggested we call it the Great Teaching. Gregory, like Zach resorting to a phrase from the Bible, said it was *the law written in the human heart* and so we should call it the Law of the Heart. But this struck me as too emotive in contemporary usage, and in an attempt to unite East and West, Jewish and Christian, and Taoist and Confucian, I suggested calling it the Law (or the Teaching) of the Way. All this was too cumbersome, however, and my friends and I settled on referring to this boundless and ancient way of thinking, feeling, and living as the Code.

As I say, though, the Code is not restricted to my old Cincinnati friends; I felt that it was something I shared with all those closest to me, and that Oriana and I had inherited the Code uncritically from my parents. There are various ways of describing it, none adequate but some perhaps suggestive. In its most basic elements it is—or was—universal from Rome in the time of Lucius Quinctius Cincinnatus to the China of his exact contemporary Kong Fuzi (Confucius), stopping by Jerusalem and India along the way.

The archaic Latin idea of *pietas* has much to do with the Code. Whereas Odysseus, Homer's hero, is chiefly known for being *polytropos*, a man of many turns or, in other words, clever, the signal epithet of Aeneas, foundational hero of Rome, is *pies*: pious, he observes the inherited forms of life, and upon their strength he founds a people and an empire, one rooted (at least at first) in toil in the land and devotion to household ancestors and their ways. The Code is expressed biblically in the divine commandments. I am not saying my cousin and I are especially virtuous. The remainder of this writing will disprove any such notion, at least regarding me. But we had internalized norms that were becoming rare, such that the Episcopal priest who presided over Gloria's burial would remark upon our observance of the Code though it was a thing that should have been ordinary and matter of course. And part of the Code entails that we may accept no praise, only rebuke if one fails to abide by it.

So I felt awkward, and Annette's arrival in no way ameliorated the feeling. On the contrary, I was still greatly embarrassed by my conduct in the night after Gloria died. Indeed, I was bound by the Code to feel this way for my undignified behavior, for the idea of dignity comes from the Code. Whatever superior social station or authority I might have enjoyed relative to my former student was wiped out and now I felt on an equal footing with her. Once I felt that way, the last mental shield against the awareness that I was keenly attracted to Annette had been broken and discarded, and I saw perfectly well that she was attracted to me, without any longer being in the least awe of me. To receive praise from a kind and earnest clergywoman while I pondered these things in my heart and sweat stung my freshly shaved face was unbearable.

And then Annette did the thing she always did that was almost charming in its tactlessness: without realizing it she spoke to me in French, apologizing that she had been unable to leave work early and then had gotten lost, and asking how I was and whether I would be free to go out with her for dinner and drinks, if I needed to do that on my last night here or if I preferred to have a quiet night in, or with my family, which she of course would also understand. Oriana glared at this woman sixteen years her junior while she spoke, causing Annette to realize her mistake and apologize profusely—in English—and introduce herself properly to my cousin.

I suppose Annette is as much French as anything else. She was born in France—exactly one week after Hannah died, which meant she had the same birthday as Hannah, fourteen years apart. At the time of Gloria's funeral, Annette was twenty-two. Her father was a Sephardic Jew, born in Tunisia. He moved with his parents to France when he was an infant. As a young scholar he traveled to Japan, and there fell in love with a Japanese woman, whom he married. Annette was born in France but spent five years in Japan when she was young and made many subsequent trips back to the country, so that she was fluent in the language. When she was sixteen, her family moved to Atlanta.

As I explained in an earlier part of this writing, I met Annette when she was a student in Chicago. She was vivacious, also scholarly and very good with languages, just like her father. Besides French and

Japanese, she spoke Hebrew well. Her English was good, considering it was her third language, but at the age of twenty-two she still had a noticeable accent. She delighted in occasions when she could speak French, and with me she would sometimes do this without thinking about it. It was not only the French, however, that put Oriana on her guard: here was a beautiful and significantly younger woman, not my wife, approaching me in a tender and affectionate manner, and this was subversion of the Code, at least as Oriana interpreted it.

But we all had a fine evening together. Annette was living with a roommate in the trendy Little Five Points neighborhood; though it was now in the process of being packed up, I was staying at Gloria's house in Druid Hills by Emory; and Oriana and her boys were staying in a posh little hotel—that is how much she hates our Atlanta family—near the Fourth Ward and Little Five Points, so we made our way in that direction. We ate comfort food at a Cook Out, Michael and Henry's favorite restaurant, and then went to the Fourth Ward Park because it's excellent for kids, with a big new playground and splash pads, which Henry loved.

Annette and Oriana seemed to get along well enough; they talked, among other things, about the strangeness of being non-white women in the South. For Annette's father is rather dark-skinned, and like my cousin she takes after her father, at least in that respect, while her other features more resemble her mother's, except that her long black hair is wavy. Atlanta by then had long since become a cosmopolitan city, a boomtown full of immigrants from all over the world. But it was also still the American South; and Annette hardly knew the city, having lived more time as a student in Chicago than with her parents in Atlanta. Oriana talked about how Atlanta was when she was growing up there from the age of nine, and she told some of Gloria's stories of the place from long before we were born.

All around us the light got thicker and ruddier over the new loft apartments that had sprung up everywhere in that neighborhood since Oriana and I were young. There weren't any tall trees around, as there are in so many parts of Atlanta, but Michael, my older nephew (that is how I thought of the boys, for I thought of Oriana as a sister), wanted me to tell him about the loblolly pines that tower and sway all across the city, and the majestic tulip trees. Of course, they have them in Jacksonville, too, but somehow they don't stand out so much and define the place. Oriana finds my fascination with trees as amusing as Hannah always did, but I talk to her sons about trees as much as I can and make up amusing stories about trees, and that evening I teased Oriana, saying I was going to make her children into tree-lovers even greener than me.

Kew called me then, having put our son to bed, and I talked to her for a little while sitting on a bench. I told her—and I genuinely believed this at the moment, or told myself that I did—that I would turn in early in order to get a good night's rest before the long drive the next day up to *Il Castello di Alta Fantasia*, where my friends were already gathered. She told me she was glad I would have that opportunity to relax after everything I had been dealing with in Atlanta.

When I hung up with Kew, it was time for Oriana to go back to the hotel with her boys. Annette said she had a book she wanted to give me back at her apartment, one she thought might bring solace and calm, if I was in need of such and had never read it (and wouldn't it be nice, she added, if for once she could recommend something to her teacher). It turned out she meant Camus's final, unfinished novel, *The First Man*: the title is a reference to the biblical line that had caught my attention at the funeral.

Oriana's disapproval of this invitation was blatant. She gave me a look I have known for as long as I can remember, the kind she used to fix on me when she was trying to decide which ridiculous thing she would compel me to do, or if she wanted to win a staring contest. But at last my cousin and I embraced, with strength and for a long moment, because we have always hated living far apart and always miss each other and we didn't know when we would see each other again. As she was letting go Oriana said, "Remember: this isn't Pittsburgh."

The Castle of High Fantasy

1

FROM THE MOMENT I DEPARTED Atlanta on the morning of Saturday the fourteenth of July, my mind was not right. Memories of the night just passed with Annette flitted in and out of consciousness. I had slept for only about an hour, towards dawn. I left Annette's apartment— I would not see Gloria's house again before it was sold—while the morning was still cool and passed the remainder of that day in disordered stupor, fraught and distracted, such that I was hardly conscious of the mountains through which I passed and which I love so well.

I began by mistaking my route. The most direct way to go from Atlanta to the cabin in the hills of southern Ohio where my friends and I convene every summer would be to travel north on Interstate 75 through the Cumberland Gap, over the Blue Grass, through Cincinnati, then arc east on country roads to the Hocking Hills. A comparable route would send me northeast from Lexington, Kentucky, cross the Ohio at Maysville, and go past Kew's hometown of Portsmouth and up the Scioto Valley before turning east into the Hocking Hills. Perhaps it's understandable, given the night I'd spent with Annette, that I didn't take the route that would have put me through Portsmouth. But it's inexplicable why I drove northeast out of Atlanta on Interstate 85 into South Carolina, then up through Asheville and Johnson City and northeast again into Virginia, where I traded Interstate 81 for 77 and made my way north. This is how I might have set out had I been traveling to Pittsburgh. The route would have added an hour to my drive if all had gone smoothly. As it was, when I approached the West Virginia line, I became ensnared in a two-hour traffic jam.

I began the drive in silence. It was not until I had passed Greenville, South Carolina that I played music. First I listened to Jonas Kaufmann sing *Winterreise*. I suppose there are few things more absurd than a man driving through the Blue Ridge with *Winterreise* (*Winter Journey*) blaring from his rolled down car windows into the broiling hazy high summer air. *Die Liebe liebt das Wandern, Gott hat sie so gemacht*—Love loves wandering, thus has God made it. I know those mountains like I know the Schubert, as something I don't remember ever not knowing. When I was a boy we would drive from my father's family in Pittsburgh to my mother's in Atlanta (back then Oriana and her mother and half-brothers lived there) every summer and most winters. I never got tired of the journey. But this time, though I was looking at the great eastern mountain forest and at wildflowers, abundant on steep banks, what did I see? I was thinking of Oriana and her boys, Gloria, my mother far away and ill. I was thinking about Kew and about Annette. When Jonas Kaufmann finished singing I let the wind be my music for a while.

But in the traffic jam I could no longer endure the heat without wind, so I raised the windows, cranked the AC, and began to play music that I did not know. I listened on Spotify to one after another song in the Ladino language, the traditional language of Sephardic Jewry. Among the first songs I listened to was one called "Nostaljia." At first I thought I grasped it well enough, since Ladino is a kind of Spanish—the Sephardim are the Jews whose ancestors were expelled from Iberia in the fifteenth century. But the language is more complex than that, the vicissitudes of history having brought into it influences from Turkish, Arabic, Greek, Hebrew, Bulgarian, French, and other tongues. The more I listened to "Nostaljia," the more unsure I became. Where I had thought the woman sang of *all of life* I later decided she was singing of *forgetting*, and where I thought I heard a song of *that world lost forever, where you can never go back*, I later thought I listened to the complaint of one who can *never escape that lost world*.

Shortly after we had finally begun to move again, I crossed out of the world of Ridge-and-Valley and came into the less linear hill country of the Allegheny Plateau—that excoriated land, its skin in so many places torn away in strip-mining. (That is the etymological meaning of *excoriated*, and Severine tells me it is still used this way in the technical vocabulary of medicine.) I pulled into the first rest stop on the West Virginia turnpike and fell asleep while the car ran, and an Israeli singer, Victoria Hanna, whose album Annette had given me the night before, sang words from the *Sefer Yetzirah* (*Book of Formation*) and the Song of Songs. I woke after half an hour: the car had run out of gas and I had to push it over to the pumps.

Afterwards as I drove I continued to listen to music almost as unfamiliar to me as the Schubert was familiar, and yet this music, the traditional songs of Sephardic Jewry as collected and rendered anew by the composer Alberto Hemsi in the early twentieth century, did sing to me, it was true music and not someone else's ungraspable art, for it had one foot in the tradition I had heard and studied my whole life, and in places it even felt a lot like *Winterreise*. Annette had also told me about Hemsi the night before. In fact, she had requested that I listen to his renditions of Sephardic music and give her my opinion on it, because she was not knowledgeable about the Western art music into which the composer had transfigured his musical heritage.

It was while I was listening to Hemsi and thinking of Annette that I finally recalled a detail of the information my father had disclosed to me in the bathroom at the funeral home in January of 1996, namely that Hannah, through her father, was of Sephardic heritage. I couldn't understand why Hemsi's music should have recalled to my mind this detail about Hannah. Perhaps, I thought, I had heard the music at her house one time. I had never been quite sure I believed in the unconscious mind—the notion had always struck me as a cheap knock-off of the world behind the world, or like a half-baked psychological analogue to literary deconstruction, which I consider to be nothing short of a Satanic lie in the vein of *And the serpent said unto the woman, Ye shall not surely die....* Nevertheless, my conscious mind, as I made my way north, seemed to be growing feebler and my behavior of the previous night—indeed, going all the way back to the evening under the locusts with Kew—seemed to suggest that my vision of life was in need of expansion.

During that drive I felt that I was sinking half-consciously into
the blue-green curves I wound through, into the Kanawha and into
long lanky gray Charleston strung along its banks; and the city looked
on that moist day of heavy warm blowing skies like it was made of
smoke, drifting here and there into sunlight and turning from ashen
to silver. How I loved that landscape, had always loved it, the way it
relaxes little by little as you approach the Ohio. The music seemed
sometimes to focus my heart in the present terrain. If it is what Kew
truly desires, I thought, then there is nothing I will not do in order to
return us once and for all to the valley of the Ohio and her tributaries,
to this kingdom of hill and water.

And yet, no sooner did this sentiment come over me than I wondered whether it was a well-grounded desire: after all, I wasn't born in
the country of the Ohio. When I was in Atlanta, in the dead of night
with Annette and a little rain sifting down through the loblollies and
oaks and magnolias to water us, did I not think that I could live happily forever in Atlanta? Or did I not think I could live in France or in
Japan and forget myself, become someone else entirely? But that was
no pure desire, either; it was more like a half-deliberate delusion, a
desire borrowed from someone else, someone who was not the father
of my son and my daughter to be born and of whatever other children
Kew would bring into the world.

Can there really be roots, identity? Is there really a personal destiny? Could Kew be right about Ireland if not about the Ohio Country—did that ancestral place await us both? It's marginal enough to
appeal to us. If we couldn't buy or inherit Kew's cousin's home in
Loop Head, maybe we could set up shop by Carrickabraghy Castle
in County Donegal, where some of my mother's people are from—
for that McPhail is really McFall, and McFall is really Maolfabhail,
legendary lords of that place. Yes, the Atlantic wind would blow away
our words, and the surf would drown them, until even the yearning
for speech would disappear. We could watch the weather dance on
Binnion and Dunaff Hill and Croaghcarragh, and listen on fair days
to a thousand larks trilling over the pastures. Thoreau said that was all
the occupation anyone should need. Isn't that prayer? Isn't that true
zazen? No, it's just a vision of life: a primitive one, cold and hard and

crystalline in its beauty, perhaps, but cut off from actuality like any vision of life.

Such visions were so easy to come by in the year of which I write, and another assailed me as I drove. I could live in Pittsburgh, I thought, and show my children Adath Jeshurun, last vestige of a world that could have been ours if it hadn't been given up before it came down to me. But now all thoughts of Pittsburgh were suspect, for that is where Annette would be living, at least for a time. Even if that uncanny repetition of my failure with Alison and Joel Stein were not coming about, I thought Kew was right: if we made some great return it could only be to the City of Seven Hills, where I would spend my middle years drinking high gravity beer with the only people on this Earth in whose company I felt truly at ease, and playing Dungeons & Dragons with them, and that would be all the more storytelling I would need to keep my heart quiet and make me at last a good husband and a good father.

The music I listened to while these increasingly insane thoughts blurred and bled together, music I at once knew and did not know, seemed to promise that all these fantasy lives—in Japan, France, Atlanta, Ireland, Pittsburgh, Cincinnati—all were true, each worth cherishing as real, each fated, and each already set down in a tale I could read any time I wanted, someone else's fiction: but never the one life to live, the life that lies beyond story. For each of those fantasy lives is a perfect, finished vision, the music said as I crossed the Ohio on Highway 33, but this life is not finished and it is not a vision of itself: it is not a story. This life is true love, and knows neither satisfaction nor end on this Earth.

2

AT LAST I PULLED UP TO *Il Castello di Alta Fantasia*. I could feel my tired hands trembling as they gripped the wheel and the gearshift. The ash on the cigarette clenched between my teeth was miraculously long, and I puffed several times after I had turned the car off and still it did not fall into my lap. I had smoked as I wished all the way from Atlanta. If Kew thought I had smoked in the car in Michigan, even alone, she would be irate. To sit in the car and see and feel and smell the smoke whorl close around me as if trapped or like some lover taking a grudging, gentle leave, and to feel the burning density deep in my lungs and fleeing hot through my nose, to feel the body work under this burden that was at the same time delight: I relaxed and felt simply alive, nothing else.

It could not last more than a moment, this forgetfulness of the filled and unfilled music composition notebooks in my basement in Michigan, of Kew and our little boy, of the City of Seven Hills and Atlanta and Pittsburgh and every far-flung place dear to me, forgetfulness even of the night spent with Annette. But for that moment there was only light, golden and rubescent, pressing down with the liquid weight of Ohio humidity, as if our Castle of High Fantasy lay at the bottom of an otherworldly sea and not halfway up a high hillside in Hocking County, or as if I had arrived on the *dying Earth* as envisioned by Jack Vance, one of the very great fantasists, so far in the future that the sun is failing and everything is so ancient it has grown sempiternal.

Gregory and Zach came up around the hill on which *Il Castello* is perched, each with a beer in one hand and a small knit bag filled with sand in the other—they had been playing the game that is called *corn-hole* where we grew up. As they would in the game, the men pitched their bags at my car and landed them on the windshield.

I turned off the car, leaving the windows down, managed to put the cigarette out in a half empty cup of coffee without spilling the long pillar of ash, got out, and walked over to my two friends and embraced each in turn. They were a comical pair, since Gregory is quite tall with a wiry champion swimmer's body, pale and freckled, smooth-cheeked, tousled hair of various light shades; Zach is an inch or two shorter than me, thickset, a man of burning dark eyes, embers rather than Gregory's elfin sparking eyes, and he's covered in dark hair from the top of his head to his toes, except for his face, which he does shave (otherwise his beard would take over his physiognomy) but his cheeks and chin are always rough and dark like a charcoal sketch. It was almost overwhelming relief to be in their physical presence. I, however, made a less salutary impression on them. Gregory said, "Jesus Christ, McPhail, you look like shit."

It is difficult for me now to recollect that first evening at *Il Castello di Alta Fantasia*. I know that I went into the cabin with Gregory and Zach, greeted Mark and Geoff in the kitchen, where they were preparing steaks and vegetables and potatoes for the grill. Geoff opened the refrigerator and gestured to its contents expansively, saying, "Behold, God's gifts for God's people." Mostly what he meant was beer. Paying little attention to which kind I grabbed—I knew only that all the beer came from the City of Seven Hills and most of it was fairly high gravity, as they say, meaning it had plenty of alcohol—I downed one can straight away in a single draft and then promptly opened a second. My friends knew I was coming from a funeral, but they were nonetheless surprised. "Long drive," was all I could say, "and a long night before that."

I was feeling guilt and remorse, and above all a great desire to *confess*. I needed forgiveness, of course, though this has become hard for us to understand: forgiveness ultimately comes only from the Lawgiver whose law one has trespassed. To use the language proper to my religion: though the sacrament had largely fallen into desuetude, I had to make a confession so that I could receive *absolution*. That is the act of making someone absolute: loosed or freed, with whatever freedom is possible in this world.

That first night I couldn't speak to my oldest friends about my feelings for Annette and my transgression. I wondered if I could ever speak to them about it. But speak I must: absolution comes only after speech. To whom, then? To a Catholic priest? There were Catholic churches within range of our retreat at *Il Castello di Alta Fantasia*. But I struggled to imagine myself going to formal confession. That mental faculty of picturing something that is not (or not yet) real—what is that but fantasy? And was I not a fantasist?

In Hebrew this capacity of the heart or mind to imagine or picture is called *yetzer*, which is nearly the same word that appears in the title of the *Sefer Yetzirah* I had been listening to on the drive up to our Castle of High Fantasy, so that you can see the idea of fantasizing and the idea of creating or forming are close. In this case, if I pictured myself doing what my friend Zach would call a mitzvah and making a formal confession of my sin, it would be the *yetzer ha-tov*, the heart's fantasy of the good, that would be active. (In Atlanta with Annette— and who knew how long before that—it would have been the *yetzer ha-ra*, the fantasy and thus the inclination to evil that held sway with me.) But to picture myself kneeling by a priest, uttering the words of sacramental confession—was this a true image of me? Was I the sort of man who does this, says such a thing, feels what one is supposed to feel in such a moment?

The answer, as it seemed to me then, was that I was not such a man. I did not *disbelieve*, and yet I was not a man of prayer, not a man to bring himself closer to God by speech either of praise or contrition. The closest I had ever come to real prayer, I thought, was translation, the space—or the silence—between languages. I could not right away speak of the matter to my friends, nor could they speak to me of such things—not yet. But coincidence was looming, and through the peculiar form of story that we were soon to play out, and the music we would make by the fire in the evenings, something indeed would be said.

3

DUNGEONS & DRAGONS IS POTENTIALLY an intricate and difficult game, and a single campaign or quest, as its sessions are called, can be as nuanced as a novel. I have lately begun to speculate that what is most like reading fiction in the role-playing game may not be the quest-like quality so much as the relationship one develops with time. A campaign spanning several days' worth of playing in our real waking time can require weeks or months of fantasy time, just as a novel you polish off in a few days of reading, at most a week or two, can report on the lives of characters, cities, even whole nations over months, years, generations.

And that is to say nothing of the time required of the author. Joel Stein's unpublished novel *Into Life* covered a span of about two years and two months. I suppose in a way it took him that long to write it—or anyway to observe his life and mine and Severine's and Alison's for that period, during which time he was not only observing but also feeling intensely. But to render it all in three hundred pages, the actual writing of the book, only took him from about the middle of November 2002 (when the action of the storyline ceases) until the middle of March of 2003, and he revised it in that time and altered a number of events or colored them to accord with the true form of life, as he told me in Pittsburgh, that lies behind the shifting veil of thought and feeling.

I cannot tell what became of my time in these Suites. As I set down the first draft of them in the old music composition notebooks during that year of failure and coincidence, I felt the writing as a struggle with time and its champions: hope and memory. To aid me in that struggle I set myself time and key signatures and tempi, just as if I were writing music. I thought of T.S. Eliot's line, *you are the music while the music lasts*. Are you the fantasy while the game lasts? And is writing quest-like in that those who go questing do not really wish the quest to end?

The frightening truth of fantasy is that we buy time with time, trade our lives for other lives: frightening, because we do not get a good deal, but we do it anyway. If all the weeks and months and eventually years contained in reading and gaming were simply added to our lives, that would be a magical gain indeed. But the time of fantasy must be purchased, I've come to suspect, at a dear price. I used to think the exchange was more than fair, a few of your real heart-beating hours for someone else's role and a whole story of life, or a few steps up a hillside in a river town for a vision penetrating to the timeless core of the world behind the world. But I came to wonder if the economy of the unreal might in fact work the other way around.

Suppose instead there is a moment when you transgress the frontier of fantasy or fiction or story—whatever you call it—and you do not return. You think you return and live a life, but you do not. From that moment, it is the world *before* the world that is your foreign country, the kingdom on the far side of fiction, past the last horizon—that is where your other, shadow life elapses that gives your real (that is, your fantasy) life its truth. You still exist, living on this inescapable Earth, this Earth beyond which, as Camus says, there is no salvation. And yet you are a prisoner here, or an apparition (Greek: *phantasia*), and you know that it is only in the game or the story that your destiny plays out. It is not you playing the character but the character who must play you in order to live, the character who must trade fantasy's infinity for your numbered real hours in order to exist. If this were so, then wouldn't it be a far crueler marketplace?

But I am not certain. I am still not certain where the borderline lay between reality and fantasy in the Dungeons & Dragons quest we played in the *Castello di Alta Fantasia* in the summer of 2018.

It is called a role-playing game. Each player fulfills the role of one player-character and the PCs, as they're called, enjoy a simulacrum of the autonomy and agency we imagine ourselves to possess in the so-called real world; they do not exist in service of the story and its world, as do the characters of prose fiction. Additional characters are controlled by the Dungeon Master (DM), who is in charge of narrating those parts of the quest which the PCs react to rather than invent or play themselves, and these non-player-characters, or NPCs, usually are confined to the story-world of their origin. The DM sketches in the world, but world-building rarely takes as high a priority as in prose fantasy: if it did, then the PCs would have less to do, and the game is really about them and their roles. So the DM is not a narrator in the way of one who would tell you about the world and inner lives of, say, Rodion Raskolnikov or Becky Sharp. However, the DM may design an entire quest and its setting, rather than rely on a prepackaged story, and Gregory was the kind of DM who designed all his own quests and their worlds.

The chief means of play is the casting of dice, so it is a game of probability on the one hand, chance on the other—if those are not finally the same. There are two strata of dice, so to speak: the twenty-sided die (d20), which is primary, and then dice of four, six, eight, ten, and twelve sides (d4, d6, and so on), which are used to determine outcomes for specific events. The d20 is the metaphysical die, the master of causation: its main function is to determine whether a potential event actually occurs. Most events in the game are of a purely physical nature, even if they play out according to so-called magic, although there are also more interesting and equally chancy moments of persuasion and perception: ideational and verbal events. The role-playing occurs apart from, yet coordinated with, the mathematical or metaphysical quality of the game: a matter of the will and personality, or you could simply say decision.

And yet, the PC is, in a sense, nothing more than a set of carefully tabulated numerical scores and statistics under headings like *armor class, hit points, initiative, speed, attack bonus, proficiency bonus, saving throws*, etc., which interact with the d20 to determine events. A PC's statistics improve as he or she moves through quest after quest, much as we imagine the course of a prosperous bourgeois life and professional career, or as some traditions teach about spiritual progress. Though there is risk and challenge in any quest, the objective is not that a PC, let alone an entire questing party, should perish. The better and more adaptive the DM, the more he or she is able to accommodate unexpected action by the PCs or uncommon good or ill luck they might suffer with the dice. So the blame for what befell us that summer at *Il Castello di Alta Fantasia* cannot all be laid with Gregory, for he was already by then as skilled a DM as they come.

Every character in Dungeons & Dragons is endowed with qualities (corresponding in the game to their numerical scores, but not expressed only in that way) under the rubrics of *race* and *class* and *alignment*. Race and class ostensibly do not mean what they mean in popular discourse. Race is closer to something like species, viz. elves, dwarves, humans, orcs, halflings, gnomes, and so forth. Each race has certain strengths and weaknesses, like distinct human cultures. These differences add flavor to the game, and it is possible to create a PC of any so-called race who is enjoyable to play, and some of the art of playing the character will come from working with his or her race's distinctive strengths and weaknesses.

As to class, that is more like profession, viz., clerics (scholarly warrior-magicians), warriors, thieves, rangers (Robin Hood types, or like the medieval Green Men), paladins (knights), mages, bards, and so forth. In theory, any race can be any class, but the unique and as it were God-given strengths and weaknesses of a race impel characters of that race into certain classes and discourage them from others. Dwarves, for example, do not make good mages, or halflings the best warriors, but exceptions abound, driven by will and cunning, as in real life. There is a good deal of generalization and determinism here, but I think it fair to say that the personal categories of Dungeons & Dragons reflected what had been for a very long time the common understanding of human nature, with its various limitations and differing inborn capacities and inclinations.

Finally, *alignment* may be a matter of choice, but once it is determined, the PC is expected to abide by basic guidelines pertaining to his or her alignment. This aspect is perhaps analogous to what I have been calling the Code. Two overlapping spectra, of three options each, are combined to indicate the PC's moral and philosophical commitment: Lawful, Neutral, or Chaotic; and Good, Neutral or Evil. Thus a character is said to be, for example, Chaotic Good, or Lawful Evil or, just as viably, Lawful Good or Chaotic Evil.

Since 1993 or 1994, when I began playing Dungeons & Dragons with the four friends gathered in 2018 at *Il Castello di Alta Fantasia*, we had been in the habit of assigning ourselves personal categories of *race* after the fashion of the role-playing game, and probably we thought of these categories as enjoyable roles rather than as the *identities* they would now be considered: Gregory, the Celt; Zach, the Jew; Mark, the Teuton; Geoff, the Englishman; McPhail, the Half-Elf (because I fit no one role). These social-historical roles or races, to use the D&D term, were based partly on our appearances, partly on our family backgrounds. We never took them too seriously; they were fantasy and play. Now that we were adult, it might be possible to give us *classes* as well, but it would be trickier to guess at our several alignments, and so I will not attempt that here. I have already related the adult appearances of my friends Gregory and Zach. But they both deserve a little more introduction, along with Mark and Geoff, before I get to the tragic matter of our quest.

Gregory, the Celt: You might call him a cleric, which is a cross between a warrior and a mage, a learned but potent sort of person. He abandoned me, Zach, and Geoff at the public high school in the suburb where all five of us lived, and went (along with Mark, his fellow-Catholic) to the prestigious all-male Jesuit high school. After that he studied Romance languages at Ohio University, not far from *Il Castello di Alta Fantasia*, then took a Master's in English Literature at the same institution. He contrived to live in Rome and Barcelona for two years before moving back to Cincinnati and completing a second Master's, this time in Education, at another Jesuit institution, Xavier University. After that Gregory secured a position teaching English and Spanish at the private school that Hannah had attended.

At Xavier, Gregory met another future teacher, Melinda, and fell in love. Melinda became pregnant, they married in a very small ceremony, really more of a backyard party, and had their first child, a son, in the summer of 2010; a daughter was born in the spring of 2012. In the spring of 2013, Melinda died of cancer diagnosed just after her daughter was born. By the summer of 2018, Gregory had been remarried for about a year to a doctor, Caroline, who loved Gregory's children to no end and seemed to understand and take pleasure in all children as if it were second nature to her, but wanted no children of her own. They were a happy family; but Melinda was the love of Gregory's life. In our role-playing game, Gregory served as the DM.

Zach, the (whole) Jew: Perhaps also a cleric, but with more emphasis on the warrior aspect of a cleric's abilities. He took a degree in history from Ohio State University, then moved to Israel and served in the IDF Special Forces for three years before pursuing a Master's in Jewish Studies at Hebrew University. All told, that was five years in Israel, at the end of which time he caught sight of a young American who had just arrived to study at Hebrew University as an undergraduate: this was Rachel, the daughter of Avigail and David, my former cello and music theory teachers. Zach vowed to himself that he would one day marry Rachel.

After completing the MA he thought of remaining in Israel permanently, but he returned to Cincinnati and hoped to find Rachel there when she finished her studies in Israel. Back in Cincinnati, Zach went to law school. By the summer of 2018, he was the only one of us making six figures. He was also, at that time, newly engaged to Rachel, almost ten years our junior and pursuing a doctorate in musicology at the Conservatory that I quit in 2001. In our role-playing game he was the only one of us who crossed the gender line, playing a mercenary female elf wizard (Chaotic Good) whom he named Justine, after the brilliant and beguiling Jewish character of that name from Lawrence Durrell's fiction. Our Justine was intelligent, the most powerful among the PCs, but haughty and off-putting in social situations.

Geoff, the Englishman: Slight of build—in college he earned the ironic moniker Fat Geoffrey—with the clean-shaven face of a rascally youth, alert and darting golden brown eyes the same color as his clean-cut hair, a man of decisive quick motion and quicker speech, strength far in excess of his build, especially since he began training in various martial arts while still adolescent. I'm larger than Geoff, halfway between Zach and Gregory in terms of stature, but when we were younger and I used to wrestle with Geoff, he'd almost always get me down in the end. Geoff, like me, came up in a family from which all trace of religion had died out, so he did not go with Mark and Gregory to the Jesuit high school. Geoff went with Zach to Ohio State, and there studied Japanese and art history. He taught English in Japan for several years after he graduated, and continued his study of martial arts there, but returned to Cincinnati without finding a clear path to a bourgeois career.

Geoff is not the scholar-type, despite possessing real intellectual ability. He is something of a wild man, the only one of us who has had a DUI, the only one of us to have spent more than an hour of his life in a strip club, and the one of us who smiles most and owns the kindest disposition. I suppose that in D&D terms he would be a sort of mercenary, some sort of drunken Zen warrior monk. But really he always wanted to do something more tactile and plastic, and so he eventually earned a professional degree in landscape architecture and started his own business as an environmentally conscious housing contractor and landscape designer. When he was first back from Japan, though, and didn't know what to do, he met a kindergarten teacher, Liz, who was a devout Catholic (she was to have more than a little influence on Kew's religious reawakening), and soon married her. Their wedding was the occasion of our first reunion in the Hocking Hills in 2009. In our role-playing game, Geoff plays a strong dwarf warrior whose motto is *Good at Parties and War-Parties*, and since this is more or less Geoff himself, his character is called Fat Geoffrey and aligned Chaotic Neutral.

Mark, the Teuton: He looks like a girl—that's what we always said when we were younger—with glorious wavy blond hair that falls to his shoulders, the gentlest blue-green eyes like the waters of some Caribbean bay gliding over white sands, something soft about his features. And yet he has always had a masculine way of moving and sitting, sort of like Zach, and though his voice is very kind, it is also firm and low. His cheeks are always stubbly. I suppose Mark looks a little like Kurt Cobain. We continued to insist he was feminine, almost as if to drop the mockery would be to forget and dishonor our long acquaintance.

Mark is the most Thoreauvian of us, deliberate and earthy. He is an immensely calm, artistic, civilized man. He went to the Jesuit high school to please his parents, but he was bored there and out of place. He then continued to stick by Gregory and accompanied him to Ohio University. There he astonished everyone by learning Chinese fluently and also managed, somewhere in the mysterious blue hills around Athens, to learn a good deal of carpentry and woodwork. In this his great passions and interests converged: for Mark is the most naturally talented musician I have met, apart from Severine, and he conceived a desire to learn to play and to construct traditional Chinese and Japanese instruments. Mark went to China on a Fulbright after graduating, during some of the same time that Geoff was in Japan, and he visited Geoff there, so that even today we still hear disturbing stories of the two of them in Osaka, Kyoto, and other parts of the country less frequented by Westerners.

When he came back to Cincinnati, Mark apprenticed himself to a luthier; but he ran out of ambition and focus and lost patience with all forms of systematic study. He has drifted through life as a sage handyman. For extra money, he played guitar and sang every now and then in the City of Seven Hills, but his primary employment was with Geoff's business, where he was able to put his polymathic practical and aesthetic competence to use. He lived that summer, and still does, in a very old barn that he rebuilt himself in the hills to the east of Cincinnati, perched within sight of the Ohio, where he was trying to cultivate the grapes that once made the area well known for wine. He also keeps bees, chickens, and goats. In 2015 Mark married a nurse, Stephanie, who cannot have children. If he wanted to, Mark could be a virtuoso musician, or write a more profound book than anyone I know, but he is at heart a man of silence.

As I say, Mark is like Thoreau—and so he is also a mirthful man, and true to this nature he played a charming human bard-mercenary named Guido (Neutral Good). This name was of Gregory's invention and, like the name of our cabin, supplied from Dante's *Commedia*: on the seventh terrace of Purgatory (the terrace of lust), Dante encounters one of his poetic forebears, the poet Guido Guinizelli, an inheritor of the Troubadours and among the founders of the love poetry that was called in Dante's day the *sweet new style*.

I played a half-human, half-elf cleric whom I had given the name Prester John (Lawful Good), after the mythical Christian king of a legendary realm in the Orient or Africa. These were the characters we had invented the previous summer, when we had taken up the game together for the first time since high school. (As the only one of us not living in or near Cincinnati, I was excluded from the various other groups my friends had begun playing in since that time, and for which they used other characters.) Over the past year the papers on which our characters' scores and statistical lives were recorded had been in Gregory's keeping. I recall a sense of awe, that first night at *Il Castello di Alta Fantasia* in July of 2018, when Gregory removed the sheets of paper containing our characters and I saw them, written in our distinct hands that I have known since we were in grade school: for that summer the year before, when we first crafted these characters, was surely more distant than a year, as far gone as the previous century or further off even than that and, beyond question, irretrievable.

4

THE NEXT MORNING, SUNDAY, I awoke from what may have been the longest slumber of my life, a dreamless span of close to twelve hours. Upon waking my first thought was whether I would go to Mass. There wouldn't be much point unless I could take communion, and I couldn't do that unless I confessed first. I would not do those things. My sense was clear: that world did not exist for me apart from Kew. When I returned to Kew, then I would reckon with that world.

But the need remained to speak somehow of what had happened with Annette. And now all hesitation was gone, I knew that I could speak with my friends about it. So I stumbled into the kitchen, poured myself lukewarm coffee and gulped it down, made my way to the great porch of *Il Castello di Alta Fantasia*, found the four men gathered around the large wrought iron table talking about school districting and property values in Cincinnati or some such sensible topic, and I held up my arms to either side as I stood in the doorway and intoned, *Introibo per sanctas fantasiae portas*—I shall go through the holy gates of fantasy.

GREGORY. "That sounds vaguely like the beginning of *Ulysses*."

GEOFF. "You have something to tell us, McP?"

I first apologized for my incoherence and exhaustion of the previous evening, then explained the night with Annette and my whole history with her, especially during the months since I had remembered Hannah beneath the locusts and fallen into despair over the writing of *The Upper Country*. I still felt awful and confused, I admitted, but was resolved to focus on the good work at hand, namely our game of fantasy.

Gregory and Mark faced me across the table, while Zach and Geoff had to turn around to look at me. Gregory raised one eyebrow and was silent. The slightest sad smile lurked in one corner of Mark's mouth. Geoff chuckled and reached up and clapped my shoulder loudly. Zach was expressionless.

MARK. "Why exactly do you feel bad?"

GEOFF. "You got any pictures of this girl? With clothes on, I mean."

ZACH. "Other people's birthdays, and funerals—man, they're not good for your marriage vows. Wasn't it at a birthday party in Pittsburgh you were having sex with that woman, what's her name, and Sevie caught you?"

McPHAIL. "Her name was Alison, and yes, it was at a birthday party."

I got out my phone and found a picture I had taken on the last night in Atlanta, showing Annette with Oriana and her boys. I handed the phone to Geoff and he turned the thing around, zoomed in to the picture, squinted very seriously as if at an obscure and difficult text, before handing the phone to Zach.

GEOFF. "You're excused, sir, I would say that's exculpatory hot."

ZACH, *handing the phone over the table to Gregory*. "There was at least one too many syllables in that word for you, Geoff, it sounded hard for you to say. But I take my hat off to you"—Zach was in fact wearing a Panama hat that somehow made him look like Bob Dylan and he doffed it to Geoff—"for using the word correctly, that's more than I would have expected. And not only that, but I think you're right."

Gregory still said nothing and handed the phone on to Mark, who made a quicker examination and said, "I guess this ruins our theory of McPhail's type when it comes to women. My earlier question stands. Not that *I* think you should tear yourself up about this."

ZACH. "Not unless you're planning to ditch Kew for this student. You aren't, are you?"

MᶜPHAIL. "She's not my student anymore. And no, she and I are both well aware of the singularity of the encounter. I have no plans even to be in a position to see her again any time soon. Everything about the situation was exceptional."

GREGORY. "There is only the exception."

ZACH. "What?"

GREGORY. "It's all or nothing. McPhail knows this. Everything is just so and cannot be otherwise. One moment is not more or less contingent than another. But never mind the metaphysics. What Mark's implying is right. And if you're not leaving Kew for your student—"

MᶜPHAIL. "She's not my student—"

GREGORY. "—then you're not in violation of the Code. Not all the way, anyhow."

MARK. "Marriage.... Jealousy, I mean, monogamy...kind of obsolete."

ZACH. "Said Master Kong, sage as usual. But that's not the whole story, Mark. McPhail feels bad, whether or not there's any point in his feeling bad or any good reason for him to feel bad. So he should do something about it."

GEOFF, *snickering, rising, and going into the cabin.* "Like what?"

ZACH. "Like *teshuvah.*"

GREGORY. "Repentance? I think Mark's point does still stand. Why? Repent what?"

ZACH. "No, no, no. *Teshuvah* is not repentance. Repentance involves pain, as I seem to recall McPhail telling me long ago—in the Latin, right? But *teshuvah* just means turning back."

MARK. "Back to what? To Kew? He is going back to Kew. There's been no real betrayal."

ZACH. "Back to G-d...or back to the Way. *Shaarei teshuvah* are always open. You can always turn back. It'll be Elul soon, the High Holidays are early this year. You've got good timing, McPhail."

MARK. "Not sure there's such a thing. Timing. Coincidence. Like Gregory says."

ZACH. "Did you run out of complete sentences out there in Clermont County?"

MARK. "There's no need to return to the Way. The Way is that from which you can't deviate. If you deviate, it's not from the Way, and if you return, it's not to the Way."

GREGORY. "Or to put it in Kew's language: All shall be well, and all manner of thing shall be well. Isn't that the epigraph to her book?"

At this point Geoff returned to the table carrying a massive Bloody Mary and handed it to me, saying, "Here you go, chief. You could use some breakfast, something heartier than coffee. Don't worry about banging your student. These things happen, thank God."

McPHAIL. "She's not my—"

GREGORY. "Can I see the photo of her again?"

I brought up the photo and handed my phone to Gregory once more. He looked at it and nodded, handed the phone back and said, "I think we'll be alright. I was worried this would affect the quest, and I think this may be a more interesting session than I'd anticipated, but I'm confident we'll rise to the occasion. As soon as McPhail can get his brains together you all can begin to *enjoy your fate.*"

If I had been hoping for explicit and unanimous clarification of my erotic dilemma from my friends, it seemed that would not be forthcoming. Upon reflection (after the Bloody Mary), I decided that was likely for the best.

5

GREGORY, THE DUNGEON MASTER. "Gentlemen, it is time. You are no longer you. Put away your phones—I'm looking at you, McPhail—for you must put away all thoughts of your so-called lives, your wives and mistresses and children and jobs, for they are no longer yours and their world is no longer yours. You possess various armaments and talismans, but among them no smart phones are to be found. As I recall, your last adventure occurred in a land called Arcadia, and you linger yet in that far country, but I find you reunited now in a different city than where that story ended. In fact, you are back in the city where you all first met each other. It is a prosperous and bustling inland city, a place of tenements perched crazily on hills and broad forums and bazaars in the bottomlands, of which there are several, for this city lies at the confluence of two rivers—like Lyon or Koblenz, Chongquing or...I don't know, Pittsburgh maybe: a literally *trivial* city, if I have that word right, a crossing—or parting—of the ways.

"It is evening of a murky summer day very like this one here in the south of Ohio, and you are gathered over drinks in a well-provisioned but nonetheless somewhat vicious establishment known as Frie's Hap."

(Here I have to point out that for this invention Gregory took the name of two Cincinnati bars—Fries Café in Clifton, which is pronounced as if it were *freeze*, and Hap's in Hyde Park—where we all commonly drank together in our youth.)

"Justine, it is you who have summoned your erstwhile companions, for you have received a communication from someone known well to you but not to these three men. Her name is Francesca Tenebroscura. She's a sort of high-ranking and successful courtesan. Very high-ranking, in fact, both courtesan and minister, top shelf stuff.

"As such an eminent person, Francesca sits at the center of a salon frequented by select artists and singers, painters and philosophers, and one or two poets. You would have heard of her, Guido, but you are, I'm afraid, too low-born to have yet been invited into her circle. With the likes of you, Fat Geoffrey, she obviously has nothing to do. But Justine she knows, because Francesca has an interest in the occult arts, and has occasion from time to time to solicit an aphrodisiac or prophylactic spell. And you, Prester John, she knows by reputation: she would imagine you to be her intellectual equal. She has, like you, an admixture of elvish blood. She's aware of your accomplishments as a cleric and the station you hold in this society. She might have liked to invite you to her salon for reasons of her own, despite your rather arid and scholarly demeanor, but that is not why she has asked Justine, along with you all, to meet her in Frie's Hap this evening. No, the reason is that Francesca Tenebroscura has decided at last to take a husband, and she needs your help to retrieve this man."

ZACH. "That's it, that's the quest? We retrieve some dude for this woman to marry? But wait a minute, she's a courtesan, but she's marrying?"

GREGORY. "Yes."

ZACH. "Just to be clear, she has sex with men to whom she's not married, that's like an overt and central aspect of her identity."

GREGORY, *gesturing vaguely at what could be entire surrounding USA,* "Stranger political arrangements have been known to exist."

ZACH. "Sucks for the women. Polyamory always starts out *sounding* good for them, and fun for the guys, but even in Faerie Land the Code will have its way with the heart, and everything else follows."

GEOFF. "I think he's saying people get jealous."

GREGORY. "That's true, but on the other hand they live in a sacramental cosmos. The kind of cosmos Kew and Liz claim to inhabit, the thing C.S. Lewis called the *discarded image*—well, they *actually* live in such a cosmos, for them it was never discarded and it was never just an image. So their stupid passions actually matter. This is the whole point of fantasy. I've taken the liberty of imaging that in such a world, sexuality and its associated passions work differently."

MARK. "Yeah, this was more or less Tolkien's whole idea...I mean, yeah, no religion."

GEOFF. "Zing! You can't beat an argument like that!"

ZACH. "Was there more, Master Kong, or are you just going to leave us with that tantalizing apothegm? I'm having trouble connecting the dots. Don't recall a lot of wife-swapping in *The Lord of the Rings*...or, for that matter, many wives."

GREGORY. "Tolkien didn't put organized religion in his mythopoeia because those people all lived in a world where the kinds of mystical and speculative truths that religion proposes are just manifest and experiential, the whole world is shot through with metaphysical aura, this sense that every little action is meaningful. They don't need religion, or for that matter literature and art the way we have those things, because every moment for them is authentic, they don't need any guarantees of the worth, the realness, of reality. They see it every day, and it flows in their blood. All religious stuff, the arts, all it does is try to tear away or penetrate through the veil that covers a reality that you all—Justine, Prester John, Francesca, even Fat Geoffrey—just live in. Maybe when you die you go to a Hades-like shadow reality that's not as thick with real being, some place like where we're sitting."

MARK. "It's like the Heroic Age is religion happening, not just religion remembered, which I guess is what all our religions are, just memories."

ZACH. "Have to admit I'm intrigued by this probably insane line of thought. To me, the world you guys are describing sounds more like the world of the Torah or the Prophets than a Heroic Age. In the world of the Torah every last little thing—some bush by the side of the path, for instance—can be *absolutely* meaningful; but in a Heroic Age you're pretty much restricted for meaningfulness to slaughter, rapine, that stuff. The thing is I actually think the world of the Torah and the Prophets was real and that this world is still that world. I mean, I've actually been there and I've been in plenty of situations that felt thick with being."

GREGORY. "That's just it, though, in this world we have to get into limit situations to feel it, you in the IDF—"

ZACH. "Not necessarily what I meant—"

GREGORY. "McPhail falling in love with his student—"

McPHAIL. "Wait a damn minute—"

GREGORY. "Once your student always your student. Or did you mean—"

ZACH. "Okay, anyway, getting far afield, my fault. Why do we have to fetch this guy, and why do we have to first meet Francesca in a brothel? I don't recall having to rescue any of you before you got married...though I recall one of you spending time in a brothel beforehand."

GREGORY. "It's no use asking me. If you want to find out, talk to her. Will you stick around and do that? You've got time to scram or try something tricky if you want."

MARK. "Guido is all for it. He's a poet, a teller of tales. Such people are ambitious for acclaim and patronage, I'm told, and this Francesca sounds like she could help him out."

GEOFF. "You don't even have to ask. Fat Geoffrey is always up for drinking, fighting, and whoring, preferably all three at once, and the higher-class the puss—"

MCPHAIL. "Indeed. Sounds like Prester John would respect her station (unlike some of us here) and take her at her word. He says we meet her on her terms, no precautions beyond basic watchfulness, lest we put her off."

ZACH. "Fuck that. Look, I don't know if it's feminine jealousy and rivalry or Justine's skepticism about figures in the court establishment (she is *chaotic* after all), but I'm wary of this acquaintance of mine asking to meet in such a place. Forget the courtesan part, she's a minister of state and she knows me. Why does she want to meet in a brothel or dive bar or whatever it is? As she approaches us, I'm going to do Detect Magic and be ready to act if she tries anything."

So, we awaited Francesca. When she arrived, she was greeted by the host himself, respectfully, even with awe, but as it were furtively, then she was shown to our table. Gregory then informed Justine that she detected no magic. "However," he said, "I need a Wisdom saving throw from each of the men—not because you're male, but because you don't already know Francesca and Justine does."

I asked Gregory what for. "Francesca is a special type of NPC," he said. "In fact, she's so special that I've invented something for her in this quest. She has a new quality I'm calling by the archaic and somewhat sinister term Fascination. McPhail isn't the only one around here with etymology—*fascination*, if I'm not mistaken, comes from the Latin for witchcraft and has something to do with a phallic amulet.... Anyway, it's like Charisma in the game, except that Fascination is entirely to do with eros and it's always active, it's not something a character can necessarily turn on or off, though they might play on it and use it, as you normally would Charisma. To put it in ordinary terms, Francesca is unusually beautiful and she has, deliberately or not (you can't tell in this case), a powerful effect on most men and some women when she first meets them. You may fall instantly in love with her. So roll your d20, please."

All three of my fellow PCs objected at first to this turn of events, this changing of the rules at the beginning of a quest. It was an unprecedented reaching beyond the DM's usual authority, to something much more like a writer's mastery of a book or a composer's of a score. I tried to bring my companions around by reference to *Star Trek: The Wrath of Khan*, in which it is revealed that Captain Kirk cheats in more or less this way, changing the rules of a kind of game, an important test, in such a way as to succeed but which also reveals a deeper wisdom about the nature of potentiality.

There was much further argument among us even at that point— the reader will by now understand why it took us three days to play a quest that most groups would burn through in half that time or less— for Geoff pointed out that Kirk is a character whereas Gregory is our DM. Gregory had then to counter with the suggestion that we think of Francesca as having long ago cast a spell imbuing herself with this new quality, Fascination, but it was an overambitious action taken in her youth, for which she has since suffered unfortunate consequences, even if by dint of her Fascination she has also come into power. The invention of new spells is permitted for the DM, or even for a PC with permission. And so, at last, we agreed to roll the die of fate, the d20.

Based on our characters' statistics, a Wisdom saving throw was something that I—Prester John, that is—was well poised to succeed in, Guido somewhat less so, and Fat Geoffrey almost doomed to fail. The image of the crude dwarf warrior hopelessly enamored of the glamorous courtesan amused us. However, Guido rolled a sixteen and succeeded. Fat Geoffrey rolled a nineteen and thereby also succeeded, though just barely, according to Gregory's calculations. And then Prester John rolled a one. In the metaphysical realm of the twenty-sided die, a one is what is called a *critical failure*. Not only do you fail at whatever you are trying to do (or not do), you fail catastrophically, pathetically (or if you are trying not to do something, you instead do it exorbitantly, wildly). Geoff laughed loud and Mark softly, Zach shook his head and looked down, muttering, "This is going to be *such* a shitshow." Gregory smiled at me like a sphinx. "Oh, my friend," he said, "I *am* sorry. This is going to hurt for you. A lot."

MARK. "So what does this mean for him? What does it mean when you roll a one on a love saving throw? Or whatever we should call it. Did you really plan this out or are you just making it up as you go along?"

GREGORY. "The DM is powerful, but it's beyond even me to control the dice or invent love. Gentlemen, we all have families and spouses, surely we can remember—"

ZACH. "Or in one case a twenty-seven year-old girlfriend, or a *twenty-year-old girlfriend*—"

McPHAIL. "Oh come on! She's twenty-two and she's not—"

GEOFF, *raising his hand like a schoolboy*, "Excuse me, Mr. DM, quick question: can you make this asshole die immediately, like in the first round of combat?"

GREGORY. "Gentlemen, please! Surely you understand that there is no more powerful force at large in the world and, some say, in the heavens themselves, than that of Eros. Whether it is ultimately a force for good or for ill I will leave you to debate. I will say only that it is no trifling matter of mere lust. Whole nations rise and fall, cities are built and razed, the lives of great men and women are made and broken for the sake of a desire that acknowledges no limit on this earth or end in this life. We are talking about the reaction to *beauty*, gentlemen, which is perhaps nothing other than revelation: an equal and opposite reaction, if you like. Beauty is *authority*, it commands and overwhelms—"

ZACH. "Aren't I beautiful?—"

At this Geoff and Mark burst into guffawing laughter, doubling over and swaying back in their seats. Just then a little breeze stirred the thick and hot air on the large deck and rustled the papers that contain our characters' statistics. I lit a cigarette, finished the high-gravity beer with which I'd chased the Bloody Mary, and I felt relaxed and fine even if far beneath the surface somewhere my heart was bobbing up and down, turning over like a buoy adrift at sea. "He means Justine," I said, "but maybe it's hard to tell the character from the man?"

GREGORY. "You are indeed beautiful, Justine, it's written down and we factored that into your stats last summer. However, the force that Fascination draws upon—desire, love, Eros—give it whatever name you like—it's what gives the poet his divine madness, her intoxicating art—this is even more mysterious than beauty itself. The world is shot through with beauty. There are many beautiful women in this land of Arcadia apart from Justine and Francesca, and Prester John has met more than a few of them and come away unscarred. But we are concerned with a reaction to a specific, unique, unrepeatable, and personal manifestation of beauty, a reaction that is finally irreducible to the calculus of cause and effect. We are concerned, in other words, with the soul's choice, the motion of the inmost self as it stumbles through this seductive world of forms and appearances. One thing, at least, there is that is greater than ourselves, that mocks our puny protestations of autonomy and our feeble lists of rights and privileges, *or* our delusions of detachment, something that makes a laughingstock of our notions of propriety and justice. And now we must determine how it will play out with our learned friend Prester John here in Frie's Hap and over the next few days as you strive to carry out your errand."

GEOFF. "Seems a bit over the top, man."

MARK. "Not all of us spent our youth seeking new ways to get a concussion in a titty bar."

GEOFF. "Excuse me, the concussion happened when I was getting thrown out of the bar."

MARK. "That's a lie. I was there—"

GREGORY. "Friends, contain yourselves. Each man bears the burdens of love according to his nature and his doom. First of all, McPhail—excuse me, I mean Prester John—first of all you lose all your cantrips and you're going to forget half your spells. There will also be some permanent subtractions from your

Constitution, Intelligence, and Wisdom scores, which will of course alter your spellcasting ability. And you lose fifteen hit points, also permanently."

ZACH. "Ah, come on, man, it can't be *that* big a deal. He'll die on the first day."

GREGORY. "I'm afraid it *must* be a big deal, Justine. He rolled a critical failure. The man is already hurting. The thing is, Prester John, you can't really sleep or rest properly anymore, or concentrate as well as normally, so it's going to be harder for you to recover from injuries and regain your spell slots after you've used them."

"However, it's not all bad news. Although Prester John will be teetering on the edge of insanity and exhaustion for the next few days, I'm also going to correspondingly increase his Strength, Dexterity, and Charisma scores. There are some perks, you know, to being in his condition. He certainly *is* not, but he *feels* like a youth again. He is more charming and persuasive, and his attacks therefore improve in potency. That goes for spells, too. You're handicapped in casting them, John, but when you do hit with an attack spell it does more damage—an extra d6 or d8 or whatever—than it otherwise would. And *all* spells you can cast a level higher than your usual. You are unhinged and weary, but you also have energy. Such is the paradox of love. Trust me: you're going to need it...."

"Now, do we want more coffee or Mary's, or should Fat Geoffrey haul the beer cooler out here before we dive into the quest?"

6

GREGORY DID SOME GOOD writing for our quest. We were in an Italian Renaissance world of feuding city-states. Many cities—like our own and like our goal, or like the Florence of Gregory's beloved Dante— were divided within themselves and plagued by internecine strife and factionalism. Francesca's betrothed, Luciano, was the scion of the ruling clan of our own city's chief rival. He was a charismatic and brilliant leader, we were told. In the event of war between our two cities—an imminent danger—Luciano would be a formidable foe. But Francesca and Luciano had undertaken to subvert the hawkish aims of our respective cities and broker peace instead, by means of betrothal. They would try to stop the romantic plan if they knew of it but, once the couple was united according to the shared rites of our two cities, the commanding factions on both sides would be forced to agree to a truce. So Francesca, despite her Fascination and its ill effect on Prester John, acquired a magnanimous quality in our eyes.

The city to which we had to travel to fetch Luciano was only a day's journey away, but we were set upon by trollish bandits, and then by the forces of a rival political faction in Luciano's city. We were also waylaid by a storm that we suspected was driven by some fell magic, though we couldn't guess whose. By the time we made it to the city on the second day out, we'd taken quite a beating with little time to rest, a strain made worse by having to protect Francesca along the way. She'd insisted on coming with us, and Guido, despite his usual charisma, failed to dissuade her. Francesca's presence also meant that there was no way for Prester John to recover in the least from his infatuation.

Once we made it to our goal, we learned that Luciano had been taken captive by the same rival faction that had assailed us en route. Now not only did we have to spirit Luciano away from his own clan, normally our enemies, but we had first to rescue him from *their* enemies (who were also ours). So we spent the third day of our campaign in a dungeon crawl, in which, despite help from some of Luciano's own soldiers (who of course didn't know we were planning to kidnap Luciano), we were again badly injured and wearied. My companions rolled well, for the most part, but Prester John had conspicuously bad luck, and it would have been bad luck even without the handicaps his erotic distraction caused.

At length we did manage to retrieve Luciano uninjured and found ourselves in a great stateroom of one of the palaces of his family, overlooking the single river that flowed through the city and surrounded by his elite bodyguard and heavily armed retainers. We were discussing how we could get Luciano out of there, since he seemed to be making no effort to supply a ruse himself, as we had expected he would upon seeing Francesca and thus realizing the nature of our mission. Zach suggested Justine would look to Francesca for guidance in this awkward situation.

What Gregory then narrated turned everything on its head. He described the scene of the encounter of this wealthy and powerful man with Francesca, and we quickly realized there had never been any betrothal between Francesca and Luciano. He was shocked and perplexed by our contribution to his rescue—and suspicious. Also, he fell under the spell of the Fascination, and despite his misgivings in the presence of armed and magically potent citizens of his city's chief rival, he made erotic advances upon Francesca, which she seemed neither to welcome nor repulse. We were very puzzled—except for Zach, who seemed to have read Gregory's mind.

ZACH. "Son of a bitch. You son of a bitch. Goddamnit!"

MARK. "What are you freaking out about?"

ZACH. "She's set us up. She's a fucking assassin and we're the decoys."

GEOFF. "I'm not seeing what you're seeing."

GREGORY. "All will become clear momentarily, no doubt, but first, Prester John, you need to make another Wisdom saving throw."

GEOFF. "Please don't tell us he's going to fall in love with Luciano now."

GREGORY. "Just roll the d20, please, McPhail."

I rolled, and again it came up a one.

Geoff laughed so hard this time—he was truly and deeply drunk by the end of this, our third day gaming at *Il Castello di Alta Fantasia*—that he fell out of his seat. We all were laughing except for Zach, who was looking at Gregory like he saw a demon.

GREGORY. "My friends, what can I say? Some men believe in a universe of random chance, others in an inscrutable fate. And still others claim to have faith in the hand of God, reaching down from heaven to guide our lives on this good earth that He has made. Myself, I am often undecided as to what, if anything, is master of reality. At least I know it is not us. People talk of decisions, making good decisions or bad. I think Prester John, being a learned man, might tell you that according to the thinking of some ancient traditions, every decision cannot but be a repetition of the original fall from grace, a fall from potential into actual; it is to fall from the world so vast that it accommodates our every last yearning to this little space where we eke out our curtailed lives as prey to the pettiest and the noblest desires alike. Isn't that right, John?"

ZACH. "Oh for fuck's sake, just do your job and tell us what happens."

GREGORY. "As you wish. Prester John, you are overcome with jealousy. You cannot endure imagining, let alone seeing, Francesca in this man's arms. You have, if I'm not mistaken, one spell slot left, at the highest level, and one attack spell. Because you have a second time rolled a critical failure, I am going to have to take over your character and say that you use your one remaining chance at attacking with a spell to try to kill Luciano. You want

it darker—(at this Gregory gestured up with one finger, like a
figure in a religious painting, seeming to indicate the Leonard
Cohen song of that title that was playing just then)—so you try
to kill the light."

There was silence from us for a few seconds as we sat there un-
moving. Then Zach began to chuckle. Soon he was laughing outright
and he smacked the table hard, nearly upending his drink. It was the
most mirth I had seen from him during the whole three days. "That's
good!" he yelled at Gregory. "Not the pun, I mean, the coincidence
with the music—that's a little too cute—but this turn—*of course* Prester John loses his shit. I think it's kind of cheating, taking over a
character like this, but what the hell, it fits. But look, DM, do us a
favor before we begin the melee: We never got a description of this
Francesca. What does she look like, that Justine and Prester John, all
of us probably are going to die for her?"

GREGORY. "That's a good question. At first I thought Francesca had
a sort of darker Celtic look about her: black hair and very pale
skin, piercing pale blue eyes—"

MARK. "Well hello, Severine...be perfect if Sevie killed McPhail."

GREGORY. "Perhaps, but some stories are stranger. My initial vision
was flawed. Francesca is, beneath elegant and delicately concealing feminine attire, rather powerfully built. Her posture and
poise and the unmistakable gracefulness with which at all times
she moves, come from an athlete's or warrior's dexterity and
unconscious bodily confidence. She is quite physically capable,
and if she were armed she would be a formidable opponent.
Her skin is not pale like Severine's, it's actually rather deep
bronze. Her eyes are a blazing green, almost electric. Her jaw is
chiseled, her nose aquiline. You may imagine that her lips are at
once voluptuous and firm. But no doubt her most remarkable
feature is the great mane of hair, which is quite various. In parts
it is almost straight, in other parts wavy, and elsewhere closely
coiled; and yet it does not seem to be a tangled mess, but to
sweep away from her face and fall and fan upon her shoulders

and down her back in a mysterious order, as if in that way emblematic of the cosmos itself. In color it is likewise various, from straw to crimson to chestnut—call it honey-colored hair, if you like, and think of all the colors honey can be—"

(Now I could not speak, so shocked was I to hear Gregory describe Hannah as a grown woman. How could he have known so well this Hannah who never had a chance to be?)

ZACH. "Okay, I think that'll do. Thank you. I'm going to try to attack her. I go next after Prester John finishes this attack, and I am going to kill her if I can...actually there's probably no chance of that, but I'll at least hurt her."

GEOFF. "What the hell for! If we give her a weapon maybe she'll help—"

ZACH. "No, you idiot. Don't you ever read anything? Don't you know by now what kind of story we're in? We've been duped from the beginning. Do you guys really not get it? We're being framed! Not that it matters now, because we're all going to die and that's the point.

"Look, Francesca's going to watch us fight Luciano and all his dudes, and then if we survive that, she's going to wipe us the fuck out and kill Luciano herself. She's not undermining the hawkish faction in our government to bring about peace—Luciano's never seen her before! He's been enchanted just like Prester John was, something that can only happen the first time Francesca meets someone. She's working for our city by assassinating Luciano and letting us—a bunch of mercenaries not affiliated with our government—take the blame. Killed while carrying out a simple kidnapping for money, that's what they'll say of us, and no one will know Francesca was here.

"It's brilliant. Our city will bring down one of our rival's top dudes without having to fight a full-blown war to do it. It's called black ops, and it happens more often than people realize. This is, if you'll pardon the expression, fantastically realistic. And just watch, Francesca is like an eighteenth-level wizard or something, I'm sure of it. Greg, can you tell us

Francesca's alignment, so I don't have to argue with Geoff for the next ten minutes?"

GREGORY. "I really shouldn't, but I've messed with the rules so much already, so who cares: she's Lawful Evil. And yes, she's a far more powerful wizard than Justine. She endowed herself with Fascination by accident in her youth, but by now she's gained control over it and uses it, to the extent it can be used, for her own purposes. Luciano is quite enchanted right now and you might actually be able to kill him and his guards."

ZACH. "Nah. Let's go out in style. Who gives a shit about Luciano, Prester John can flail at him or Guido can sweet talk him. I've got like ten hit points left, but I'm going to hurt Francesca before I go down."

And so it was that we died. I continued my bleak rolling, failing in my spell-attack on Luciano, so that in my next turn I had to go at him with my hand weapons, with little result. Fat Geoffrey comported himself valiantly and strew his foes about him, until the final round when he, too, rolled a critical failure, and Gregory narrated his gruesome death.

I was on my last legs at that point, and I had used my last chance at spellcasting to attack Luciano. When it was Luciano's turn again, after my last attack hit but failed to do much damage, he cut me down, and Gregory told of a disgusting and vicious end: Prester John was brutally *unmanned* before Luciano delivered the coup de grace.

Guido, though a skilled and agile fighter besides being a charismatic bard, tried to escape rather than negotiate or fight. "I alone will survive," Mark exclaimed, "to sing to the world of this sorry tale and bring honor to us all!" But he failed his Dexterity check as he was trying to climb out a window and was strangled from behind, his throat crushed and his neck broken by Luciano's elite bodyguard.

As for what happened to Justine—it was evil. She could do little against the woman who had captured Prester John's heart and disordered his mind. It turned out just as Zach foresaw, Francesca was more than Justine's equal on the elf wizard's best day. Francesca overwhelmed and captured Justine in a spell that froze her, suspended a few feet off the ground. Justine failed in her next saving throw to get out of the spell, and Francesca seized one of the bodyguard's pole-arms. With this weapon, shrieking ecstatically, Francesca danced—artistically, Gregory told us—around Justine and hacked off her limbs. To end it, Francesca disemboweled her victim in a single stroke and turned the polearm, which she set magically ablaze at its end, toward Luciano. Then the fantasy, as far as we were concerned, was over.

7

A LITTLE DOWN THE HILLSIDE at *Il Castello di Alta Fantasia* there is a large circle of flat, grassless ground containing a fire pit. Every night we had spent at the cabin over the preceding ten years we had made a fire there, unless there had been pouring rain—and even then Mark had sometimes tried, for much like my former friend Joel Stein with cigarettes, Mark claimed to be able to build a fire under the most adverse conditions. The very first fire we built there, ten years before, burned high, and Geoff, who was to be married two days later, was driven by his anxiety on that occasion to leap over it many times throughout the night, a feat of whiskey-fueled athleticism none of us has attempted since. Sometimes we would cook food over the fire, but usually we just drank and played music around it late into the night.

These four men were the only people with whom I regularly made music anymore. A gentleman ought to be able to delight his friends with music. This was in fact one of the first things about the Code that we all hit upon, when we were in high school. By the summer of 2018, Zach was an accomplished amateur fiddler; Geoff brought a mandolin or a guitar; I brought a guitar that had belonged to my mother or a giant old Hohner chromatic harmonica that belonged to her father, John McPhail; Gregory brought an accordion, a lap steel, or a dulcimer; and Mark was liable to bring any of several instruments, including a guitar, a banjo, a sanxian (the Chinese banjo), or a pipa (the Chinese lute) that he had made himself. For our session on the last night at *Il Castello di Alta Fantasia* in July of 2018, we brought down to the fire my harmonica, Geoff's guitar, Gregory's accordion, Zach's fiddle, and Mark's sanxian.

When it is a matter of traditional or folk styles of playing, and of playing those styles with deep learning, precision and feeling, Mark was the most versatile and talented among us. When you heard him play, you wondered why he had achieved no recognition. But ambition was something so foreign to Mark that whenever he felt pressure to be ambitious about something, he would become physically ill. When he played, he disappeared into the music, he became the music. The idea of yoking his playing to some desire for approbation or financial success that existed apart from the man who was one with the music was inconceivable for him. I admired my friend, but I had always found his attitude untranslatable to literary art.

I was the first down to the fire ring on our final night. I built the fire and sat by it and smoked, feeling out of sorts and still surprised by Gregory's description of an adult Hannah who never was. Clearly I was wrong in thinking he had never met Hannah: there was no way he could have come up with that description unless he had. The revelation was a blow, calling into question regions of memory which I had felt were soundest.

Now there was the question as to why he had used Hannah to describe the D&D character, and why he had used her to slaughter us. But I decided, sitting by the fire I had kindled on that most familiar of Ohio hillsides, that I didn't want to ask him. There was about the whole incident the same feeling of omen and admonition that I had experienced at intervals, with increasing intensity, since remembering Hannah under the honey locusts in October. I felt that if I brought it up we would become engaged in a theological and metaphysical disputation that, for once, was not an appealing prospect.

Instead, I watched the smoke from my cigarette mix with the smoke from the fire and drift up to the canopy of tulip trees and sassafras and oaks and maples. It was such a pleasure, I thought, but I should probably stop smoking, except for the occasional pipe maybe. Smoking is an odd way to savor and celebrate botanical life, but that is what the practice had come to signify for me. The tulips (yellow poplars) especially grew very tall and straight and seemed to stare down at me and confirm this judgment: surely, they seemed to say, the whole of the Law declares that there is right use and ill use of the creatures of this Earth. They had their problems, these trees: disease, storms, human predation. But in their looming over me they were exactly right in their place, and these trees at least were healthy.

My friends slowly made their way one by one out of the cabin and down the hill with their instruments, like the dwarves with their sundry instruments arriving at Bilbo Baggins's house at the beginning of *The Hobbit*. We had been playing some of our usual songs during the past few nights, including "The Water is Wide," perhaps my favorite in recent years. I could still hear Geoff's voice (he is the best singer among us):

> *The water is wide, I can't cross over*
> *Nor have I wings with which to fly*
> *Build me a boat big enough for two*
> *We both shall row, my friend and I*

As he sang I thought of the words Jesus is reported to have spoken: "Greater love hath no man than this, that he lay down his life for his friends." Was friendship, not romance, the heart and end of true love? If that was so, then it was an idea our culture had lost long ago. But the way Geoff had sung the song mixed such an ideal of friendship with the more familiar pathos of the broken-hearted and weary lover, for he also included traditional lines:

> *I leaned my back against an oak*
> *It seemed to me a trusty tree*
> *But the boughs they bent, the trunk it broke*
> *And so my love was false to me*
> *Love is most fair, love is most kind*
> *Shows every joy when love's first new*
> *But love grows old and love grows cold,*
> *Fades faster than the morning dew*

Zach was the first to come down to the fire ring after me, carrying his fiddle and bow in one hand and two beers in the other. He handed me one of the beers, saying, "The other forty beers you've drunk here don't seem to have worked but I thought one more might do the trick."

I took the beer and said he was probably right. He set his own beer down and picked up the stick we used to prod the fire and began tracing in the dusty ground around the fire pit with it. After a minute I got up to see what he had written. It was two words in Hebrew, from the twentieth chapter of Exodus, usually translated into English as *Thou shalt not commit adultery.* Then he glanced up at me as he swept away the writing and said, "Eh? How's your Hebrew coming along? You should be working on Hebrew, not Hawaiian!"

He was remembering the Hawaiian grammar books and song-books and dictionaries he had noticed scattered in the back of my car. In that season of my life I was almost always working on one or another language, and although I had not been thinking in particular of Severine, recalling her when I drafted an earlier Suite of this writing had put me in mind of her current abode, a place that had long fascinated me for its mixture of cultures and its complex history. I wished to study the language because I consider it one of the most beautiful I have ever heard, alongside Irish, and as with Irish I also wished to study Hawaiian because it was an endangered language. I felt I was living in a time when my own language was failing: *woman* did not mean *woman* anymore; *man* did not mean *man*; *love* did not mean *love.* I couldn't do anything to save English, it seemed to me, but I could maybe save some fraction of the spirit of these languages, Irish and Hawaiian, to which I was mysteriously drawn—these languages which my own native language had almost driven out of their native lands, doing with its putrescent pop culture what earlier armies of conquest had achieved far less perfectly.

McPHAIL. "You know Jesus did exactly what you just did. With the woman caught in adultery. He wrote something on the ground, in fact it's the only time he's reported to have written anything, and then he wiped away what he wrote."

ZACH. "Yes, I know. And he tells the woman he doesn't condemn her and then to go and sin no more. Well, McP, go and sin no more. The most important thing is always *shalom bayit*"—(by this Zach meant *the peace of the household*, the harmony of husband and wife)—"And you can still have that, you still do have that. I said *teshuvah* earlier because it means movement, as you know, not self-torture. The Psalmist says that a sacrifice G-d will not despise is the contrite and broken heart. But I think the point of a broken heart is that it means movement, change. Like with this thing"—he tapped the fiddle strings with the bow and they quivered and sounded—"you can have movement and harmony at once, in fact you need both together, the one doesn't exist without the other. You're at a turning point. Gregory is right that everything is a turning point, everything flows. Mark would say something incomprehensible about the Tao being a river without banks or whatever. I think the point is a river flows, and it curves and bends, too."

McPHAIL. "And a river can sing. Let's tune." I blew an A on the harmonica and Zach started tuning the fiddle to my instrument. And I went on: "Funny you mention turning point or change. I've been wondering lately about going in a totally different direction." Craning my neck back to see the tops of the trees in the last of the light, I said, "Like back to school and study one of the natural sciences. I have these moments like Virgil in *The Death of Virgil*, where he's sick of his art, thinks it has less of the earth and truth in it than a halfway decent treatise on sylviculture or husbandry.... You know what else I was reading in Atlanta? Rachel Carson's sea trilogy. Now those are perfect books. If I could write like that, a perfect flow of prose but no web of *ideas and opinions*—"

ZACH. "Hey, you do what you have to do to write. But that's the stupidest part of that Broch novel. The whole thing is a self-refuting thesis. I never understood why you thought it was so brilliant. Look, McPhail—and it's so funny we still call you that, isn't it?"

McPHAIL. "You all thought it up, you said it was my *true name*. You thought the aural pun was amusing, and it is, it's turned out to be appropriate."

ZACH. "No, because.... Look, what I was going to say"—and he started now to punctuate his speech by bowing double-stops and then some increasingly complex riffs—"is that natural science is a noble pursuit, but for you it can only work if it lets you write. You are a man of the book. You belong to a people of the book—or two peoples of the book. Since earlier to help along our quest you already quoted the greatest story ever told by Jews—by which of course I mean 1980s *Star Trek*—I'll steal from Spock in that same film, and from Kohelet, to say that of making many books there is no end. And yet it is your first, best destiny. Anything else would be a waste of material, human and written."

Now Gregory came down the hill, bellowing something at us in a screeching fake singing voice, "*Tras de un amoroso lance / y no de esperança falto / bole tan alto tan alto / que le di a la caça alconce*"—lines from a poem by Saint John of the Cross, called *Falconry* usually in the English title. The Spanish means *Launched upon a romance, lacking no hope, I flew so high, so high, that at the last I caught the prey.* He was grinning.

ZACH. "I think the omniscience of DM-ing has turned you cynical."

GREGORY. "Of course not, just getting my Spanish ready to sing."

On this night we would play through the traditional Sephardic songs I had insisted on the first night that we learn. Gregory, who had by far the best Spanish, would help me sing them.

Mark and Geoff came down soon afterwards, bearing their instruments and whiskey, and we tuned up and drank a little. Then we played, and for that while at least my ill feeling was all purged from me. Our music was mournful, yet detached, for that is the effect of Mark's sanxian. It has a deeper, richer sound, more tinged in pathos, than a modern American banjo. It sounds less metallic and more primitive, to my ears, and there is almost something inhuman or otherworldly in its hollow twanging. A sanxian is made with snakeskin, and the scales—each distinctly visible—on the body of Mark's instrument were black and gold, and they flashed in the firelight, the gold scales like white lightning and the black scales like moonlit water.

By the time we reached our last song of the evening, the one which had grown on me most since I discovered it on the drive up to *Il*

Castello di Alta Fantasia, a time that seemed many months distant—by then I was so tired and depleted that I might have finally achieved something like what Mark is able to do with his music, the world had dropped away and I had fallen into the sound, and there was no English left in my mind, I was no less and no more than the simple words.

La rosa enflorese, we sang, *en el mes de Mayo*—The rose blooms in the month of May. *Mi alma s'escurece, sufriendo de amor*—My soul darkens, suffering in love. The nightingales sing, sighing love—*Los bilbílicos cantan, suspirando el amor.* Passion is killing me, my sorrow grows.—*Y la pasión me mata, muchigua mi dolor.* Come quickly, my dove, come quickly to me—*Más presto ven palomba, más presto ven a mí.* Come quickly, my soul, for I see that I am dying.—*Más presto tú mi alma, que yo me voy morir.*

No life, no beliefs, no memories, no plans, no truths but the music, cut loose from the world.

We Incarnate Something

1

As I DROVE NORTHWEST AWAY from *Il Castello di Alta Fantasia* on the morning of Wednesday the eighteenth of July 2018, I noticed in the first village I passed through, at about ten in the morning, a man smoking a pipe on his porch. It was a glass pipe: he was smoking meth the way his ancestors in that place would have drunk coffee or smoked a pipe of tobacco during a break in the morning's agricultural or other manual work.

The man observed me with dead eyes as I drove past. We must have been about the same age. In fact, I thought here was a man—and I knew there were millions of others like him—whose life had been destroyed somehow, disappointed, robbed of meaning and purpose, and he had turned in that despair to a drug or combination of drugs that allowed him to carry on living, though it was a sort of living death or death in life.

He looked like my cousin, Gloria's grandson Ryan, conspicuously absent in Atlanta; or like my friend Mark: lean, square-jawed, long and tousled dark blonde hair and classical features that would have been quite attractive under other circumstances, in another place and epoch. And the man's chosen drug (if the language of choice is fitting here) and its degradations could have been my cousin Ryan's fate if he had not turned to a far harsher asceticism and renunciation, one which would not even permit him to attend upon his grandmother's declining years or burial rites. Perhaps this man too, the one I drove past on his porch trying to inhale some last sad simulacrum of life, he too, like Ryan, might have lost something original, a father or mission or desire, some original *yetzer ha-tov* or marvelous Buddha mind.

And then soon I was thinking not of my cousin Ryan, and not of Kew's brother somewhere not far from that ruined porch pitched in his own struggle with the same world of addiction, disappointments, and disadvantages, but of my cousin Patrick, Oriana's younger half-brother, who had lost his life almost four years before to a massive opioid overdose. Oh, roads of Ohio, fiddle-curved, what did I think of then, while I drove along you to the only home I knew, or away from the only home I'd known.

On the day after Thanksgiving 2014, I stood in Fort Clinch State Park on Amelia Island, Florida and watched an *Ohio*-class submarine put out to sea. Kew was with me, and Oriana. That autumn was unusually cold in the Southeast. Though in back of us and before us across the mouth of the Saint Marys River on Cumberland Island in Georgia was a green landscape, the weather was little different than what would have been normal for the defoliated Ohio River country of that season, making a juxtaposition of temperature and palette that I found disconcerting. I was wearing a wool coat and I had turned the collar up against the north wind. The feeble sunshine was bright but pale.

It was Kew who had noticed the long black object slinking into the glaucous Atlantic flanked by small escort ships. As soon as Kew pointed out the submarine, wrenching us from our collective silent reverie, I noticed the sound. They are nuclear-powered, the *Ohio*-class, and very quiet submerged, but maybe going at the surface in shallow coastal water you can hear them better. I know it was not the small escort ships I heard; it was not a loud noise but subtle and deep. We had been walking desultorily around the outer wall of the fort, but as soon as I realized what Kew was pointing at in the ocean that had just come into our line of sight, I bolted for the shore to get the best view possible of this rare event. I heard my wife and my cousin following and laughing hesitantly, and Kew saying, "He's like a small boy...."

I told them, when they had come to where I stood transfixed on the beach gazing at the submarine, that there were eighteen *Ohio*-class vessels in the Navy. They had two home ports, one in Washington

State and one at the Kings Bay base, up the Saint Marys River over there. These things deploy for six months at a time, and their movements are always secretive, I said. Nearly all of them, at any given moment, are lurking under the sea somewhere, so to see one going in or out of port is unusual for anyone who doesn't live right by one of the two bases. The chances are that that thing is full of nuclear warheads. They carry twenty-four Trident missiles. All eighteen boats used to carry a nuclear armament, but a few have been converted to carry cruise missiles with conventional warheads. Still, between them they've got something like half of the military's entire nuclear arsenal, fifteen or sixteen hundred warheads in over three hundred missiles. But those Trident missiles were made to carry a dozen warheads a piece, three times what they've got now. Even with the treaty restrictions, that one boat, I said, could turn every square inch of Europe from London to Istanbul, into a pile of ash.

Kew and Oriana weren't laughing anymore when I finished conveying this information, and they looked at me grimly. I don't know what it is about the South, especially the lowland South, that makes me so apocalyptic. You would think such moods more likely to overtake me in the rusted-out cities of the North, where I've spent my life. But Pittsburgh, Cleveland, Cincinnati, Toledo, Detroit, Chicago, Milwaukee: in those places I feel easy, familiar, adept. Maybe it's because the North is *post*-apocalyptic.

Or maybe it's because when I was nine or ten years old, only a year or two after the Cold War ended, my father and I read together a book called *Alas, Babylon* by a man named Pat Frank. The book was published in 1959 and my father read it a few years later, when he was about twelve years old, during or shortly after the Cuban Missile Crisis. The title, I remember my father explaining to me, is from the Christian Bible. It comes from the eighteenth chapter of Revelation, in which the angel who visits John of Patmos says, *Alas, alas that great city Babylon, that mighty city! for in one hour is thy judgment come*. The identity of Babylon in the text is complicated, both a woman and a city—a City of Seven Hills, to be precise. Some have interpreted this Babylon to be Rome, others Jerusalem. The angel calls the city a whore, mother of abominations, and one who has perverted kings and whole peoples—civilization and adultery again go hand-in-hand.

In the novel, the phrase *Alas, Babylon* is a code used between two brothers, one of them an officer in the Air Force. When the officer sends a message with the phrase to his brother, who is living an aimless life in a backwater Florida town, the brother in Florida knows that nuclear war is imminent. The book shows the inhabitants of that backwater surviving the end of civilization. In particular I remember the description of nuclear bombardment. The protagonist stands outside his home and sees glowing red-orange light in different places on the horizon—incinerated cities and military bases (including possibly the one where I saw the *Ohio*-class submarine put to sea). When I read this description with my father, I experienced a pleasing sensation of beauty. And I discovered again, about five years later, when I read Revelation for the first time a month or two after Hannah died, that the end of the world, when it is something described, something you see in fantasy, can be beautiful, and that beauty can bring solace if your own life has become painful, when you feel your own inner world ending.

It is uncanny to think that my catching sight of that *Ohio*-class submarine and running—Kew was correct—like an excited boy to the seashore, is what put us, if only for a few moments, in a better mood on that cold, clear, un-Floridian day. For the world, or a world, had in fact come to an end, that is why Kew and I had on very short notice spent Thanksgiving with Oriana: eight days before I saw the nuclear submarine, Oriana's half-brother Patrick had died just short of his twenty-eighth birthday from an opioid overdose. He was to be interred the Saturday after Thanksgiving. As I recall, this was the time when the notion of an *opioid epidemic* was just coming into wide circulation, though the epidemic had in fact been underway since the 1990s.

"Why do you know all this?" Kew asked me, as we sat in the cool sand and watched the submarine grow distant in the northeast, none of us wanting to cut our way through Black Friday traffic to return to Oriana's house, where we would find my mother, and my aunt Caitlin (probably drunk), and Oriana's other two half-brothers,

Cormac (Patrick's twin) and Sean, as well as of course Oriana's husband and two sons, and later on more of my mother's relations, all gathering for the wake. Before I could answer, Oriana said to Kew, "It's because of his dad."

I came to consciousness of the wider world in the last years of the Cold War. I remember watching the fall of the Berlin Wall on television with my parents and asking them what it meant. When I was a boy, my father had a penchant for cartography and military history, and for the intricacies and details of the Cold War, and this he passed on to me as he did the names of the trees in the City of Seven Hills. My childhood was filled with histories, geographical and historical atlases, and books that explained the workings of war in all times and places. One of these books that I grew up poring over was *Jane's Fighting Ships*, which is not, as its title might suggest (this is what Kew said on the beach), a book to interest young girls in the Navy, but a massive compendium of maritime powers, listing with specifications every class of military ship in service in every navy. I remember we owned the *Jane's Fighting Ships* for 1990, which would have been about the year my father and I read *Alas, Babylon* together.

I said, "Sometimes I think that that thing—that one and all the others of its kind prowling around the oceans ready, at a moment's notice, to wipe out nearly all the life on this planet—I think it's the secret mechanism of this world, the embodiment of some truth about ourselves, our fallenness or delusion, that none of us usually thinks about, something that we're actually trained to put out of our minds, and that ignorance is part of the problem." I was pointing to the submarine when I said this, and in doing so I was also pointing up the coast, the long Atlantic seaboard, tidal and ambiguous for hundreds of miles before it becomes rocky and discrete in that corner of the country where Oriana and I were born.

Oriana must have cast her thought up along the coast as well, because she said, completing my own thought, as she often does: "I still think of that trip, in fact I've been thinking about it a lot this past week." Kew didn't know what my cousin was referring to, so I gave a circumspect rendition of the story that goes more or less as follows.

2

IN THE SUMMER OF 2003 I drove down to Jacksonville to visit Oriana. On the previous two such summer visits to Oriana, Severine had been with me. This time I was alone, and though Oriana was living with a roommate, she was in a sense alone as well, for this was the summer when she was divorcing her first husband Cal. Oriana had been married to him an even shorter time than I had been married to Severine. Cal, it turned out, was violent and manipulative. He became physically abusive after he and Oriana married, and he still posed a threat in Jacksonville that summer, though he'd been legally restrained from approaching her. Oriana wanted to take a road trip somewhere neither of us had been, so we went up the coast to Savannah and Charleston. We were gone for over a week, and during that span we lived large. I had inherited a modest sum (long since dissipated) when my grandfather in Pittsburgh, Isaac ben Meir, passed away that April. I paid for everything, and I have never spent money with greater pleasure. We deserved it, I felt—Oriana deserved it, after what she'd been through.

What I remembered most as I related this to Kew on the beach in 2014 was the feeling of escape, the sensations of that low-pressure sky, that low country, and that low and turning season of our lives. No region, no shores of this world, could be more alien to my sensibility, and yet in that time no place seemed like it could be more sad and beautiful, more becoming to us.

We arrived in Savannah simultaneously with a tropical depression. The rains over the old town in those last days of July 2003 could not keep us in—Oriana being the kind of Floridian who attended hurricane parties on rooftops—and we wandered about that mystical little city. When we got too wet we ducked into the cathedral, dedicated to Saint John the Baptist, to dry out. Inside, Oriana wondered if the only other time she had been in a Catholic church was the occasion of my marriage to Severine in the Immaculata atop Mount Adams in the City of Seven Hills, and she asked herself aloud, while we sat dripping in the otherwise empty pews, if she should start going to church.

I don't know if it was her divorce that gave her such a thought, everything that she'd gone through with Cal. This young woman who had grown up with me, just ahead of me, always leading the way and teaching me, this kind and generous and sweet person who only wanted to salvage from her chaotic background a good and ordered life, this sisterlike friend who was one day to sit beside me on a beach while we watched a boat full of nuclear missiles slink into the gray Atlantic swell, this woman who has stood beside me at one too many funerals and who sat soaking in a Roman Catholic church wondering if she should get up and go into the confessional—but there was no priest present and she was not Catholic—she had been made to suffer and even to inflict upon her own being evil wounds which, when I thought of them, filled me with rage and a poisoned feeling in my gut, like I'd swallowed a meteorite full of some radioactive alien metal.

When Oriana said that about going to church and even to confession, I knew that we had come into the cathedral for a more significant reason than to get out of the rain. There was beauty in there of a kind hard to come by, and which we needed. But I couldn't fathom, then, how she, cheated and downtrodden, felt she must confess sins. I didn't understand this impulse of my cousin's until Patrick died, and I sat on that cold windswept beach watching the *Ohio*-class submarine and Oriana made a similar comment, this time to Kew, about the need Oriana felt in that dark moment of her brother's death to visit a church and somehow communicate or acknowledge her sense of remorse. Kew said that she thought she understood, because she thought that all sorrows—not only those that seem to come from misfortune—come in fact from failure, and that no failure belongs to one person only, that we rise and we fail together, and so when your life splits apart at the seams, or the life of someone you love, even when life is destroyed, though it may be none of your doing you still feel it as failure, your very own.

But in Savannah, in July of 2003 in the Cathedral of John the Baptist, rain sweeping through the town, I had nothing wise to say to my cousin. I asked instead if she would go to an Episcopal church, since that was the denomination in which she had been raised. Anyway, she had been baptized in an Episcopal church. For when our grandparents married, when John McPhail joined his line to that of Katherine Scarborough, the Irish with the English, McPhail gave up his religion—almost, Oriana and I have always thought, with relief and gratitude for the chance to escape from the Irish Catholic ghetto of Boston, as it was in those days. And we owe that union to the World War that brought John McPhail to Georgia to train as a paratrooper, the war that transformed the United States of America into a superpower, the most powerful nation ever to stalk the Earth with such things as *Ohio*-class submarines. In response to my question, Oriana sighed and said, "I don't know," and we sat there a little while longer in bedraggled and bemused silence before slipping back out into the rain to make our way to the hotel, there to change into dry clothes so we could go get drunk on expensive wine.

But on our way back to the hotel we went in the wrong direction at first, away from the river, and in this way stumbled upon a structure we did not expect to find, the Congregation Mickve Israel. We thought at first, in the gray and swirling confusion of the rain, that it was another church, built in a slightly less sumptuous Gothic Revival style than the cathedral. But we quickly learned that it was a synagogue belonging to a congregation that had been founded by Sephardic Jews in the early eighteenth century. Two days later, we would discover a similarly ancient (by American standards) and originally Sephardic synagogue in Charleston. But I would forget about this for a long time. I did not even remember my discovery of Southern American Sephardic Jewry when I gave a version of this story to Kew on the beach, on the day after Thanksgiving 2014. I would not remember finding these two synagogues with Oriana until I wound my way out of the Hocking Hills back to Michigan from Ohio in July of 2018.

3

I TOOK MY TIME on that drive. I was not as depleted as when I had left Atlanta, but my mind was if anything more muddled. On the north side of Columbus I stopped at a park and sat by the banks of the Olentangy River and tried to think. I was returning to Kew and her world—to a suburb in Michigan, to my little son already learning to talk, to the Catholic Christian religion and our friends in the parish. I must ready myself.

When I returned to my car I reclined the driver's seat for a few minutes, lit a cigarette, and resumed listening to Pierre Fournier's recording of Bach's Suites for Solo Cello. This was like a decompression chamber or an airlock between the world of *Il Castello di Alta Fantasia* and the world of Kew and Michigan and the Church. In my regular home life I didn't listen as much to the kind of music that I played with my friends in Ohio, and on my way home Bach and other classical compositions for cello were all I permitted myself to hear.

Before stopping in the park, I had paused the music at the beginning of the Fifth Suite, in C minor, which is the most melancholic of the Suites and has been my favorite since I first heard it as a child. I started thinking of my old music teachers, Avigail and David, and their daughter Rachel, trying to remember if she'd been born yet when her mother introduced me to this music. And I was thinking, when I resumed the drive, of how Avigail, the one who taught me cello while her husband taught me theory and composition, had guided me through the Bach Suites with such care for nearly the whole time I was her student.

For a hundred years, since their rediscovery by Pablo Casals, the Suites have been the heart of every cellist's repertoire. Avigail sought to instill in me an appreciation for the inexhaustible wealth of interpretive possibilities that the Suites seem to contain. She recommended to me, above all, three recordings of the Bach Suites. The first she made me listen to and fully comprehend was that of Casals. There is no more passionate, romantic playing to be heard in the whole canon, she said—and skillful, even if we now call it *ahistorical*. But Casals did not just rediscover and study this music, my teacher told me, he fell in love with it and committed himself to it body, soul, and mind.

I had not heard another cellist play the Suites like their foster-father, Casals, until I heard Alisa Weilerstein, whom I've already mentioned in these pages, play all of them in a single session. What I realized upon hearing and watching the greatest cellist of my generation play Bach's Suites was that what I prize most in the interpretation of music, as in the composition of literary works, is some sense of *difficulty* that goes beyond the technical. No matter how elegant the writer's sentences—and elegance is nonetheless the chief aim of prose, in my mind—I want in reading them to perceive instinctively that they were achieved only with difficulty and in this way are distinct from everyday, utilitarian speech and writing. And though she will have nearly perfect control of her interpretation and comprehensive intellectual understanding of the music, from the performer of music too, I wish to perceive—and again, this can only be an intuitive, irreducible perception—that her interpretation is a sort of trial, and so distinct from a merely intellectual understanding of the music and anything that might be said only *about* the music.

Avigail also impressed upon me the importance of understanding Pierre Fournier's recording of the Suites—the one I listened to as I departed from *Il Castello di Alta Fantasia*—which was a much more reserved, even austere but still not historicist interpretation. But when I had committed that idea of the Suites to heart, Avigail paused our lesson one day to explain to me something about Fournier. He was a Nazi collaborator, she said, or perhaps sympathizer, or merely

complacent—in any case, he performed many times for the occupying Germans and for the Vichy government and received substantial
payment for his art. Shortly after the conclusion of the Second World
War, Fournier was briefly suspended from performing publicly, but
he suffered no more serious consequences and lived to a ripe age,
respected as one of the great masters of his instrument.

I asked Avigail how that made her feel about Fournier and his
interpretation, and she said it was still among her favorites and that
the music, she thought, existed in some way apart from its makers
and hearers. "But," she said, "I always think about what sort of man
he might have been when I listen to his music. I believe we have to
forgive," she said, "whatever we can bring ourselves to forgive. It takes
a lot of practice, like this thing," and she tapped very gently with her
bow on my cello. This was at the end of the summer, shortly before
the Days of Awe, when I was fourteen years old.

On that same day, Avigail gave to me what was at that time a
rare recording of the Soviet Cellist Daniil Shafran's performance of
the Suites. This, she said, was her favorite of them all. He was the
most poetic cellist, she insisted, other than maybe Jacqueline Dupré.
And she told me Shafran was Jewish. Avigail always made sure I understood who among the great performers in the Western classical
tradition were Jewish. It seemed to me, back then, that she was trying
to convince me that this was a family of which I was a part, or could
be a part if only I would do something or be something—but I could
never conceive of what that something was, though I sensed it was in
some way bound up with the music. I knew that she was telling me
something more than what she said or played, but I could not speak to
her about it, nor could I answer her in my playing: much that was distinct and unique and precious for her was a single vague mystery for
me, and that included my own Jewish heritage, the Jewish heritage of
the musicians she told me about, and some Jewish essence or expression she perceived in the tradition of absolute or abstract—wordless,
non-representational—music itself.

Other Jewish cellists she told me about around that time were
Gregor Piatigorsky and Emanuel Feuermann. The latter was important to her as the artist she most wished she could hear interpret all

of the Suites, but unfortunately we have no such recording from him. Feuermann was a virtuoso and something of a gallant, Avigail told me. He was born in Galicia. Not long after my teacher told me about him, I would learn that Feuermann in fact came from what is now Kolomyya, Ukraine, and I then confirmed with my father that his father's parents, my great-grandparents Meir and Raissa (one of whom the reader may remember from Adath Jeshurun in Pittsburgh), were born in Kolomyya. Feuermann was perhaps the most talented cellist ever to live, Avigail told me. He ended up at the Berlin Conservatory, but came to America in 1933 when the Nazis dismissed him from his position there. His career and his life were cut short by a botched routine medical operation in 1942, when the man was thirty-nine years old.

On the drive from Columbus to our house in Michigan I listened to recordings made by all these Jewish musicians: Weilerstein, Dupré, Shafran, Feuermann, Piatigorsky. And I recalled whatever I knew about them and their music and how I first learned about them; and I was still thinking, too, about Oriana at different times in the past, and about Annette, and about the quest that Gregory had written for us. The quest began to take on meaning, though still vague: something was coming to me and to everyone. Even when something drastic happened, that probably would not be it. Something worse—maybe years away, maybe taking years to unfold—was coming to judge the heart of life, the heart consumed in the *yetzer ha-ra*. Judgment was coming upon a game rigged from the start.

When I arrived home, Kew and our son were playing in the back yard. I had expected a scene like one imagines from a stereotypical film or a commercial, my little boy running up to me joyously, calling Daddy! Daddy! and extending his arms asking to be picked up. He had done it plenty of times before. But given my mood, the clouds of foreboding and guilt I trailed, it's perhaps not surprising that he stopped short of me, scowled, then turned away shyly. It was some time before he was at ease with me again and delighted by my presence.

4

THERE WAS MUCH TO DO upon my return to Michigan. Though we rented our house, we were responsible for its upkeep and maintenance at the direction of the landlords, who allowed us to deduct expenses thus entailed from our rent. My own negligence had allowed our yard to fall into a state of chaos by that summer, and the landlords wanted me to clean it up. In fact, they encouraged me to completely relandscape the place and gave me leave to do whatever I wished as long as I improved it. That was the catch—as it is in any context—this idea of *improving*. Kew and I wanted to make the place more in line with the native ecology of the Upper Country, so I planted and sowed all sorts of native grasses and flowers, and tore out various shrubs that had no business being there and were failing anyway. If I could not put my life or my passions in order, I could at least bring a more natural and wholesome order to our immediate surroundings.

Though they had given me no explicit guidelines and certainly had not warned against the new landscape I devised, what I came up with apparently did not pass muster with the landlords. However, it was only after compensating me for the time and materials I had expended in reordering the yard that they came to inspect the work. Their pronouncement, to use their own word, was that it was too *wild-looking* and not sufficiently *gardeny*. I had to redo nearly the entire yard, now at my own expense.

Previously neither Kew nor I had given sustained thought to owning our home. Now I found myself considering my friends who seemed to be happy owning their homes. There was Severine in Hawaii with her carefully cultivated mango trees; there was Zach on a trendy street in Mount Auburn with a trendy house so much larger than he and Rachel needed that he rented out part of it and made good money doing so; there was Mark out on his farm with his vines and luthier's woodshop; and I had not one but two friends, former colleagues in Chicago, who had turned their entire yards into vegetable and herb gardens.

After some reflection, I thought that my ideal was to own some place large and old, spartan in its furnishing and half tumbled down— like in Dodie Smith's book *I Capture the Castle*, in which a genteel English family fallen on hard times lives in an old castle; or like the English naturalist writer Roger Deakin, who lived in an Elizabethan manor built on the site of a much older castle that had a moat he could swim in every day. I could use a moat, I thought, and a vast estate most of which I would let grow wild, like Aldo Leopold's farm in Wisconsin where, as he put it, his chief crop was silence. My demesne would have mature native trees and grasses on the grounds, and, except for edible and medicinal crops, only flowers and shrubs of the Upper Country, and I would go out into the yard and listen to the world and do nothing else.

And yet, one sweltering afternoon in the first week of August, as I rested from brutalizing the yard I had just crafted and contemplated the outlandish plants—suitably *gardeny*—and the ridiculous amount of mulch to make them more presentable that I now had to install, it struck me that I was in danger of succumbing to the very sort of puritanism that so infuriated me in every other area of culture. Surely not every action incommensurate with an ecologically sustainable life was a sin worthy to induce self-excoriation? But even supposing it was so grave a matter, the idea of sin is not supposed to be that it is a crime, but an error: straying from the Way. If there is no means of returning—confessing the deviation to that which is greater than the human heart and thus able to forgive it and summon it to return—if there is no possibility for true reconciliation (which is free: not transactional, not blood money), then there is nothing ethical about such a code.

If a moral system, a whole culture, exists to provide order without which human life degenerates into savagery and debasement, then it must also provide means of repairing that order when it is inevitably broken. Neither of the two extremes, libertinism and puritanism, fulfill this basic task. Oddly, both libertinism and puritanism, I thought, wiping the sweat from my face in that yard in Michigan, were sweeping through my culture. The former was breaking it to pieces and the latter was preventing any self-repair. And so a hardness and bitterness, I felt, was leeching through society, sapping all humor and joy in one niche and clique after another—in fact forming those groups, based in identity, which is to say in resentment and outrage and refusal of forgiveness. But the necessary balance is quite simple. Zach had re-enacted it on our last night at *Il Castello di Alta Fantasia*: if there is not *Go and sin no more*, then there is not joy.

And I had no joy then. I was burdened with unconfessed mortal sin—we could never seem to get to Sunday Mass in time for me to go to confession beforehand. And since the previous October when I had remembered Hannah under the honey locusts, I had been launched upon a quest of retrospection. Both of these conditions served to turn me inward, and I have always believed this is wrong. The Code to which I thought I adhered revolves in some degree on the attainment of harmony and balance, what the Greeks called *apatheia* and *ataraxia*—detachment and equanimity. Only in such a way can you be really present in your life. To be cast backward and inward upon yourself by memory and shame is to be cut off from the present.

And yet what are we apart from memory? How can we occupy any relation, fulfill any role, except by meeting obligation and, if we fail to meet it, feel that failure? What this means for presence I wasn't sure, for we are necessarily turned critically upon ourselves in the effort to live rightly. There is no selfhood that is not governed: *autarkeia*—self-government—is another crucial moral term. It's interesting that this term came to mean self-sufficient, or content, because whoever governs is also judge (Greek: *kritês*). I knew, though I did not wish to admit it, that it is not judgment of oneself that brings contentment: it is forgiveness. And that brought me to the strangest truth of all: no human being can forgive sin, whether his own or another's. It is the Way itself which (or Who) must accept one's return.

I stared at the native white pine towering up from my neighbor's yard, a tree I often looked at to bring me solace. It was a thriving and magisterial tree, a creature of maturity and wisdom, which seemed to hold out to me something like hope—though I have never known just what that is. But I know presence. The white pine was present, a presence in my life, and if there was one thing I was sure I believed, one thing that must unravel this mess of self-awareness and forgiveness, it was the awesome potency of real, living presence.

5

IN THE WEEKS DURING which thoughts like the ones just reported sprang up and grew like tangling vines, I was also preoccupied with finding new employment, something I'd not got around to doing since being let go at Saint Brendan's. One day shortly after my return home from Atlanta and Ohio, I suggested to Kew that I might be done with the literary world and with teaching, and that I could return to school and take an advanced degree in one of the natural sciences so as to do something different with my life.

Kew did not care for this suggestion, chiefly because she did not like for me to use language such as *my life*—she thought in terms of *our lives*. We began to argue. "You're a writer," she said later that evening after our son was asleep, "you study languages, you read, you drink black coffee and smoke cigarettes when you can get away with it. Don't go against your own nature. Write the fantasy. If the natural world is what you care most about, there's no better genre for bringing it to imaginative life and charging it with symbolic power. You could write *The Upper Country* in three months—or less. You could write it before the leaves turn, if you wanted to. I don't know why you don't."

Kew also suggested I go to our church and pray about my writing and the future course of *our life together*. Despite her insistence on mutuality and the togetherness of living, she also recognized that I should go in the middle of the day and by myself, so as not to be distracted. Our church held Mass every day at half past noon, and unusually among Catholic churches by this time the pastor offered confession during the half hour before each mass. For several weeks after I returned from the South and Ohio, my schedule was simple and clear. I woke with our son and spent the whole morning with him while Kew slept in or worked, then I biked to the church while Kew put our boy down for a nap. I stayed through Mass and then remained for a time afterwards in silence. On my way home I bought ingredients for dinner and cooked them after working in the yard or around the house.

This routine might have borne fruit, given more time; it might have reoriented all my thinking. But I could not discipline my mind and pray, and I could not bring myself to go to confession. Each time I rode to the church—I always biked through the baking and broken city streets, perhaps as a kind of penance—I was firm in my conviction on the ride there that I would confess my sins and then receive communion at Mass. But it was as if the exertion relieved me of the need—and gave me an excuse to tell Kew I had not arrived in time. As soon as I took a seat or knelt in one of the ancient creaking pews near the confessional box, my conviction—indeed all faith of any kind in a reality beyond the immediate—evaporated completely. The best I could manage—or that I could let happen, for to intend it was self-contradictory—was the peace of having no thoughts at all. But even this solace soon failed me.

In our parish there were a number of women in their twenties, thirties, and forties who were mothers of children ranging in age from infants to teens. Most of these children attended Saint Brendan's, where I'd been teaching the upper school students. Their mothers, all of them energetic and somewhat charismatic people, were devoted to the Catholic Christian religion in its more traditional forms, and they were Kew's natural social peers. She befriended them quickly when we arrived in the area, or they befriended her, and after every Sunday Mass we would socialize with them for a while. Their husbands were always present as well, of course, but I rarely found them to be as lively as their wives or have much of note to say—apart from one or two incidents like the one reported at the beginning of this writing, when one of them would make a remark I found disturbing.

I was conscious of no animosity towards any of these people; indeed, they struck me as kind, sincere, and generous. But for the most part the women did not work outside the home, and those who did worked in no intellectual or artistic career. Their husbands likewise pursued ordinary middle-class careers, which, though dull and office-bound and perhaps objectionable to some of them, they accepted with equanimity as part of their station in life and concomitant with their duty as provident fathers and husbands. I regarded this as noble in its way, one of many possible expressions of the Code, but it was not my role.

While these families welcomed us warmly upon our arrival in Michigan and respected Kew and me for our intellectual careers, they also, I believe, suspected us for the same reason of being potentially unreliable. My one published novel, some of the mothers quickly discovered (their husbands were not readers), took the divine and transcendent seriously but it was, after all, a species of fantasy fiction: a thing of dubious value to this group unless the author's last name was Tolkien. There were one or two of them suspicious even of J.K. Rowling's fantasy, though I informed them that the British author was on record declaring herself a practicing Christian. Evidently, she was the wrong kind. It was clear to me that being a certain kind of something—in other words, occupying the niche of an *identity* or, as I thought of it, a *brand*—this was important to the mothers and fathers (but especially the mothers) of these young families. And this, as I conceive it, is anathema to the Code, the opposite of the roles which the Code supplied.

Kew's creative work was innovative and inquisitive, but it could not have been more influenced by her faith and by her scholarship as a medievalist. These friends of ours at church prayed for a holy cultural renaissance and proclaimed their admiration for works of art that had once upon a time been revolutionary, but they seemed unable to accept even the most mildly experimental work in the present. So Kew and I were, I suppose, both appealing and a little intimidating or somehow orthogonal to the ethos of that parish, and that I was perceived (incorrectly) to be Jewish added to our intrigue.

On Tuesday the fourteenth of August at the noon hour, I sat in a pew near the confessional, wishing to confess, not confessing, thinking of my cousin in the Cathedral of Saint John the Baptist in Savannah on a summer day fifteen years before, wishing to confess and not confessing—she never did, never became religious in any way. I was conscious of the fact that the next day was the Feast of the Assumption of Mary, an ancient feast of great solemnity and holiness in traditional Christianity. I would come to Mass with Kew and our son, and if I did not receive communion then (something I could not do until I had been to confession), it would be conspicuous. I could abstain from the sacrament for a little while, as I had done since getting back from Atlanta and as Kew would do sometimes if she missed confession, but eventually Kew would wonder why I couldn't find the time to get in the confessional.

I had almost steeled myself to rise and receive the sacrament of reconciliation, as it is formally called, when one of the young mothers just mentioned—this was the first time I had seen her without any of her family—entered the pew in front of me and knelt. She did not do this without a glance and a smile over her shoulder at me. Of all the mothers I have been discussing, this woman was the friendliest with me and Kew, the most intrigued and least intimidated. She was also the one I found most attractive, by a fair margin, and the wife of the man who had made the remark about Teresa of Ávila's Jewishness reported at the beginning of this writing. She was a few years older than me, but looked young, and her oldest child (she had four altogether) was already in the upper school.

No image of this woman or feeling about her had ever entered my mind when she was not visible to me, but whenever I was looking at her I could not be unconscious of her physical appeal. My fellow-parishioner had a voluptuous figure and long, thick, curly dark brown hair. In fact she looked quite Spanish, perhaps Sephardi. She carried herself in a way that I thought of as feminine and at the same time very assertively present.

In the first Suite I mentioned that the phrase *alta fantasia*—high fantasy—appears twice in Dante's great poem, the first time in the seventeenth canto of the *Purgatorio*. In the beginning of that canto,

Dante wonders at the imagination, which is synonymous with the mental faculty called fantasy: it is the mind's storehouse of images and its capacity to envision, to behold images. What astonishes the poet is that imagination can so steal our attention, our consciousness, that we become insensible to our actual surroundings. But what, then, the poet asks Imagination, can move you, if the senses are giving nothing to work upon?

He supplies the answer himself: A light moves you, Imagination, a light that comes from Heaven, taking form by itself or guided by a heavenly will that seeks to aid the lowly human being. I say lowly for he is in thrall to the images presented to him by the imagination—as I reported at the beginning of this writing, I was in thrall to images of a fantasy Hannah ... until I was not. But here the great revolution occurs. Until this moment in the Western tradition, fantasy—those enthralling images—was at best suspect, at worst demonic. Now Dante declares that at its most meager fantasy arrives by the senses, but at its best it is divine dispensation, an intervention that does not condemn the man but raises him higher. This is why the images Dante now sees—at the end of the *Comedy* he will call the entire poem by this phrase—are *high fantasy*; they come from on high and for an instant they elevate the man to that lofty source.

Whosoever looketh on a woman to lust after her hath committed adultery with her already in his heart.... So declares Jesus in the Gospel. In my heart then, as I prepared to confess my adultery with Annette, I committed further adultery with the woman kneeling in the pew in front of me. I shut my eyes shortly after she took her place there, and with all my powers of imagination, as we say, I envisioned sex with my fellow parishioner. I was hot and sweaty, grimy from the ride to the church, and in the stuffy air of the building I only seemed to sweat more: but I imagined that I had worked up a sweat not by cycling through the desert of a ruined American city but in vigorous, full-throated sex with this woman. How I would love to go at it with her until my muscles were sore as if from a workout. I didn't want to think these things. I had shut my eyes to prevent the thoughts, but that very sensory deprivation seemed to inspire the fantasy all the more intensely.

I probably knew that would happen: every action brings equal and opposite reaction. Or in other words, it was just the dynamic Dante acknowledges. First imagination was fueled by the senses, then it rampaged to the point where I was almost senseless: no high fantasy, but an altogether mundane one. Now, in addition to confessing the night I had spent with Annette, I would have to also describe what I had just been doing (ideally if not actually) with my fellow-parishioner.

I desire not to desire, I thought. But could that be right? Did I not desire rather to desire rightly? To transfigure my desire? For I had given my heart and my mind to the religion that *was* desire, utterly personal—as attested by the tabernacle containing the consecrated bread, the body of Christ, which I faced. There is nothing the Catholic Christian is meant to desire more than that real presence. And it seemed that I *was* desire. There was a line, I recalled, in a Tom Waits song about that: *Time is just memory mixed with desire.* Time, or the self, he could have said. The song is called "The part you throw away."

So what was the point of confessing? If I was only myself, some tiny little agency pushing a soul around, back and forth and up and down in the world, a soul I had to somehow get *saved*—if I was that and nothing more, then there was no point in confessing. In that case all I would be confessing was that existence was a sadistic game: Here are your desires—which is to say, your self—and here is happiness; you must destroy the former—your self—to obtain the latter. But of course that is exactly what every religion tells you to do. On the terrace of lust, Dante had to walk through fire, and he was morbidly afraid.

I knew—even as I did not cease my mental coition with the woman in front of me—that if the self is what is overcome, then the true reason to confess had to be that I was not in fact that little, wanting, desperate self. I was all to which and to whom I was bound. I was Kew and I was Annette; I was Severine and Hannah, my mother and father, Joel and Gregory and all the rest, everyone and everything, the low gray moving skies of the Upper Country and the heavy thick life-giving air of the Ohio Country, and the damp luminous dream-giving air of Ireland, even the curvaceous brunette in front of me whom I barely knew from Eve. And my confession would be no more and no less than the admission that we all composed one flowing pattern, we all existed in relation or not at all, and my part of the pattern—or the part that I *am*—had gone askew, erred from its appointed way.

That was all grand. Nevertheless, I could not rise, could not disentangle myself from the images of sex. For the images pleased me. I have always believed that the man and the woman coming together is the sacred symbol of reality. Now the woman in my fantasy changed, she became Annette and then Severine—and now this was memory as well as fantasy. Perhaps I should try to imagine this protean woman as a filthy, emaciated figure staring out from a photograph taken at the liberation of a Nazi concentration camp. *For to be carnally minded is death; but to be spiritually minded is life and peace....*

I couldn't make myself do it. Here was my last opportunity to confess before coming back to the church with Kew for a great holy day, and I had spent the time adding to what I had to confess. There was no way out of this spiral—no way that I could find for myself. And so I prayed for the first time in my life. I mean it happened on its own, I didn't have to try to think or feel something, the words surged up in my heart: *Lord Jesus Christ, Son of God, have mercy on me, a sinner, and deliver me from this fantasy. Mary Immaculate, Mother of God, obtain for me mercy, that I might be delivered from this fantasy.*

And my prayer was answered. The images of sex vanished, and these tortuous ratiocinations that accompanied them without dispelling them. In their place came no words, no thoughts, but an image arose of the mature white pine growing a hundred feet or higher over my neighbor's yard, a perfect tree, and I saw it beneath the low, gray, moving skies of the Upper Country that I love so well. My heart ceased its racing. My senses were active and acute again, and when I heard someone leave the confessional I opened my eyes, stood up, entered the confessional, and recited the formulaic words, accusing myself analytically, as if I described some ruined landscape, mined and polluted.

I received my penance and exited the confessional without looking at the woman who had occupied my thoughts until just minutes before. I didn't look at her even when she walked up to receive communion in front of me, and the scent of her fragrance mingled with the taste of the sacrament. While cycling home I concentrated only on the taste of the host, which I had let melt on my tongue, and I looked forward to seeing the great white pine to whose image I owed what little peace I had found that day in the church.

6

WHEN I RETURNED HOME, I saw that the street in front of our house was blocked by a large crane and several other vehicles being used to fell, dismember, and cart off the mature white pine in my neighbor's yard. How many coincidences of thought and feeling, life and death, was this now since I'd stood under the locusts with Kew and remembered Hannah? For a while I remained there with my bike in the street and watched the dismemberment and butchery.

After I finally put my bike in the garage and the groceries in the fridge, I went into our backyard and found Kew sitting on the grass with our son watching the tree come down. She told me the assault on the white pine had woken her and the boy from naps; she also told me that she had known in advance it was going to happen, having spoken to our neighbor the day before. It seemed there was nothing wrong with the tree and it posed no danger to any structure. Instead, our neighbors wanted to put in a larger garage and what they called a *party patio*. The white pine was to be removed for this purpose.

Kew was as outraged and saddened by this event as I, but I could tell as she informed me about it that something else was bothering her, something very deep, for there was a haunted look about her, and I asked her what it was. She said we should go inside and she would show me online. At this my heart skipped a beat, and I foresaw what was to unfold—or half of it: the second half I ought to have foreseen but did not.

I had left my laptop out on the kitchen table before heading to Mass, and Kew had needed to get on the internet for some reason after our son had been awakened by the tree-felling, and her own laptop was upstairs so she had opened mine to use. I had left the browser open to my email, and she saw a message from Annette in my inbox. Kew opened the message and read of Annette's recollections of the last night she had spent with me in Atlanta.

Kew had no sooner done that than one of the young mothers in our parish about whom I wrote in the previous movement of this Suite called Kew to share her distress over the sudden explosion of a new sexual abuse crisis in the Catholic Church. Kew, still reeling from my infidelity she had just discovered, could hardly speak to this woman, but the woman interpreted her shock to be reaction to the Church scandal. Nor was this totally mistaken, for, as Kew was now explaining to me, the prospect was grim.

She was visibly shaken and I could tell, now that we were inside and not staring at the rapidly vanishing white pine, that she had been crying. But we spoke to each other calmly while our son played between us. I looked at Kew sitting on the sofa, her belly protruding, and the late afternoon light shining scarlet in her hair. I felt like an idiot, a juvenile, an unserious person, some incontinent character in yet another novel droning on about petty domestic problems of the *yetzer ha-ra* and the nebulous abstractions of the intelligentsia while the actual earth all around choked and sputtered and groaned to be free of this libidinous dust called the human. I hoped this was not the climax of the eerie season of life that had begun when I remembered Hannah to Kew beneath the locusts back in October. I should have been careful what I hoped for. Were I writing the novel of my choice, I would spare myself what was yet to come.

"I think you can sleep in the basement for a while," Kew said, "after you write to your ... *student* and cut off relations with her. I'll watch you do it and send the email, and that's the last I ever want to know about it." When I tried to express my sorrow and shame, Kew told me to shut up. "At least let me tell you," I pressed, "that I just confessed my sin to a priest." But Kew shook her head.

Now Kew explained what she had really wanted to show me online, the second part of the day's revelation, which I had not anticipated. On that day, the fourteenth of August, the day before the Feast of the Assumption of the Blessed Virgin, a grand jury convened by the Commonwealth of Pennsylvania released to public scrutiny a thousand-page report detailing an historic atrocity of ongoing and widespread sexual abuse and predation perpetrated by the clergy, along with a systemic cover-up perpetuated by the hierarchy of the Roman Catholic Church. It was immediately clear that similar inquiries in any jurisdiction of the Roman Church would discover the same horror, and that before long it would become clear that the cover-up and denial reached all the way up the hierarchy.

In the coming weeks, the only closeness Kew and I could experience would occur in our mutual research of this new scandal: a closeness of revulsion. This was not like in 2002, when the *Boston Globe* initially exposed sexual abuse and the cover-up. It was easier now to read harrowing reports online. The grand jury report was soon made accessible. It was enormous, and the acts it documented so graphically beggared the imagination. Most of them were from long before, but it didn't matter, they were still real and present, because so was the culture within the Church that protected the criminals. Kew and I turned to these reports the way an addict turns to his drug, and the effect was just as degrading.

The scandal has passed now, as every momentous outrage does (including the one I have yet to report in this writing); it has passed into the background nothingness of our time, the time of the *dying Earth*—like memories of winter amidst yet another record-breaking long, hot summer, or like a spent lover, sated (as he thinks) for now. But the power of memory is mysterious, and I can recall with vivid feeling the despair and the fear that the abuse crisis held for us. Kew stood to lose her ancestral religion. She felt bereft as if she were watching the whole world end, for she had grown up in the Roman Church, however carelessly; she had built her academic career around figures who stood at the heart of the Catholic European heritage; and devoting herself to the religion more deeply after the miscarriages had been a comfort. Now, she felt, she had allowed herself to find solace and truth in what she was beginning to see as nothing more than a mendacious nightmare of organized hypocrisy and cruelty.

As for me, I was at risk of ruining our marriage. It was not in the first instance anything to do with Annette—for example that I still thought of her and imagined what my life would be like if I were with her and felt sorrow for my treatment of her (I never went behind Kew's back and contacted her again, partly due to the rather brilliant way Kew forced me to word the email to Annette). No, what I felt was a weight drape itself upon me, some cold, dark, poisonous metal pendulum begin swinging from my heart. The nightmare of inescapable repetition. For just as I had doomed my marriage with Severine by forsaking music—not by some drunken tangle with Alison at Joel Stein's birthday party—so I feared my marriage with Kew would founder if we lost the thing greater than ourselves that we shared. I had nothing like that with Annette, or with anyone else. A man can abandon his children and every human thing dearest to him. But a man cannot cast off the yoke of God. He can lose it only by losing his faith—by having it ripped away, which is what the scandal threatened to do to me. And if I lost that, then something like my passion for Annette could indeed ruin my marriage.

Kew, for her part, chiefly felt anger and disgust. The Irish are not given to brooding melancholy, as she says, and perhaps this was Kew's salvation. Still, she thought something was intrinsically and uniquely wrong in the Catholic Church—apocalyptically wrong, in the fullest, biblical sense of the word, for from this time Kew began poring over Revelation, or, as it's called in the Greek that Kew read, *Apocalypse*. She told me that she saw four kinds of evil at work. There was the atrocity itself, and though much of it appeared to have happened before the 2002 exposure, it also appeared to be a systemic practice that was returning, like a cancer that could not be eradicated. Then there was the methodical and longstanding cover-up by the hierarchy. Third was the unfolding—*spewing* was Kew's word—official response, an endless series of pathetically vapid, insipid, banal, insincere, condescending statements and evasions couched in the most asinine PR language, made by bishops and other prelates. And fourth, Kew said, was how much that outrageously inadequate response seemed to appease so many of the laity.

After the fourteenth, when I had confessed, I did not set foot inside a Catholic church for a long time. It was one thing, I told Kew, to read of the evils of the Church in the past or in far-away places, even if those were places we also knew, such as Ireland. But this was different, at least for me, I was the father of a son—the vast majority of the sexual abuse was wreaked upon boys, a fact that went unaccented in media coverage—and these heinous crimes had been going on a long time, but they were *still* going on, and now I was personally and voluntarily bound up with the Roman Church.

But Kew did go to Mass that Sunday after the fourteenth. She went by herself, and there met the young mothers I mentioned earlier, including the one about whom I'd entertained uncontrollable fantasies immediately before confessing my liaison with Annette, and also the one who had first informed Kew of the grand jury report. During and after Mass, she said, there was little spoken of the scandal. The only person, in fact, to mention it was the one who first brought it up to Kew, but already by then this woman's attitude had become defensive: she was worried the scandal would harm the image of the Church.

"They're *mothers*," Kew told me, "women with young *sons*, of all people the ones you would think would be outraged by this."

"Those women," I said, "have staked their whole identity on being *Catholic mothers*."

"That's true," Kew said, "but there are some things too horrible to forgive, and anyway what actually is the point in having a so-called identity?"

"We all want to be part of a group," I said, "a clan, a clique, a tribe. It's how we've learned to fight our way through existence, these little platoons and sects and cohorts."

"Well," Kew said, "I don't think I want to be part of this tribe anymore."

That night, Kew watched a film, *Miss Meadows*, which was released a few days before my cousin Patrick died in November of 2014. Kew watched this film solely because she knew that at a certain point the protagonist, a woman vigilante, shoots a Catholic priest she catches molesting a young boy. We had watched the film once before, when it came out, after we had returned to Chicago from Patrick's funeral. Why *Miss Meadows* had failed to impress at that time with regard to the Roman Church, I cannot say. Sometimes I think that before we had children, and before Kew had miscarried, much was abstract and theoretical for us that would later become real, substantial, living. We were complacent in those days, and newly elated by the success of my first novel. But we were no longer complacent on that night in August of 2018.

I could not watch the film with her, and I didn't think she wanted me to, so I descended into the basement. Reading the reports of sexual abuse had deranged me, to the point where I myself almost felt assaulted or threatened. I had once before seen a man in my condition, I thought, a man haunted by a specter, and I perceived a need to set down that image. I began by sketching the first few movements of this Suite in my old music composition notebooks, which put me in mind, as I intended them to, of Oriana and that side of my family. I dug and dug in the bedrock of my mind—like Bastian in the book of *The Neverending Story*, when he has all but lost his mind—until I was able to turn this disease of memory to my advantage: to find the image I required though I did not desire it. Then I composed the following movement of this Suite.

7

ON OUR FIRST NIGHT IN SAVANNAH in 2003, when we were drinking wine and listening to the rain make faint music on the windows of the restaurant, my cousin Oriana said something disturbing. She was even then worried about her brothers. The twins were sixteen and her brother Sean was fourteen at that time.

"I don't know when was the last time any of them were happy," Oriana said. "Can you remember the last time you saw them happy?"

"It was our last summer at the lake, the night that Grandpa had his . . . thing."

Oriana sipped her wine very slowly, it was a blood-red wine, and by some trick of the light I thought for a moment that her eyes were the color of the wine. Then she nodded slowly.

In August of the year 2000, Oriana and her family and I and my family for the last time visited our grandparents in the cottage they owned on one of the many small lakes scattered among the Pocono Mountains in the northeastern corner of Pennsylvania. John McPhail and his young wife Katherine Scarborough (Gloria's sister) built this cottage with their own labor in the early 1950s as a place of solace and retreat, but not far from the career that had taken John McPhail to Binghamton, New York, in which highland country neither he nor Katherine knew anyone, but where they would remain for most of the rest of their lives. The cottage was small and primitive, but graceful. At first, my mother always recalls, there was no running water or electricity. In the autumn of 2000, my grandparents sold the place and removed to Florida in order to be by Oriana and her family, and there our grandparents passed away two years later, within two weeks of each other. But Oriana and I grew up spending a significant portion of our summers at the cottage.

The lake on which it was situated is about two thousand feet above sea level. Shaped like an arrowhead, its waters are always black and cold, or so they are in my memory. It rarely got very warm there, even in the middle of summer. Great dark fir trees flourish all around the place, and maples and birches, spruces, pines, and oaks. The lake itself is now densely lined with cottages, though the countryside is sparsely populated, off the beaten path, and when John and Katherine McPhail built their cottage it was among the first to go up on that remote shore. On the lake our grandfather taught Oriana and me to fish, and he taught us how to sail using his small pontoon boat. He also taught me to play guitar and harmonica. Katherine, whose last decades were marred by rheumatoid arthritis, taught Oriana how to make fruit pies from scratch, and how to can and jar in late summer, as she had done every year when she had been healthy.

To his dying day, John McPhail had a full head of hair. In the latter part of his life it was a blazing mane of white that swept back away from his deeply weathered and wrinkled face. His was a stoic and often silent appearance and presence, and it could be intimidating. Certainly Severine thought so: on my last visit to the lake I took her with me. We were by that time unofficially engaged. On this visit to the lake my grandmother Katherine gave me her engagement ring—not a common article in her time—to give to Severine. Everything about the visit felt ceremonious and foreordained.

One evening toward the end of our time there, my father, always inquisitive and even reverent about history, made the surprising decision to ask his father-in-law, my grandfather John McPhail, about his experience in the Second World War. A hush fell over the table, even among Oriana's unruly brothers. My mother locked eyes with her sister Caitlin and I saw a small, suppressed terror in both women; my grandmother just looked sad, and turned her large pale gray-blue eyes—my mother's eyes, and later my son's—down at her ruined hands.

My father knew the risk he was taking. He thought that John McPhail might not have long to live, and my father wanted to record John's stories before it was too late, just as he would attempt to do with his own father. I would go on to learn that my father succeeded in this aim when I read the notes that he wrote up from this dinner, but Oriana and her brothers and Severine and I did not hear all of it ourselves at the time.

My grandfather began by describing *Operation Varsity*, which dropped thousands of American and British paratroopers, among which he numbered, on the east bank of the Rhine in Westphalia on the 25th of March 1945, the Feast of the Annunciation: smiling in a strange way—I can't say whether he was remembering his forsaken religion fondly or ruefully—my grandfather said he'd always found the coincidence funny. *Operation Varsity* was successful, but hard. After difficult campaigning, John McPhail was fighting through the streets of Münster, and his platoon was pinned down by a sniper ensconced in the steeple of a medieval Catholic church in the center of the city.

When my grandfather arrived at this point in his narrative, he underwent a transformation. Already he had been speaking by stops and starts, incognizant of his daughters' insistence that he did not have to say anything. Now, his eyes grew wide and he looked straight ahead at no one, instead of at his plate or sometimes at my father, as he had been doing. His hands, already gripping the wooden table so hard that his knuckles were turning as white as his hair, somehow began to shake without releasing their grip. And tears began to stream from his eyes, though he did not blink. My mother asked me and Oriana to take Patrick and Cormac and Sean outside. We objected, but Caitlin McPhail (as she was once again calling herself, after divorcing her sons' father) could put the fear of God into you with a single glance, so up we rose and made our way out of the cottage with the twins and Sean and Severine trailing behind us.

But what occurred then, for us, was an awesome and happy evening, though it was so simple. The sky was clear, the air very fresh. We walked and walked, all the way around the lake by the open nighttime sky's light—the starlight that has become so rare, it seems—an unlikely combination of ages, eleven to twenty, laughing and joking.

We knew it was our last time at the lake, that in some way it was the ending of a generation we were witnessing, the ending of an epoch and a world, but it did not feel like the end of anything.

By the time we got back to the cottage it was fully dark. We saw that my parents and Caitlin had made the usual fire in the front yard—that is, the yard by the water—and we could rejoin them if we wanted, but we had no such desire. Instead, we lay on our backs in the back yard—the side of the cottage facing the dairy farm across the dirt road—and looked up at the Milky Way. I have never seen it so clear, so perfect, as I saw it that night. Severine lay to my right and I held her hand. My cousins lay on my other side, first Oriana, then her brothers the other side of her. We did not have to say anything, we all knew a contentment as clear and untouchable as the stars we looked at. After a little while though, Patrick said to his sister, "What do you think happened to Grandpa tonight?" And Oriana answered, "I think he was seeing something ... that wasn't there. It was something he saw a long time ago, in the war, and he was seeing it again and it scared him."

She was partly right, as it turned out, according to my father's notes; but there was more to it than seeing. What John McPhail had described at the dinner table, after the younger generation had departed, was first one of his comrades shot down in the street by the sniper. The wounded man was crying out madly, and the lieutenant ordered my grandfather and one other man to try to drag him to safety. The wounded man was someone my grandfather disliked. (I would later learn the story from my mother: John McPhail and the wounded soldier had been in love with the same woman, Katherine Scarborough.) However, the reason that he did not want to retrieve the man was that he was very afraid. But he carried out the order with his fellow-soldier, while the rest of the platoon tried to distract the sniper with covering fire. This effort was unsuccessful, and John McPhail was shot. The sniper's bullet passed through John McPhail's shoulder and his left lung and almost pierced his heart. At the dinner table, fifty-five years later, in the cottage he had built with his own hands, my grandfather wept and screamed uncontrollably, reliving the pain and the fear.

8

ALMOST AS FAR BACK as I can remember, I have found the ending of summer and the first phase of autumn, from around the middle of August through September and into October if the weather is warm, to be a time of unease, misgiving, and turmoil of the heart. A season of raw nerves, it feels like a turning point equally of foreboding and forgetting.

Everyone with whom I share the Code agrees with me in this feeling, but we have differing explanations as to why it arises. Kew thinks that anyone with a scholar's soul, such as she or I have, she says, is responsive viscerally and intellectually to the way the summer leans into the beginning of the academic year. This surely has something to do with it. Gregory, Mark, and Geoff, however, relate the nervous feeling of summer's end and autumn's start to the onset of football season, a sport which dominated the boyhood consciousness of those men.

The most mystical theory was proposed by my friend Zach. In the late summer of 2002, when I expressed my sense of summer's decline to Zach (who was too patrician to ever be into football, though he has always celebrated baseball), shortly before he returned to college and before I went to Pittsburgh with Severine and attended Joel Stein's fateful birthday party, Zach said that I felt the way I did about it for the same reason he did: because I had a Jewish soul that responded to the ending of the Hebrew year, the month of Elul, which is a time of inner searching and, as he was to remind me at *Il Castello di Alta Fantasia* in the summer of 2018, a time of *teshuvah*, turning back to the Way.

The Jewish new year begins with the Days of Awe, a time when the earth and all that is on it is suspended in judgment. On Rosh Hashanah, the first day of the year, God decides the fate of each man and woman, whether he or she will live or die in the coming year. But there is a period of ten days—the Days of Awe between Rosh Hashanah and Yom Kippur—before that judgment is inscribed in the Book of Life or the Book of Death, when atonement may be made and judgment reversed. In the secular year 2018, the Hebrew month of Elul (i.e., the last days of the Hebrew year 5778) came to an end on the evening of Sunday the ninth of September.

I was conscious of the end of Elul at the time, and I was thinking of Rosh Hashanah as it was formerly known, *yom hazikaron*—the day of remembrance—and the story of the biblical Hannah, which is recalled on that day in the Jewish liturgy. Her story is one of beseeching God for a child—a son in this case—and Hannah's gratitude when she conceives Samuel. Her very name means *grace*, the special favor of God. That year, Rosh Hashanah happened to begin on the evening of the day after the Feast of the Nativity of Mary, whose parents Joachim and Anne (that's really the name Hannah again) were also childless. Joachim offered a sacrifice at the Temple for a child, but the sacrifice was rejected. At last, though, they did become the parents of Mary, whom Catholic Christians call Immaculate.

But on that Sunday when Rosh Hashanah began, Kew and I were also reminded, as we were every Sunday in that epoch of our lives, of the doom that seemed to be falling on the Catholic Church. And we were filled with sorrow, for we would not go to Mass for Mary's feast. Out of this crisis came a new interest on Kew's part in my Jewish heritage, an interest that happened to coincide with the penitential month of the Jewish tradition at the time of my own need for repentance.

Kew came into the basement as I was preparing to go to sleep— I was still sleeping on the futon down there and had no idea when Kew might relent and allow me to return to our bed. The sight of her standing there, quite pregnant, was painful; for I find nothing more erotic than the sight of a pregnant woman, and Kew above all. She was glorious, and some otherworldly luster in her hair, flashing in the lights she had turned on, seemed to lend a warmer hue to the old music composition notebooks on my desk.

"I want the God of Abraham, Isaac, and Jacob," Kew said, "I would even become Jewish if it gave us some... tradition, some belonging in which to raise our children, to be a family." As she said this, she began to move her hands over her now hugely swollen stomach. She spoke more, haltingly. "But I don't know, maybe not... I don't want... an identity *or* a role. I want something.... Look, I have to bring this child into the world, and that takes... something that affirms what I know in my bones and my blood that you and I are."

"What is that?"

"Symbolic."

"I don't understand," I said. "Is a Christian symbolic—or a Jew?"

"No, I mean as a man and a woman. We incarnate something."

Then Kew's mother called from upstairs needing help finding some medicine she had forgotten to take, and I talked no more with my wife that night. But I was nonplussed. For Kew had quoted a film, one which she knew meant a great deal to me—though she did not know fully why that is. For hours I was sleepless with the memories that I now record in the last movement of this Suite.

9

LESS THAN A MONTH after filing for divorce with Severine, in December of 2002, I moved into a small apartment, a nondescript place on the fifth floor of a large complex perched halfway down the hillside Riddle Road descends from the plateau on which the University of Cincinnati sits to McMicken Ave. on the edge of the Mill Creek valley. The apartment had a tiny balcony, accessed by a sliding glass door, on which I could just fit two chairs and a table for an ashtray. The balcony looked east, up Riddle Road, which was lined on both sides, there just ahead of me, by pear trees that turned white in early spring and scattered their petals like snow—in one of the three springtimes I watched from that apartment (I disremember now which it was) I saw those white pear petals begin to fall, only to be covered by a thin, ephemeral snow.

I loved that little balcony in that apartment and would sit on it for hours, even in winter, smoking, reading, studying, occasionally looking up the hill toward Riddle Road Market, where Severine worked after she had renounced the violin, and toward the house where we had lived together, though it was invisible even from my elevated vantage. A honey locust on Riddle Road grew just a few yards away to the level of my balcony. I lived in the apartment alone. For friendship I would drive to Columbus or to Athens, Ohio to visit the men whom I now meet every summer at *Il Castello di Alta Fantasia*, or to Pittsburgh to visit Joel Stein.

All of my friends were still home for the holidays, so I had spent New Year's Eve 2002 in Gregory's parents' home, just as I had done on New Year's Eve 1995. All five of us who were gathered on that previous occasion, and whom the reader met at *Il Castello di Alta Fantasia*, were present; but present as well this New Year's Eve were several other men and a number of women, including Severine. Just after midnight, Severine and I were going upstairs to the top floor— the party occupied the ground floor and the basement, as Gregory's parents and siblings were elsewhere for the night—and we were going upstairs in order to have sex. Our divorce in no way dampened our desire for each other, a fact which would remain problematic and irresistible for about four or five months longer.

But we were divorcing, after all, and it was not by some uncommon or unexpected fluke that I managed to say something on the way upstairs that infuriated Severine. There was a brief altercation in the upstairs hallway where no one could see us or hear us over the music, and Severine concluded this argument not by her usual means of confounding me with a dramatic or gnomic statement, but by punching me in the face. I fell to a sitting position on the floor of the hallway, and for the long remainder of the night we did not speak to each other.

The next day in the apartment perched over Riddle Road my jaw was sore—Severine has always been physically strong. As I huddled in my coat on the high balcony painfully smoking cigarettes, I considered that my life was in ruins, that I had ruined it, particularly with respect to women and the form of marriage that constitutes a significant part of the Code. I was lonely and it seemed that I deserved my loneliness, did not deserve to be forgiven anything.

Joel Stein had recently insisted I watch *Der Himmel über Berlin*, and Joel had given me his DVD of the film when I had seen him less than a month before in Pittsburgh and told him of the despair that had settled over me since filing for divorce with Severine. (Little did I know then that he had already begun turning that story into a work of fiction, just as I began composing in my old music composition notebooks, shortly after they happened, all the events and thoughts which fill these Suites.) So now I watched the film, without the subtitles in an effort to improve my German.

I have already had occasion to mention in this writing, when I was thinking about the philosopher Max Picard, that the German word *Himmel* means both *sky* and *heaven*. For this lexical reason it is fortunate that *Der Himmel über Berlin* is not called *The Sky over Berlin* or *The Heavens over Berlin* in the American release, but *Wings of Desire*. The film is about angels and what it means to be an incarnate being, a soul joined seamlessly with a body. It is also about a city that is beautiful and beloved despite division and past desolation, and it is about the sky or heavenly realm over the city and how a city looks from that vantage, and it is about childhood and storytelling, and it is about the endless richness of ordinary sensory life.

There is a moment when Peter Falk—yet another Jewish figure, my former cello teacher Avigail might note, to emerge in these pages—playing himself (and who, I remembered on that New Year's Day, plays the grandfather in the frame story of *The Princess Bride*) declares the goodness of such ordinary sensory things as the combination of black coffee and cigarettes outside in cold weather. He says this to Damiel, who is one of the guardian angels, so to call them, of Berlin. At this point Damiel has not yet become a man, not yet become incarnate, but soon he will, because he is in love.

The film opens with the image of a hand writing the first lines of a poem (the *"Lied vom Kindsein"*—"Song of Childhood"—by the Austrian writer Peter Handke) and the voice of Bruno Ganz, who plays Damiel, reciting the lines. The poem will be read in its entirety over the course of the film. It begins: *Als das Kind Kind war*—"when the child was a child." After the first few lines of the "Song of Childhood," we hear a cello play a long low D. It was from the note on the cello that I trusted the film and woke to full attention. But it was when Solveig Dommartin (who would die of a heart attack in January of 2007 at the age of forty-five) appeared on screen at the twenty-five minute mark of the film, that I began to surrender completely to the images I was seeing and the words I was hearing: it was then that I began to break down before the film. Solveig Dommartin plays Marion, the young woman with whom Damiel falls in love, and he gives up his angelic nature to be with her. Solveig Dommartin looked exactly like Hannah.

We first see Solveig's character Marion performing on a trapeze, for all I know some of the same moves Hannah practiced. At first she is in black and white, but by the end of the film, when she is united with the angel Damiel, they are both in color. It is only once Damiel has made his sacrifice and committed himself to this world that the film presents us with color. Solveig Dommartin was bilingual in French and German, and in the film she plays a French trapeze artist performing with a small circus that has come to West Berlin—it is 1987 or thereabouts, and we see plenty of the Berlin Wall. Marion speaks German, but the film gives us her thoughts in French. Marion is young and pensive, I suppose she does not quite know what she wants from life or where it will take her, and she is alone; yet she is content in her solitude and flux.

At the end of the film, after the circus has shut down and moved on without Marion, the young woman, obeying an obscure intuition, leaves the concert she has gone to hear—Nick Cave and the Bad Seeds—in an old theater and she goes to the adjoining bar, where Damiel is sitting. The man is incapable of speech. Marion delivers one of the great poetic utterances of cinema, a monologue that I immediately thought was comparable to General Löwenhielm's speech, which I had just read in Joel Stein's copy of *Babette's Feast*. (Joel had given me Isak Dinesen's fiction, which I mentioned in conjunction with the lecture that cost me my job at Saint Brendan's, at the same time as the film.) Marion's speech is sometimes called a *Liebeserklärung*, a declaration of love. But at no point does Marion simply say *I love you*. (Thirteen years later I would learn from reading Joel Stein's copy of *The Star of Redemption* that Franz Rosenzweig says this is just what the lover does not say: I love you. Instead, Rosenzweig says, the lover, who is like God in this way, always speaks a command, even if it is not explicit: Love me.)

What Marion offers is an interpretation of grace and fate; and yet she upholds a kind of selfhood, or decision. Throughout *Wings of Desire*, we have heard, in the "Lied vom Kindsein," a gentle wonder at contingency or coincidence, how things happen to be: why am I this person rather than that one? However, Marion declares, *Mit dem Zufall muss es nun aufhören*—Coincidence must come to an end now. We see her and Damiel in profile, until she begins to speak of *Entscheidung*—decision—and then she is speaking to the camera. We are more than the two of us, she tells me as I sit there alone on the futon in my apartment, we are the whole world. *Wir verkörpern etwas*—we incarnate something. Then I see her again in profile, and she says to Damiel, *Es gibt keine größere Geschichte als die von uns beiden, von Mann und Frau*—"There is no greater story than that of us two, of man and woman." Shortly afterwards, in the final scene, Damiel will reflect that it is only his astonishment (*Erstaunen*) at the two of them together, at the man and the woman, that has made him a human being: body and soul joined perfectly. He sees in himself joined with Marion a perfect image (*Bild*) in which he will live out his days. Damiel thinks this as he watches Marion spin high up on a rope, the last color image we see, and he thinks, *Ich weiss jetzt was kein Engel weiss*—"I know now what no angel knows."

Since I first heard Marion speak her *Liebeserklärung*, so much of what I have done has come from a need I have felt to understand what she meant by *incarnating something*. In that image of the man and woman together and in her words, I have been sure, there is some secret to understanding the world behind the world. But it was not until I sat late one night on the futon in that basement in Michigan— the same futon I sat on while watching *Der Himmel über Berlin* on the first day of 2003—that I began to understand that what Marion says about story is equally important. I wondered if she meant the story of love when she says the story of man and woman, and I thought that *if* that is what she means and *if* she is right, then it must be because that story is the only one that has no end, or none that we can see. Even the story of Revelation, as it's restated in *Die unendliche Geschichte*, anchored in Bastian and the Princess, has no end but only a return to this Earth and escape from the world of fantasy.

But in reality, fantasy is not always so easy to escape. After *Der Himmel über Berlin* had finished playing on that winter day in 2003, I fell into a doze—it was not true sleep in which one dreams, I am sure. What then happened was a kind of visionary moment. Perhaps it was akin to what happened to my grandfather John McPhail in August of 2000, or like what happened to me staring at the woman in the pew in front of me in August of 2018. I heard the door to my apartment open and I awoke—or thought I awoke—in alarm to see a woman enter—Solveig Dommartin, as she appears in *Der Himmel über Berlin,* or Hannah as she would have appeared if she had lived to adulthood—Hannah as Gregory described her at *Il Castello di Alta Fantasia.*

This woman sat beside me on the futon. I did not know delight, or not that only. We did not speak, there was no *Liebeserklärung* from her or from me. But we made love, and it was perfect lovemaking. I cannot explain what I mean by that phrase, and I recall nothing of how the vision ended: one moment the real, living, substantial Hannah was astride me, ecstatic, and the next I was awake, sober, tired, dressed and alone on my futon in a small apartment perched over Riddle Road. I rose and stepped out onto the porch in my bare feet, lit a cigarette, and looked at the tall honey locust garishly illuminated by the streetlights.

The Upper Country

1

"BE USEFUL FOR ONCE and come up here and fuck me."

Thus Kew texted me as I sat in the basement on the night of the nineteenth of September, which is when Yom Kippur—the Day of Atonement—came to an end; and so ended as well my exile in the basement.

When I went into our bedroom, she was sitting on the bed, eyes blazing more gold than green, like those of a wild animal crept up to the edge of a campfire. "I'm tired of this" was all she said. When, uncomprehending, I stared at her, she shook her head as one does at children or idiots and gestured impatiently at her midsection. "What do I have to do," she said, "spell it out in Hebrew or Hawaiian? I'm ready to give birth and I want your help to move things along."

Kew's water broke the following evening, and our daughter was born in the early morning of Friday the twenty-first of September 2018. A week or so later I consulted old notebooks and journals to determine if my hunch was correct, and I saw that it was: in the small hours of the morning on Saturday the twenty-first of September 2002 Severine discovered me with Alison at Joel Stein's birthday party in Pittsburgh. And so the tide of coincidence and memory that marked this strangest of years—the last year I conceived of myself as a writer—rolled on, its meaning less and less clear, or my ability to descry it drowned in the fatigue of caring for new life not yet grown enough to know or care about so-called meaning.

2

My PARENTS WERE SUFFERING from lung and heart conditions that had forced them both to retire early and had seriously restricted their movements. But when my daughter was born their health had stabilized; however, still at some risk to themselves, they came in the first week of October to stay with us for over a month. I put them up in the basement, on the futon I had owned since I split with Severine.

One morning shortly after my parents arrived from the east coast, at about five o'clock, when I could not go back to sleep after my daughter had awoken to nurse, I went downstairs to make tea and found my mother already at the task. She told me some of the medication she took made it difficult for her to sleep. But she was an early riser anyhow. This woman, who had always carried herself so stoutly and confidently—I see this in my cousin Oriana's forthright comportment as well—was now stooped and frail, her long wavy hair entirely white. Not two years before she had had still as much deep golden hair as white, had stood upright and vigorous, and had passed her spare time doing things like canoeing in backwoods Maine.

I wondered if the confusion I had experienced over the previous year had anything to do with the suddenly blatant fact of my parents' mortality. *Tree people* Hannah had always called my parents. The odd phrase summoned for me an image of strength. The image reflected both ways: the strength I beheld in my parents, who imparted to me the Code, I saw in trees, and the strength of mighty trees I found in my parents. When I was first learning Old English, in the autumn of 2002 (when Severine and I were falling apart and Joel Stein was beginning to write his novel to find out if life was worth living or if, as he put it once, it was worth dying), I came across these words in the poem called "The Dream of the Rood":

> Syllic wæs se sigebeam ond ic synnum fah,
> forwunded mid wommum.

Here is how I would translate the words: *Fantastic was that tree of victory, and I was guilty of sin, cut deep by defilement.* The tree is the Cross of Christ, and this poem was one of my first serious encounters as an adult with the image of the Crucifixion, but what I first thought of when I read those lines was my parents, for they were my great twinned tree of victory in life.

Now I saw my mother's hands shake and she strained to pick up the tray with our tea things on it. She cursed quietly, so I picked up the tray and carried it to the little screened-in back porch where we could talk without disturbing anyone. I thought, as I went, that my mother's days now were few, and that when she died there would be nothing like the solemn ritual and piety that her aunt Gloria's passing had occasioned.

It should have been one of the coolest hours of the day, well before sunrise, yet the temperature on the porch was seventy degrees, according to a little thermometer hanging on the wall: the antique had once hung in the McPhail cottage in the Poconos, and perhaps for that reason my mother scrutinized it and grunted ruefully. Then she breathed deeply and said, "This air reminds me of September afternoons in Cincinnati, when it's still warm and humid but the reek of autumn has set in."

"In other words," I said, "this air belongs a month earlier, in a climate warmer than the one where we're sitting, and a generation ago, when I was a boy."

She had brought a book up from the basement, and now as we sat down she waved it in front of me in this way she has of asking a question by merely pointing something out. When I was a boy she would get me to name animals and flowers and trees in just this silent way. The cover of the book showed an image of a peacock and peahen embracing while perched on a blossoming bough, so I could see why my mother, who had spent her entire career working with wildlife, had been intrigued by the book. But the title was in Sanskrit, for this was my Sanskrit copy of *Ritusamhara*. I was hoping my mother had not noticed the book that this one had been sitting on top of, a collection of James Tissot's watercolors. That book was to be a gift for her, since in her illness, which so greatly restricted her outdoor life, she had taken up painting in watercolors for the first time in many years.

"It's a long poem," I told my mother, "by an Indian man called Kalidasa who lived in about the second century. The title means the gathering or garland of the seasons, although it can be a little ominous to my ears now, because *samhara* also means destruction, or I guess you could say the birth and death of the seasons."

"Destruction! How prescient. The seasons certainly aren't what they used to be. We're losing them. I can't imagine an October morning like this when I was a girl, in the same climate. We'd have been more likely to have snow by now."

"Yes. And I think that if we lose the seasons as we've known them, we lose a lot of the poetry of life. As for *samhara*, I don't know the deep roots of the word, why it would mean harmonious bringing together and absolute scattering. But I guess there is a very deep awareness in India and China that these sorts of pairs are what our reality is made of: birth and death, darkness and light, man and woman. The idea is you just can't have one without the other. So maybe that has to do with *samhara* being a coincidence of opposites, as philosophers say."

"You get this affinity for words from your father. And my aunt had it. Not me."

This is true. And because for my mother words only ever have one meaning, or one meaning at a time, she is often silent and prefers silent places and work, or anyway she likes such things that don't involve language. By that autumn in Michigan I was beginning to see the nobility and wisdom in this point of view, which had always before struck me as narrow.

"So is the poem about animals?" my mother asked.

"Not exactly. It's full of the natural world, though. And very beautifully, I think. Traditionally it's supposed to be the earliest and least accomplished of Kalidasa's poems, but it's my favorite. It's about the traditional six seasons of India. It glorifies the seasons by casting them as backdrop to archetypal lovers—or it glorifies the lovers by depicting them in response to all seasons. The man and the woman in a garden, the garden of all creation. It's a primordial poem.

"*Ritu* is the word for season, and it means basically a rightful or appointed time, something due and fixed. It's related to the Latin *ritus*—our word *rite*—but actually it's also related to Latin *ars*, which in English is *art*. The Latin *ars* means something fitted, joined, appointed, composed, made appropriate. That's what art was in India or Europe for thousands of years. It was the representation of the sacred order. What makes the seasons beautiful and meaningful is that they repeat, but not in the same way. They circle in a spiral, like going up a mountain. And I think that's how we perceive the eternal, the sacred. I think it's why we have memory."

"I wonder if Gloria would have agreed with you."

"I think she would have," I said. And I wondered if the seasons are the Maker's art, wrought according to the laws he set himself (as I set tempi and key signatures in my old music composition notebooks). Are the seasons the music of the skies that we are now altering, rendering unreliable and discordant? Do the seasons make up a story? It would be the story of consummation in repetition, *The Neverending Story*; or like the musical octave: the same again but different. The old lore of number and proportion, Spenser's *musica universalis*, now skewed to dissonance. But it is supposed to be only at the end of time that an art more than human—a divine music—shall, as Dryden wrote, untune the sky.

What kind of time, though? We used to have more than one word for time. In French the word for weather and time is the same, and that is the only kind of time I think we still have in English. But in classical Greek, that time—the time of weather rather than the seasons, the time that is nothing but the linear onslaught of change—that was *chronos*; and the time of eternity, spiraling musical rightful time—that was *kairos*. When, near the end of Revelation, Jesus says the time is at hand, the Greek word is *kairos*, the time of apocalypse and the time of the other world, time that is always coming round again like the seasons.

And I thought of the Latin *serere*, which means to sew, and gives us the English *season*; ironically the word comes from the same root that gave *saeculum*, from which English gets *secular*, the world *before* the world, the world that does nothing but pass away: the world where there is no more Hannah. Always still, I realized, sitting there with my mother in Michigan while she watched the first deep red glow on the horizon, my thoughts keep coming back to Hannah. Is there still Hannah in some other world? I had wanted to know this since I was fourteen. Studying a dozen languages and adopting an ancient religion had granted me no answers. And yet, if there is another world, then there is Hannah; if there is Hannah, then there is another world. I thought I knew that much.

Whatever has been, is always, said Severine to Joel Stein on a September night—not too warm for once but rather cool—in Pittsburgh sixteen years before, two months before our marriage was swept away in the endless nothing of *chronos*. Hannah lives in the world behind the world, I thought, whose undying time she felt pulse in her body in those days when she did leaping somersaults on a trampoline: and whose endless passion play she could see, lying next to me in a basement in Ohio, when we watched *The Neverending Story* and *The Princess Bride*. And so, I thought, if I must bid the seasons and all rite and foretime farewell, then I must bid farewell also to Hannah and to everything that has been and is—or was—always.

I could not share these thoughts with my mother, because she will not think about the world behind the world. For a long time the fact that I had not been able to share these kinds of thoughts with her had troubled me, since for me these thoughts are deepest feeling. But I could share the silence with my mother, and the mild morning, and the good strong tea she makes. We shared the season.

3

WE USED TO RUN, Gregory and I, like no one we knew. It was wild running. It was dangerous, but we didn't stop until we were the captains of our respective varsity cross-country teams, at which point it would have been a more serious matter—for the team—if we injured ourselves. And we would be injured: usually by tripping on rocks, because mostly what this wildness involved was running in the creeks, a leaping course from limestone to limestone.

Hunley Creek, Clough Creek, Little Dry Run, Five Mile, Eight Mile, Nine Mile, Duck Creek, McCullough Run, Sycamore Creek, and Horner Run, Hall Run and Big Salt, Sugarcamp Run and Wolfpen, the East Fork and the Little Miami all the way to the Ohio. They're all right here if I want them, on the USGS maps that I tack onto the walls by my writing desk wherever I live.

By that autumn when my first daughter was born, I had become obsessed with the maps, as if they were precious relics retrieved from a lapsed world, a symbolic story whose meaning has been lost or the rubrics to a liturgy that has been hollowed out by unbelief. And like those old inscrutable tales and gestures and symbolic orders, the maps on my walls told me something unlike anything I could find on a screen, even looking at a digital image of great accuracy.

The maps were becoming old and discolored, wrinkled at the edges, but to my eyes they were of surpassing beauty. They are mostly green, for the widespread deciduous canopy; also rose, for certain municipal built-up areas; the roads are purple, open spaces white, and the streams and rivers pale blue. Except within the rose-colored areas, each individual building appears in black: I could pick out where I lived and where Hannah or my friends from *Il Castello di Alta Fantasia* lived, and where I walked alone by the conservatory and among the cradle hills. Across the maps the wide band of the Ohio meanders, but what unifies these maps is the topography, indicated by dark red contour lines denoting elevation at intervals of ten feet, always rising from (or descending to) those creeks and streams whose names I never forget. What I see first when I glance at the maps is that wild boyhood running.

Gregory, a born runner, could almost always beat me in a regular race, whether on a track or in the woods. But for all his elfin speed and agility, I was more sure-footed in the creeks than my friend, as if I had instinctual feeling for those places, and so there I usually paced ahead. But sometimes Gregory would overtake me just before we would enter one of the many large concrete culverts that allowed the creeks to follow their natural course zigzagging beneath the roads. Sometimes the culverts were long and bent in the middle, where they became dark, and sometimes they contained a low level of water so that we had to run hopping from one side to the other (in a flash flood they were lethal spaces); and they were graffitied by kids we never saw. Gregory would put on a burst of speed and daring just before a culvert so that he could be the first out the far side, yawping and howling barbarically. Rarely we would emerge to discover other kids lurking, usually getting high and once or twice making out. A berserk Gregory, even when he was just nine or ten, put fear in the heart of any grungy stoner.

When he passed me like this I would let him stay ahead when we ran back up through the neighborhoods. There we ran lawlessly, cutting through yards and jumping fences, usually shirtless even in cooler weather (shirts were a hindrance among all the branching honeysuckle), like two maniacal medieval flagellants terrorizing the complacent burghers of southwest Ohio. We were stopped twice by police and written up in the local papers, but in truth we were free and absolute, and held dominion over all those little waters and valleys.

We ran the creeks all through spring and summer and autumn, Gregory and I, but it is in the cooling season, cross-country season, that I'm most drawn to remember our wildness. We ran for our cross-country junior high and high school teams every autumn for six years, between 1994 and 1999. Those seasons laid down memories of running at a deeper level. We raced in the spring, as well, for our track and field teams, but the track could never claim our hearts as the hills and woods and streams did, when we coursed through them among the other boys, and the girls' teams cheering us at stations on the way and waiting at the end. And so when summer ends and the year declines, my senses send me back to that place and that epoch and my old companion and rival, all our cross-country seasons mixed together in one whirling time.

I remembered all this, more or less, to Gregory himself. He called me on the last of those unusually warm days in the second week of October. Gregory always calls me at this point in the calendar, because Melinda's birthday (the reader will remember this was Gregory's first wife, who died in the spring of 2013) falls at this time. We don't speak often on the phone, but every year since Melinda died, without fail in the second week of October, Gregory has called me. We don't speak of Melinda in particular; in fact, Gregory never acknowledges outright the reason for these rather precisely timed calls. He does not need to. The more critical he is of me in these conversations, the more I can tell Melinda is on his mind. In the October 2018 call, he was only slightly more critical than usual when I had finished my unprompted and unpremeditated remembrance of our youthful running.

GREGORY: "That's some impressive nostalgia, McPhail. You doing alright?"

I said, "Oh you know, strikes and gutters. Kew found out about my affair, I'm taking forever to rewrite *The Upper Country*, we're having some sort of household religious crisis, but we have this amazing baby girl, very healthy and loud, and my parents aren't great but at least they could make it here."

GREGORY: "Are you going to baptize your daughter?"

McPHAIL: "We already have. It was the only time any of us have been in a church since the middle of August. I don't know if we'll ever go back. And yet.... The water has been thrice poured, the child anointed, the words pronounced, the worlds symbolically joined. I believe it, and yet I don't."

GREGORY: "Yes, well, the Code is strong with you. So what's this malingering book supposed to be about?"

McPHAIL: "I have this idea that this country is forever divided, or that the real Civil War never truly ended, and so in *Repentance of the Gods*, as I'm sure you remember in exquisite detail, it's this alternative history of North America, and it's an epic war between a North settled by the ancient Roman Empire that never fell, and a South settled by the Greek eastern empire that also never fell. I set up the series so that the hero and heroine are poised to move at the end of each volume to a different alternative history of a war-torn North America. In *The Upper Country* it's supposed to be a North America that's mostly French-speaking, the idea being that France won the Seven Years' War. Now the couple is fated to play out their love in this version of history, and once again they're separated by the great continental division.

"In *Repentance of the Gods* there was no Christianity. But in *The Upper Country* it's our timeline to the eighteenth century, so the division isn't linguistic and racial, like in the first book, it's an old-fashioned Catholic-Protestant thing. But what happened is that I started writing a totally different book, I guess it's the third book in the series, because it's back in our real world.

"I took the night of Hannah's death as the beginning. Now the book was going to start on New Year's Eve 1995. An entire life, an epoch, a world, hinges on a moment—let's at least say it does. And say I decide against the beer and the role-playing game. I go to the party and Hannah answers the door, I kiss her then and there and she doesn't slam the door in my face. In fact, it turns out to be a decent night. A little awkward at first, but after all I'm a known and welcome person in the house, a family friend—it's how love used to go, arrangements like that.

"At midnight, or just a minute after, it's been a secret this whole time that I kissed Hannah at the threshold. I manage to get her away from the crowd, for a few seconds no one can see us, and with the momentum of that shared secret to guide us we kiss again. The brain is part of the body just like the eye or the hand or the heart. It responds bodily to the things of the body. And what happens next is that Hannah doesn't die, she doesn't fall to the ground unconscious, a few minutes into 1996. This is still the inflection point of my life, but everything moves in a different direction. Eventually Hannah and I marry.... But I couldn't figure out where it goes from that premise."

GREGORY: "Of course not, you idiot, you're supposed to be writing alternative history not an alternative autobiography. I didn't realize how indulgent this writing has become. No wonder you've been going out of your mind and became enamored of your student—"

McPHAIL: "She's not my student—"

GREGORY: "Still exonerating yourself! Look, McP, you'd be fine if you'd just forget your real life. Quit trying to write the book behind the book and stick to the fantasy you're good at. It's like you've forgotten what storytelling is, or like you think it's broken somehow. It isn't. It's the same as ever. It comes from ignorance, darkness, nothingness. It glitters with the brilliance of the nothing, McPhail, and it never ends. Story is wonder, a world, it opens up and out, it's discovery. It's not a fucking confession.

"Think about D&D. The reason it's good and fun is that it isn't narcissistic. You get *away* from yourself in fantasy. Seriously, if you want: lay down your life to save it. If you don't discipline yourself to leave yourself out of your writing—I mean in any direct way—you'll drive yourself insane with longing for what could have been but wasn't. Because that's what our so-called inner lives are—just desire, lack, non-being. Forget it.

Your job is not to crave the possible, it's to long for the *impossible*. That's why you're a fantasist. It's the impossible you need to learn to believe in, McPhail."

McPHAIL: "But isn't that... impossible?"

GREGORY: "I'll tell you what I think. What's cruel about life, but also its only hope, is that our wishes are not fulfilled, not even infinitesimally. What happens is only what we *can't* foresee. All that desire, that sense of another world, it's nowhere, not even the littlest bit real, and it certainly isn't potentiality sifting like sand in an hourglass into the world of actuality, or whatever mumbo jumbo the philosophers come up with.

"What all that desire morphs into with each passing year is the sense of the *failure of life*. But true fantasy, the higher form of what we played in the hills, has nothing to do with that, it's not wallowing in memory and it's not speculation, it just flat out *is not you*. It's the discovery of another actuality, which to us in this world is not potentiality but impossibility. Art is the way to make that discovery. Religion was too, once upon a time, when it was vital and new. Anyway, that's what art is, and it's *not representation*.

"Writing anything down means it's from another world. Clarissa Dalloway is as unreal as Bilbo Baggins. Neither of them is a representation of anything, they just are what they are in their own worlds. You need to love your own one real life and you need to love your writing; but writing your life is not living. If you'd write real fantasy, then you'd live. It's not too late for you, McPhail, either to write or to live."

McPHAIL: "Maybe you're right about art not being representation. But then how come back at *Il Castello di Alta Fantasia* you made that NPC, Francesca, an adult image of Hannah?"

GREGORY: "Because you'd been talking about this other writing you've been doing, writing your life without Hannah, as you said, and I wanted to show you that wasn't real *and* I wanted to show you how dangerous it is to desire what could have been."

McPhail: "But how did *you* know what could have been? You never met her."

Gregory: "Of course I met Hannah. The last time I saw her we must have been thirteen. I was going to sleep over at your house that night, but first Hannah's family was visiting. We raced around your neighborhood. You could never beat me—not unless I let you—but she could. She passed me by on that giant uphill, passed us both, like we were standing still."

4

WATER DOES NOTHING BUT FLOW and fall, yet it is power. That day in the second week of October when I spoke with Gregory, Hurricane Michael was battering the Gulf Coast, yet another freakish storm, herald of the new normal. For many days after I spoke to my friend I was haunted most by what I had said to him about my daughter's baptism. By the time of my thirty-seventh birthday, when I had written most of the first version of these Suites in my old music composition notebooks, it was my own baptism that loomed in memory. And so on that day of cool clear sunshine I sat on a blanket in our backyard, my month-old sleeping daughter bundled up on one side of me (a few tufts of her surprising quantity of hair, exactly the same color as Kew's, sticking out from under her wool cap) and a pint of Guinness on my other, and set down this tale as briefly as I could.

By the beginning of 2016, Kew had brought me around emotionally to joining the Catholic Church, and teaching fiction and poetry (including to skeptical Annette) showed me just how essential a Western, which is to say largely Christian, tradition was to my chosen art. It was almost as though if I were to be a writer, then I must be a Christian, and the most archaic and deeply rooted sort of Christian I could be. The roots of my words had to go far back and skip nothing along the way. I must be an *incarnational* writer if I would know and put on paper something of the union and beauty of body and soul.

There was nothing, however, about the Christian religion in America that appealed to me in any form I had ever encountered.

In America Christianity struck me as a totally artificial, superficial, and usually hypocritical imposition, an alien and exploitative ideology grafted onto the land. But in Britain and Ireland, anywhere in Europe, things were different. More accurately, the landscape was different. And since rekindling our relationship shortly after Kew's move to Chicago in the summer of 2011 (from Oxford via one year in South Bend, Indiana, the reader may recall), Kew and I had spent a portion of every year in England, visiting her friends there, and in Ireland, where as I've stated some of Kew's distant relations owned an old cottage which they let us use. Kew was able to bring me around to joining the Catholic Christian religion—as distinct from merely entertaining it intellectually—because she was able to show it to me in Ireland, and there I was able to experience it as something out of doors, something sunk into the very rock and mixed with the tides of the Atlantic.

In County Kerry, where Cnoc Bréanainn rises, she was acquainted with an old priest, an elder friend of her second cousin or some such connection. He was a wizard-like man, unlike any other priest I've ever met (Irish or not), who traipsed around Kerry smoking a pipe, and he was one of the few people there who still spoke any Irish. Persuaded by Kew, this priest, though past the age of eighty, agreed to baptize me in a peculiar but licit way in the early spring of 2016: with ice-cold water at the break of dawn in the ruins of Kilmalkedar, at the foot of Cnoc Bréanainn in Kerry.

The name of the ruin is more accurately spelled something like Cill Maol Céadair, the church of Maol Céadair, a name meaning ... well, what exactly? The Irish *maol* (a word appearing in what is supposed to be the original form of my mother's maiden name McPhail) denotes baldness or flatness, but in the early Christian period it connoted a servant, perhaps in the sense of an ascetic who had taken the tonsure. As for *céadair* or some such word, it means the cedar tree. So Maol Céadair was the Servant of the Cedar, for Jesus was said in legend to have been crucified on a cross (that would be the same *sigebeam* or *rood* mentioned in the second movement of this Suite) made from the wood of a cedar.

The man Maol Céadair was supposed to have been originally from Ulster, perhaps not far from where the McPhail—or rather the

Maolfabhail—originated. (As for the second part of *Maolfabhail*, it seems to be a word for traveling, roaming, journeying—*fábhall*—thus perhaps the name means a wandering scholar or monk.) Maol Céadair is supposed to have built his church jointly with Saint Brendan. That building no longer stands, but perhaps some of its gray stones, color of Atlantic storm, are part of the ruin that is there, which dates from the twelfth century. And so I had requested to join the Church, to myself become a Servant of the Tree, among the stones of Cill Maol Céadair. After I was baptized, Kew and I followed the path from the ruins to the top of Cnoc Bréanainn, along the Stations of the Cross described in the dream I had of Joel Stein on Christmas Eve.

What I found, almost immediately upon returning to America— Chicago at that time—was that I no longer had any access to that elemental ancientness of Christianity, even though Kew and I attended the most sumptuous and traditional church in the city. That was just the problem: it was in the middle of a giant American city, and like many Catholic churches in that city it had been built in the ornate Polish Cathedral style, as it's called, and this—unlike the gray Atlantic stone of Kerry piled into altar and temple—had nothing to do with anything in my heritage and I *felt* that somehow. It was like going to church in a museum.

But among those stones on the windswept fringe of Ireland it wasn't like a museum, it was something original, mysterious, and ascetic. By the time of the scandal in August of 2018, after which, except for my daughter's baptism, I no longer wished to enter a church, I was probably looking for an excuse to beg off from the religion. At least, I was in America. But I was left with the memories of my baptism in that primitive dawn, at the limit of the Old World. There was something in that moment to which I had to remain true, but I no longer knew how to do that, or how I could make it something that might be passed down to my children.

In the Christian religion it has been said from the beginning that we are baptized into Christ's death, and so also into his rising from the dead—for the Christian religion is yoked at every moment of its story to the idea of the *felix culpa*, the descent in order to rise even higher. Now the waters of baptism seemed to have become for me only an entry upon what was dead, on what was past or passing away, not on anything to come. I began to understand what Kew had meant when she said she had lost a whole world. This was not solid metaphysics; still, it was how we felt. I had only to imagine my little boy or even my baby girl abused by a priest to curse all metaphysics to the end of time.

5

Severine called me, sounding worn yet excited, two days after I composed the previous movement, to inform me that on my birthday she had given birth to her first child, a daughter. We couldn't talk for long, of course, but one thing Severine did tell me then was that she and her husband were going to have the child baptized. Severine, like her mother before her, had remarried a man who was Catholic by heritage. I told her it was fitting to baptize a Navy brat, and she seemed to agree. After we had talked, I knew what I wished to be the last account of Severine that I would provide in these Suites—the only account, I finally realized, that makes sense of why I have always thought of her as floating down the watercourses of the Ohio valley and finally far out to sea as a Naval officer and island-lover.

I entered the ninth grade at the end of the summer of 1996, nine months after Hannah had died. In those days, the middle school and high school grades of our school district were all together in one building. The orchestras, however, were distinct, though both were under the direction of a man named Paul Ostermann. On the first day of practice, Mr. Ostermann introduced a student who would be playing with us, despite the fact that she was only entering the eighth grade. This student was a violinist, and because of the level at which she played, it was deemed appropriate for her to join us. This was longstanding policy, and I had spent my middle school years playing with the high schoolers. It was also Mr. Ostermann's policy that twice during the school year all of the students in the orchestra auditioned with Mr. Ostermann to receive their positions, just as they would in a professional orchestra.

Severine, our new eighth grade student, promptly won the first violin position, despite the fact that an older girl, Hilary, was also a violinist of soon-to-be professional caliber. Severine remained first violin for the remainder of her high school career. Likewise I was the first cello: this meant that Severine and I sat facing each other. I thought she was a sphinx, aloof and terribly dark—even her eyes, blue and electric like the heart of a very hot flame, were somehow dark, or cast shadows mixed in with their light. But as soon as I heard her play her instrument, even just to tune it, finger exercises and etudes to warm up, I knew that at least as far as music was concerned we moved in the same world.

At first this was the only way I knew Severine, these glances that she always returned. This was not like with Hannah; however intrigued I was, I was not in love instantly with Severine, or at least I did not think that I was. But there was a mystery I had to solve, which was why she had not joined the high school orchestra when she was in the seventh grade. I didn't remember seeing her around school at all the previous year, but she was apparently not a new student. I soon learned that Severine had spent most of her seventh grade year in the hospital or under close medical and psychiatric supervision at home as she struggled with anorexia. The disorder almost claimed her life. The story, as I was eventually able to glean it from Paul Ostermann, was that it was the violin that saved Severine. Indeed, she had to almost die in order for her father to be willing to purchase a quality violin for her and the lessons she needed from a true master. By the time she returned to school for eighth grade, Paul Ostermann was convinced she would one day enter the ranks of the virtuosi.

All I knew was that I wanted Severine's friendship, and slowly throughout that autumn I did my best to win it. Devoting myself fervently to the cello and my studies of music theory and history, as my parents wished me to do anyway, was my primary means of relating to Severine. But we also began to roam on foot around the suburbs where we lived, in a way not unlike how Gregory and I ran through the yards and gullies and creek beds. It was by the side of one of those creeks that what I finally understood in the autumn of 2018 to be my formative image of Severine was born.

On Saturday, the first of March 1997, it was unusually warm in the Ohio Valley and the air therefore saturated with twice its normal moisture for that time of year. Thunderstorms settled in over the City of Seven Hills. It rained heavily through the weekend, but the stalled system brought three times as much rain in areas all around us, all over the middle and upper parts of the Valley. The downpour resulted in the worst flooding in generations. School the following week was closed for several days as the waters of the Ohio, the Licking, the Little Miami, and all the smaller tributary streams of our dendritic country continued to rise after the rain had moved on. I went with my father to look at the high water in the center of the city, and we went up into Ault Park (where Severine and I would one day hold our wedding reception and perform one of our most successful duets together) and surveyed the flooded valley of the Little Miami. But the moment I record here occurred that Sunday afternoon, after Severine and I practiced together.

We set out, despite the rain, to walk from my house to Stanberry Park in Mount Washington. At that point no one realized the flood would become so bad when the waters from upstream made their not so gradual descent. But I think that when Severine and I saw Clough Creek raging underneath Hunley Road where it crosses Clough Pike, we had some presentiment of what was to come. I had never seen anything like that water, not even in the closest encounters Gregory and I had had with flash floods. The surface of the torrent was churning just inches below the bridge as it burst from the culvert in its mad rush for the Little Miami—where it would find too much water to join, and so the water would climb still higher and spill over the bottomlands. Clough was brown and gray and white and wild, and it was shockingly loud.

Severine and I paused on the sidewalk, gripping the handrail and leaning over the creek, transfixed. As it is written in Genesis, there we were, a man and a woman between the waters above, that fell upon us, and the seething waters below us. We did not speak for a few minutes, and when we did we had to shout.

"It's like it's alive and it will never stop," Severine said. "When I was sick, it was like the whole world was dead, or it had stopped somehow, time was frozen. I was frozen, too, I was stuck. Then I discovered that sometimes when I play I can feel like this water. I don't think I could stand always feeling that way. But right now it's good."

She looked at me and said, "Right now is good, isn't it?"

6

IN THE SPRING OF 2004, a particular species of cicada that leads a subterranean existence for seventeen years before emerging aboveground
to procreate surfaced and flourished for some weeks in a magnitude
of several billion individuals across southwest Ohio. The creatures
covered the surface of the earth, whether built or natural, like a biblical plague. At no time in the day or night were you unaware of them.
The destination of these autochthons was the arboreal canopy, and
they achieved their goal in wave upon wave of rising life, but when
the time for death drew near the insects fell back to the earth, where
their spore had been dropping all along in a kind of sticky rain. So
you would see people walking on a sunny afternoon with open um-
brellas, and in the wealthier quarters of Cincinnati women, wary of
the creatures becoming entangled in their hair, carried tennis rackets
around to swat at them as the cicadas flew clumsily from tree to tree
or plummeted. Restaurants offered cicada dishes. In the vestibule of
my apartment building mounds of cicada carcasses accumulated and
the reek of them was ubiquitous indoors and out.

But the aspect of this phenomenon that persists in my memory
most tenaciously has nothing to do with all that: it is sound. The cicadas made a constant, loud, complex sound. Many people referred to
this as song and claimed to hear something poetic, a sad but mighty
effervescence of the *carpe diem* spirit in an otherwise disgusting creature that came into the air and the daylight only to sing and mate and
soon die. Others called the din noise or even cacophony, which latter

term literally means an evil sound. The cicadas themselves could certainly seem evil, I supposed, with their growing stench as more and more of them died and the weather grew hotter and stickier with the swelling springtime, and their corpses piled ever higher or clogged the sewers, weird counterparts to the fallen leaves of autumn.

The difficulty, I found, with thinking of them as evil was that if I pursued that line of thought with any rigor I eventually arrived, as already suggested, at the biblical plague of locusts, and in that context it is not the insects which are evil, upon whom the judgment of God rests, but the people against whom the plague is sent. But in any case I was never sure that cacophony was appropriate to describe the combination of the distinct noises the male and female cicadas made unceasingly as they sought each other in the boughs: a high constant whirring and a lower, more jagged and raucous chorus that heaved and quieted rhythmically. That complex sound subtended and permeated and rose above all life in that high spring of 2004, an immanent *musica universalis*. It was difficult to sleep at night.

For the first time in many years I recalled the cicadas of 2004, and the thoughts and events I now describe, in the early morning hours of Saturday, the twenty-seventh of October 2018. My sleep had been much interrupted by my daughter, whose waking in the night to feed had also this time woken our son. After the last time I succeeded in putting him back to bed, at about four in the morning, I gave up on sleep myself and descended as quietly as I could to the living room. A terrible nervous feeling clung to me—in my spine and in my gut. It was as if I feared I would discover my father dead on the futon in the basement, having had a heart attack in his sleep. Or perhaps it was more a feeling of having lost something, or forgotten something of grave importance. Whatever it was, I couldn't understand where the boding had come from, for my sleep, too little and interrupted though it was, had not been troubled by bad dreams.

I needed music. Crammed among our bookshelves I found my headphones, and I put them on. I also picked up the book, lying atop the stacked books, next to my headphones. From my phone I played Alisa Weilerstein's newest album, a recording of Haydn's two cello concerti and Schoenberg's early, romantic composition, the chamber piece and tone poem (as such music is called), *Verklärte Nacht*—Transfigured Night. It is an unusual program, explained by Weilerstein thus: the music of both composers, though separated by 150 years, is all associated with Vienna, which city the cellist's grand-parents, who were Jewish, fled after the Anschluss, and so escaped annihilation in the Shoah.

Weilerstein does not speak to this point, but Schoenberg was Jewish. Though he was assimilated, Schoenberg recovered his Jewish heritage later in life, partly in defiance of the rising tide of Nazism. He claimed that he had always thought of himself as a Jew, despite his youthful conversion to Christianity (which back then was, as Heinrich Heine once remarked, the ticket to entry into European social and in-tellectual life), and Schoenberg described his formal return to Judaism as the natural culmination of a lifelong spiritual inquiry and yearning.

The conversion, or recovery of his Jewish heritage, impacted his art as a composer. It also produced one of the rarest documents in re-ligious history, a written statement of teshuvah, witnessed and signed by a rabbi of the Union Libéral Israélite and none other than Marc Chagall in Paris in 1933, where Schoenberg fled when Hitler came to power. All that was long after the composer had written *Verklärte Nacht*, but who is to say the future turning and returning of one's soul is not present in all that the soul makes, in youth or in age?

As I was listening to Weilerstein and the Trondheim Soloists begin to play *Verklärte Nacht*, I opened the book I had picked up. When I realized which book this was and saw what it contained, my heart skipped a beat. For I saw what Kew had been doing, trying to go back in time and recover something of ours that I had lost and tarnished. She had been trying to do something which, since August, I had imagined accomplishing with my Jewish heritage but had feared was impossible, or at best a kind of pretense or role-playing game. Kew was trying to recuperate and remember—to truly live again—a kind of passion and revelation.

Among the pages of the book, functioning as a place-marker, was a photo Kew had taken in the spring of 2004, when she and I were finishing our undergraduate degrees. Kew was a student in the Classics Department as I was, and we had crossed paths many times in the preceding three years, without interesting each other. But that was changing quickly in the spring of 2004. In fact, the photograph I held in my hands was taken after our first night together. It showed neither Kew nor me, but the dawn as it descended slopes of the high ground on which the university sits. The view was of the tall honey locust that grew just outside my balcony perched over Riddle Road, and beyond the honey locust the street, flanked by pear trees as it ascends to the university. On the back of the photograph Kew had written *Transfigured Night*.

This small, dilapidated image was marking the place of the poem "Verklärte Nacht," which gave Arnold Schoenberg the textual inspiration for his composition of that name. The book was an antique volume of the poetry of Richard Dehmel. Kew had bought the book the day before she took the photograph. We had gone to a used bookstore, Duttenhofer's, near the Classics Department and the conservatory. Afterwards we had gone out with friends to a bar down the street, Christy's (which no longer exists), and then I'd invited Kew and her friends back to my apartment to recite the poetry and drink more. Only Kew took me up on the offer.

At my apartment, Kew and I read some of his poems and talked about how erotic they were, how much in love with love. We were as versed in the hermeneutics of suspicion as anyone who came up through the university system in that time, but Kew was not suspicious of love, as so many people seem to be suspicious of it today, seeing in it no more than the machinations of hierarchy and deception: for her it was glorious and sometimes awful, but anyhow a force of nature or something Godsent, not something one could choose or deny. And she spoke of love as a thing of the body and one's real, substantial, limited place on the Earth.

Sitting there in my apartment, I found "Verklärte Nacht" in the volume of poetry and said that before we read that one to each other we had to listen to Schoenberg's string sextet of the same name. I then got up to open a large bottle of Chimay—"she may or she may not," Kew said, punning on the name of the beer and grinning at me—and poured it out for us, and put on the only recording I then possessed of the music, the Leipziger Streichquartett's.

"You'll have to turn it up to hear it over this din," Kew said, gesturing with a nod to the hollow roar of the cicadas that was coming in through the balcony doorway, where only a screen separated us from the insects and their chorusing.

While the music played, we talked of our past romantic and sexual lives: this seemed natural in the wake of reading Dehmel's poetry. I told Kew about Severine, *the wife of my youth* as scripture says, and I explained that although Severine and I had continued to see each other sporadically for about six months after we filed for divorce, in November of the previous academic year, I had not since the end of that strange time been intimate with anyone, nor had I intended to be. It was a celibate and solitary life I'd been leading in that apartment that looked on the pear trees and the honey locust—a life unlike that of our fellow students, Kew said.

In fact, I could not believe she was sitting there, on the futon where on New Year's Day 2003 I had experienced my vision of Hannah as Marion from *Wings of Desire*. Now, as I listened to Weilerstein play Schoenberg, I remembered that I could not believe how beautiful and desirable Kew was that first time she sat there. Her dress was low-cut and form-fitting, a vibrant blue-green, and although it was hot and there were the cicadas to worry about, she had not put up her great mass of flame-like hair and it rolled and flowed all down her shoulders and her back. She looked to me like some Celtic warrior goddess. And there was something in the confidence of the way she sat there, at ease in my space, that said to me she knew this was all scripted, we were moving, she and I, through a preordained choreography.

It was true what I had told her, that I had been celibate in the previous twelve months, but while I was pouring the Chimay I glanced at her sitting there looking at the CD case and I was overcome by the urge to sleep with her. I realized, however, that since the dissolution of my relationship with Severine I had forgotten how to initiate sex. Was I supposed to say something first, and if so, what? I was not so stupid as to have missed that Kew wanted the same thing I wanted, but it was clear that she was waiting for me to play my part. At least the book of poetry had given us a pretense for sitting next to each other on the futon. But it was absurd: How could I, already having burned through a marriage, be confused about this kind of thing?

When the Leipziger Streichquartett fell silent, we read Dehmel's poem that had inspired the music. To be honest, I don't much care for the musicality of the poem. It is sing-song and saccharine: too pretty. But the idea of it is beautiful. I thought so then and think so now. A man and a woman walk together on a winter night *durch kahlen, kalten Hain*—through a bare, cold grove. They have only very recently become lovers, it seems, for the woman confesses to the man that she is carrying a child, but it is not his child. She says she wanted *Lebensinhalt* and *Mutterglück*—fullness of life and a mother's happiness—but *Nun hat das Leben sich gerächt: nun bin ich Dir, o Dir, begegnet*—now life has avenged itself, now I have met *you.*

The man is very much in love, and so something happens which you could call a conversion or an epiphany, a kind of revelation which provokes a decision: *das Weltall schimmert*, he says, the universe shines, and each of us has kindled a warmth in the other, and that warmth will transfigure the stranger's child. *Du hast mich selbst zum Kind gemacht*—and you have made me into a child, he says, and embraces her and they are no longer walking through a cold, bare woods but through *hohe, helle Nacht*—high, bright night.

It had been my turn to read the German and Kew's to translate it. When we finished we were looking at each other, and I thought that if words were necessary before action they were no words other than the poet's—and so hers. In a single motion I tossed the book aside and more or less dove upon her. It could not have been the most graceful motion. She had long since slipped her shoes off but I still wore shoes and socks, everything. I was on top of her, kissing frenziedly and then pulling her dress down, which she seemed very enthusiastic about, when she suddenly pushed me back up and I thought I had made a terrible mistake. But she was in front of me in no time tearing my pants away, at which point my shoes became a hindrance, though only briefly.

It was an athletic, fearless abandon of lovemaking. The year without sex, and my consciousness of that interval, vanished the moment I felt Kew's breathing and moving beneath me, and from that point I put myself into it wholly, not haunted—as I had been afraid I would be—by recollections of Severine, but capable of a complete effacement of the self as I have heard some people say happens in prayer, a pouring out of the self into pleasure that transcends the individual because it is mutually willed, at once escaping the body and sunk deep into it—just as I had imagined and foreseen while pouring out the Chimay.

Kew knew her part as well as I knew mine. And that, I have always known, is what good love-making requires, at least if it is love-making, the creation of shared delight, and not simply having sex, the mere taking of pleasure. It's in our roles, so the Code insists, that we exist and exert for others. Kew and I had left two dim lights on by which to read the poetry and we never got around to turning them off. It was late enough when we started that people would soon have been straggling home from the bars, and if it hadn't been for the cicada chorus someone drifting down Riddle Road would have heard the telltale sounds and looked up and seen everything, for we also never got around to closing the long blinds in front of the porch's sliding glass door. The futon was new then and in good repair, but by the time we had exhausted each other it had somehow become broken, and we fell asleep naked and sweaty on the floor.

7

My former Pittsburgh friend Joel Stein experienced the cicada emergence of 2004 in Cincinnati. It was the only time he came to the City of Seven Hills. Alison (or, rather, my unfaithfulness to Severine) had long since come between us, and the fiction Joel had made of that, not to mention Joel's new Jewish vision of himself and his sudden need to leave Pittsburgh. But we loved each other still and he felt like he had to see me in my natural habitat, as he put it; he felt he must swing by on his way home to Minneapolis to begin his new life in his hometown.

Joel met Kew the weekend after the one I described in the previous movement, and his verdict upon her, at the moment he and I parted company for the last time, was minimal and prophetic: "She's a Celt like Severine, but with bigger tits and a bigger smile; she's also smarter and more ambitious and will be more successful than you." After that statement I had no further inclination to speak with Joel, though despite all bitterness I missed him in my life, for he was my last connection to Pittsburgh.

We continued to communicate through a few long handwritten letters. The last of these was dated Friday, the twenty-second of October 2004—my twenty-third birthday, the last autumn I lived in the City of Seven Hills, while working on my Master's in Classics. Kew had already moved to England by then. Joel writes of a woman to whom he'd become engaged, Rivka, the daughter of a longtime family friend (this kind of thing is exactly why he'd moved back to

Minneapolis). He wished me luck and made it plain that our acquaintance was at an end.

Naturally I thought of that last meeting with Joel and the last letter from him, after I had remembered Kew and our first transfigured night—that springtime night was a pleasant and a wondrous recollection and served momentarily to displace the feeling of baseless terror with which I had awakened. But when I thought of Joel the feeling returned, so powerfully in fact that I had to stop listening to Alisa Weilerstein. In the predawn silence my mind flew back to the Friday before my thirty-sixth birthday, the previous October, and the strange series of realizations, coincidences, and events that had occurred since that day when I remembered Hannah to Kew under the locusts at the end of our block. I had felt increasingly sure that some story had begun on that date, under the trees, but I had lost the plot, as they say, just as I had floundered in rewriting my now horribly overdue novel. Everything had sort of fizzled out.

At least the season has finally turned crisp, I remember thinking as my family began waking up. Since I was awake first, I cooked a large cozy autumnal breakfast for us all, though I had little appetite myself. I told everyone I wanted to watch the Notre Dame-Navy game that evening (they were playing at Navy on the West Coast, I remember) but if we had no other plans, maybe we could take a walk as a family if we bundled up my daughter sufficiently.

By the middle of the day it was only about forty degrees, and misty, very damp, seeping cold, and my mother didn't think she should go out in such weather, nor did Kew want to take the baby out. Kew's mother was never able to walk far. So I went out with my son, who was always eager to be out of doors, and with my father, who was the same—three generations of the menfolk, as Kew noted, and all the womenfolk staying behind, very old-fashioned.

While we were walking, my father glanced at a news update that appeared on his phone, stopped in his tracks with his mouth hanging open in silence, a fine rain bedewing the screen of the phone and his mass of curly hair the same steely color as the sky, before finally conveying to me the information that a white nationalist named Robert

Bowers had shot and killed eleven Jews during the morning service in the Tree of Life synagogue on Wilkens Ave. in Pittsburgh.

Behind my father, a block away, I could see the locusts where I remembered Hannah in October of 2017; the trees showed only a few yellow leaflets remaining on their boughs. I asked my father if he had ever been to the Tree of Life synagogue, or with any of the congregations that used the building. He said he doubted it, but it was possible. I continued to push my son in the stroller, and we said little, too shocked to speak.

I thought of everything I had weighed, everything I had done and left undone, since that Friday the October before when I remembered Hannah for the first time in many years. It seemed to me walking next to my father and pushing my firstborn child in a stroller that I had been trying to record a music secreted in the palimpsest bedrock of time, a music of memory and immediacy echoing each other in my obsolete consciousness and along the parochial fringes of history. I had never asked for this music. But I had thought it might sustain or give solace, even life, to just one other person.

Now the time had run out, the symphony was plummeting through the last discordant remnants of the Code and the forgotten roots of words into silence. It seemed to me in that dim midday that only in the pure music I had long since renounced, the absolute music that reaches into the world behind the world, can the artist master time, set a time signature at will and free of words. But even that was illusion, wasn't it? For only in performance—the body swaying with inhalation and exhalation, the fingers weaving over the keyboard or the bow parting the air amidst a cloud of rosin dust like a bridal veil over the emanating sound—only then is the composer's time realized, only then—in time.

I wanted to believe that singing in my veins and sinews from one autumn to the next there had been many kinds of music that made up one great music. Who then was the composer, and for whom did he compose? Or was I no more than a poor chronicler, one who'd been given too much time to set down and had turned even that into self-indulgent drivel? I thought of my family's graves in Adath Jeshurun and knew at last that I had lost them, that I was cut off from the stream of history and memory, and there was no more to say. As those eleven Jews in Tree of Life were silent, so I would fall silent, I would become silence.

But my task in the composition notebooks was not quite finished. The music of coincidence had one more theme to conclude. And without this conclusion, my restless, vain heart could not have set itself on silence: for I had to find out that silence was not the final end, but a part like other parts, ordered and balanced in the whole composition. Only in silence can the artist escape the last temptation of the idolatry of egotism that we call identity: the idolatry of imagining oneself, fantasizing oneself, as an artist.

I would watch that Notre Dame-Navy game (and text Severine afterwards, jeering at Navy's total defeat). After the sun had gone down in Michigan and that horrible sabbath come to an end, watching the game brought a granule of solace: this repetition of autumnal Saturdays spent with my boyhood friends in the City of Seven Hills. But first, when we had returned home and I had put my son down for a nap, I opened my old university email, something I checked very infrequently, and saw a message from Joel Stein, sent the day before my birthday. I could hardly believe my eyes.

I went into the basement and, while my daughter was watched over by her grandparents and Kew and our son napped, I read through the message several times. It seemed that during the Days of Awe just passed, an acquaintance had mentioned to Joel my novel *Repentance of the Gods*, and he had been attracted by the title, which he found appropriate to that time in the Jewish year. When in a small independent shop (still the only venue from which Joel purchases books) he saw *McPhail* on the cover, he decided to acquire the book, and he had finished it a few days before sending the email, almost fourteen years to the day since he had last written to me.

Now he wrote saying that he thought he perceived something about my book which as far as he could tell no critic had picked up on. He thought I must have taken *The Star of Redemption* to heart—yet it was not so, for when I wrote the novel I hadn't read that book, though I possessed Joel's own copy he'd given me in Cincinnati on the occasion we last saw each other. Nevertheless, in my fantasy I had imagined a world that contained Judaism but no Christianity, where the pagan empire of antiquity had never lapsed. And it was a much more brutal, rapacious, Nietzschean world even than the one that had really come to be, the Jews in it more dispersed and assimilated even than they were in this world after the Shoah. And Joel thought this had been lost on the reviewers. Nothing could make clearer to him, Joel said, that the biblical view of humankind was fast vanishing from the culture. But Rosenzweig had known, Joel said, and I clearly knew, that Judaism and Christianity depend on and engender each other, that they are entwined in the dialogical marriage upon which the fate of the world rests.

Not that he had a very *personal* interest in such things any longer, Joel said. He explained that after moving home he had eventually gone back to school and pivoted in a completely different direction from the literary aspirations of his youth or the philosophy he had studied in Pittsburgh—his PhD was in biochemistry, which was his father's field. His father was now retired, and Joel had taken over the same or a very similar university position. Joel's research, he said, had moved from text to world.

He had married Rivka, and they'd had a daughter—the only child that, for health reasons, Rivka would be able to bear—now twelve years old. They had given her the name *Chana*, which would of course more commonly be spelled *Hannah*. The full teshuvah to orthodoxy he had envisioned for himself when he left Pittsburgh was not something Joel strove to maintain after Rivka's cancer was discovered shortly after she gave birth (this detail reminded me of Gregory's first wife Melinda, but Rivka had decisively beaten her disease). For Rivka's illness plunged Joel into a crisis of *kavanah*—the intensity and pure, focused intention of the heart in prayer, a kind of self-effacement that is at the same time attentiveness, concentration, and deepest feeling.

In the midst of this crisis, Joel said, he had taken to canoeing in the Boundary Waters, and it was only there that he knew *kavanah*. "There," he said, "and it was actually a frightening moment, because I thought I had become lost and it was getting cold and dark—I finally knew *where* I was, and until I knew that, it was like I'd had no capacity to concentrate. To study and to learn, yes, but not to really be *doing* what I was *thinking*. A Jew is supposed to feel this in Eretz Yisrael, but you know I have always agreed with Rosenzweig about Jewishness and the land. After that day up north, I stopped thinking about my Jewish identity—in fact, I stopped thinking about identity at all. I just don't think there's any such quality of being. The world's a desolation. The Fall is real, always. We're all shattered and scattered every which way. We have a role, just one role now, and it's to wake up to where we actually are. The natural order as it exists in the place where I actually live—that was my *Lernen*, my holy study, from then on."

At the end of his email, Joel had included his phone number and invited me to call him. I dialed his number, and he answered promptly. But after identifying myself, I could not speak. Joel was shocked as well, it seemed, for he was silent with me, until we both spoke at once, saying, "In Pittsburgh—"

Now the reader may imagine how it is to hear the voice of an old friend, a voice not heard in fourteen years, a lifespan even—Hannah's lifespan. The voice of a friend you looked up to as one who could set in writing the true shape of things behind the veil of thought and action and feeling, but who renounced that gift. The voice of a friend whom you had betrayed.

"I wrote to you my story, but what have you done," Joel asked me at last, "since those days in Pittsburgh?"

I spoke slowly and quietly at first, but gradually more quickly and confidently. Chiefly I spoke of such things as have appeared in these Suites. It was hard to speak of what had happened in Pittsburgh, as though the memories we retained of that place seemed farcical or unserious now, the very sort of juvenile distractions and follies that, as I reported early on in this writing, Severine and I once escaped—so we thought—by contriving to be served wine underage in a café atop Mount Adams, by marrying, by abandoning art or place for the sake of something we had thought of as freedom.

But when Joel did finally speak of Pittsburgh, I was struck, even over the phone, by the familiarity of the cadence and timbre of his voice. I recalled just that pattern of sound from so many years before in Pittsburgh, in Ritter's or Kelly's or Blue Lou's in the middle of the night, with Alison or Severine chiming in when they could get a word in edgewise. And this sensory recollection did not seem frivolous, it seemed on the contrary to get to the very heart of reality.

Joel said he felt the same while I was speaking, but he thought I was melancholy. "Escapism is tough," he said, "because the more you try to escape the world, the harder you have to look at it, look right through it. I've chosen to go the other way, to stay on the surface, because it's easier that way. Only the prisoners with nerves of steel escape. And sometimes they're caught when they think they've made it to freedom, and sometimes they die trying."

"I used to want to escape in my writing," I said, "but I think the reason I'm stuck with the novel is that I'm losing that old desire. Now I'd rather figure out how to actually be here."

"That's how it's been for me," Joel said. "The most astonishing thing, I've realized, is that we don't actually know how to live here on the Earth. No other animal has this problem. This has become the great lesson of the Eden story, for me, the expulsion from Paradise. It's the one true story, the one *undeniable* story, the Fall—ultimate humiliation, sometimes I think a kind of green terror. For me, the only way to deal with it is to just try to see what's really there—not what could be or was or ought to be—and to think about how we can carry that into the future or how much of it we have to let go. Maybe your fantasy is really there, but then again maybe you have to let it go."

"God knows we have to let a lot go."

"Everything, I think, eventually. Every story except that first story. But you know I think there's some weird consolation in that story. Have you ever heard of a painter named Tissot?"

"Tissot!" I couldn't help shouting. By now I should have been expecting coincidence, but still this was astonishing—and delightful. Affinity is delight. It was affinity, I decided, not coincidence. No more coincidence. *Mit dem Zufall muss es nun aufhören....* With relief I saw it was so: for I saw that Joel Stein was my friend, even now, in the present. How many people know or care a thing about a James Tissot? Yet here I was, picking up from the futon the volume of Tissot's watercolors that I had given to my mother and expressing my surprise to Joel.

"Good taste is best held in common," was Joel's way of agreeing there was no coincidence. "I'll tell you the truth, McPhail," he said, "I do value science—in an existential way. It's detachment, like meditation or contemplative prayer. No ego. But sometimes I need consolation, and that's a *feeling*. A strong one, deeper than the ego, I hope. And I get that in the late paintings Tissot made, inspired by his visits to the Holy Land. Above all, I get it from his picture of Adam and Eve being expelled from Paradise."

I found the image he meant in the book I had given my mother. "What do you mean by consolation?" I said, as I sat down on the futon where I had first made love with Kew more than fourteen years before, and where some fantasy Hannah visited me in a dark hour. I wondered if those were moments of consolation, and I thought that if they were, my life ought to be full of such gratitude that it would be almost crushing.

"I think it's a kind of faith in the createdness of the earth and all that is on it, but also... this will sound weird, McPhail, but also in that silly little watercolor I see the forgiveness of the Earth, and of us. I see redemption in the createdness of all things—especially the man and the woman. More and more I think you'll see people despair of the end of the world. But if you ask me, for a Jew or a Christian that can't be the whole story, because a Jew or a Christian knows the world does not end because it *was* not made: it *is* created, in every moment. Every week we relive the six days—and the seventh, this day, the sabbath. And this is true even when one is looking the Fall square in the face, like in Tissot's painting—or like on this terrible Sabbath in Pittsburgh."

"Wasn't that Rosenzweig's idea?" I said, "Isn't it what we need in order to be a serious people again, that kind of faith and consciousness?"

"We are not a serious people, that's true," Joel said. "What is seriousness, earnestness, righteousness? That is a question we fail to ask because we have forgotten it can be asked."

When he said this, I could almost close my eyes and see my old friend hunched over a cup of coffee in the small hours, waving his hands and invoking anyone from Augustine and Nagarjuna to Walter Benjamin and Joan Didion, cigarettes smoking in the ash tray.

"I'm looking at Tissot's image of the expulsion from Paradise," I said. "I, too, have looked at this image a lot, and there's something about it that breaks my heart. Maybe it's that we're looking at a hillside. I guess Paradise, for Tissot, was a matter of up and down, a rugged terrain rather than the walled zoo and pleasure garden like philologists say the word denotes. This hilly land also happens to be the topography of my mind. In the upper right-hand corner above Adam and Eve there's a muted vague unfolding distance, like you see from most hillsides in the Ohio Valley, or standing anywhere in the Allegheny Plateau, or maybe somewhere in the Blue Ridge. But the distance reminds me of the endless landscape of fantasy, as I've glimpsed it in works of fiction—those books where it's as if I can peer at an even further horizon from within a story that is already itself just beyond my horizon.

"But what matters more than any of that," I said, "is Adam and Eve standing there, down the hill from the three angels. You'd think those angels with their swords of flame and commanding gestures pointing away would dominate the painting, but they don't for me, I always look at the right-hand side, to that distant view and to Adam and Eve below that vista—it reminds me of Faërie, but within the logic of the painting it must be our fallen world."

"That's not just Eve," Joel said, "that's Kathleen Newton—the love of Tissot's life. She must have been a passionate and romantic woman. And she was Irish—your type, McPhail! You know the story?"

"I think so. She arranged to marry a man, and did marry him— liturgically, but without consummation—only to divorce him because of her involvement with another man. She had a daughter by that second man but refused to marry him. Then Tissot met her, and she became his lover and bore him a son. But she contracted tuberculosis, and when she was like twenty-eight or something, she took her own life by overdosing on laudanum because she couldn't handle Tissot's sorrow at her impending death."

"Yes, and he never got over Newton. He dabbled in occult stuff after her death in an attempt to communicate with her departed spirit. And then, about three years after she died, he had a vision or a vivid half-waking dream, in which he saw two old vagabonds, a man and a woman, in the ruins of a cathedral, sitting dejected in their poverty and exhaustion, and Christ crowned with thorns comforting them. Tissot eventually painted this vision. You see I've become totally obsessed with the guy. Anyway, it led to his religious reversion. I've been obsessed with that too, ever since Pittsburgh. I can't talk to my colleagues about this, McPhail, or anyone at the synagogue. But I swear that if there's any other story in the world besides the Fall, it's the story of teshuvah, return, conversion.

"Well, look, the thing that's sort of crazy, McPhail, is that I think it was just the same for Tissot as it sounds like it is for you and your Hannah. What I mean is that it wasn't until about *fourteen years* after she died that Kathleen Newton, or memories of her, became Tissot's Eve."

I was silent for a moment in the face of this mystery: the mystery of *number*, which is to say story or *time*, which is to say *music*. At last I said, "They look modern. The way Eve brings her hand to her furrowed brow and looks back over her right shoulder, up the hill to Paradise, unable to understand what's just happened. And Adam, whose face in profile we can barely see, looking back over his left shoulder, he's rueful and wry, equally uncomprehending of the cause but perhaps more aware of or resigned to the fate that awaits him and his helpmeet. There's less fight left in him. He looks like any young man today, a bit scruffy, not bulging with muscles like some classical Greek figure. They're disheveled, a young couple, hungover, walking away from an ill-fated party in the small hours—"

"—In Pittsburgh, Pennsylvania," Joel said, "in September of 2002?"

My friend laughed. His laughter began low and slowly at first, but it grew by rhythmical increments, it welled up from beneath his heart and echoed and boomed—I was going to say across the phone lines of the Upper Country, across Minnesota and Wisconsin and Illinois and Indiana and into Michigan, but there are no such phone lines anymore, so I will say that Joel Stein's laughter ascended into the firmament, in wave upon invisible wave it rose into airless superplanetary space until it struck upon a communications satellite and was reflected down to me in the basement in Michigan. He laughed and laughed, and it was good to hear him laugh like that. It is among the great songs of this world, the laughter of an old friend.

Joel in his laughter was telling me that the Holy One, blessed be He, enters no heart that He does not first break. Joel in laughter that had not succumbed to the wound of years was telling me that here my music could rest for a while with the image—not frozen, but happening always—of the man and woman leaving the garden, alone together, descending the hillside. Joel in his laughter was telling me that we have been plucked from the places of our desolation and preserved so that we may tell the man and woman's story of exile and return, the story of love. The laughter of my friend rang in the heavens and it rang down on Earth, saying love has no end in this or any world, so we go back to love's beginning, *the beginning that we tell stories about because we do not remember.*

Gleditsia Triacanthos

ON FRIDAY, THE NINTH OF NOVEMBER 2018, my father and I walked early in the town in Michigan where I wrote the first drafts of these Suites in old music composition notebooks. My parents were returning home to the east coast the next day, so it was to be our last walk together for an unknown length of time. My mother was not well enough to accompany us in the weather: the world we walked in had been transfigured overnight by snowfall, and snow was whirling when we walked out the door. The streets and houses, cars and trees, made up a landscape at once opaque and—in the fleeting, roaming sunbeams that burst through the low, moving sky—dynamic, blinding splendor.

Snowfall always changes the world, my father said, especially the first of the season, but in this case it was stranger because of the foliage still in the crowns of the oaks and blanketing the yards. My father spoke of how winter had always excited him, today even as it did when he was a boy. It's the most mysterious time, he said, when what has fallen and rotted is secretly transforming into new life. "I love the way autumn smells," he said, "but also winter's cold clean watery smell of fresh snow, so this is the best of both."

We walked into the center of town and stopped into a Dunkin Donuts to get coffee. Back on the street I wished for nothing so much as a cigarette to accompany my black coffee in the cold gray weather, just as Peter Falk extols in *Wings of Desire*; but I would not smoke around my parents. Instead, as we walked down the large highway that bisects the town, I told my father of the strange vision, so to call it, that I'd had when my daughter was born, only the second time in my life when I have known such a waking dream (the first, as the reader will recall, involved Hannah and was of a very different nature).

There was some complication at the moment of delivery and my daughter could not be placed right away at her mother's breast. My daughter was examined on the heated pediatric table they set up, and after the pediatrician pronounced her safe and healthy and withdrew, there was a little interval when the delivery doctor and nurses were still busily attending to Kew and no one was by my baby girl.

I went over to her and offered her the little finger of my left hand. Her cries were feeble, but the tiny creature was obviously much distressed. Grasping my finger, as a newborn will, seemed to calm her. And in the moment when she took my finger, I saw imagery in my mind as vividly as if it were really there before me: I saw the girl grown into a young woman, with long curly dark blonde hair like my mother's when she was young, and Kew's green eyes, and my daughter was looking around and smiling. What she was smiling at was a green world, a forest, but it was covered in snow. There are sources, I told my father, for the natural imagery, this rare but not impossible coincidence of opposites—a book I read in middle school, maybe a scene from *The Search for Spock*, but what that doesn't explain is why I should have had that vision just then, and of my daughter fully grown.

After relating this anecdote, I realized that we were making our way toward the Jewish cemetery, and as we went my father spoke, as he had done several times in recent years, of his desire someday to visit the places in what is now the Ukraine that his family left to come to the New World. And he spoke of the progress he was making in learning the Yiddish that that family spoke. I asked him if he had any interest in studying Hebrew or visiting Israel.

"The land of Israel, and the Hebrew language—that's all sacred. I lost all taste for the sacred when Hannah died. It's true," he went on (perceiving my surprise), "that was a turning point for me. You didn't know this because I didn't tell anyone about it, but I had been going through a kind of midlife crisis, I was looking for something more than what I could see. You could say I had been moving in a religious direction. I thought about talking with your grandparents about it, because I knew I'd have to make their final arrangements someday, and when I thought about how they'd renounced their religious heritage, it made me question how that affected my own life.

"But I knew after Hannah died that we aren't here long, and I thought I had to be very careful about where I focus my mind, and never waste words or time on anything I wasn't sure was really there,

really in me and around me—my family and my work, that's what
was worth it, that's all I knew that couldn't be denied: not opinions
and speculations, not even science. The Yiddish—that's really there,
that's part of me, I can remember some of my family speaking it when
I was a boy. It's a way for me to go back, a little. But Hebrew? That
was never for me. I know it troubles you, but as you and your kids get
older you'll learn better how to figure it out, what's really there for
you, it'll come more naturally to you, show itself to you."

When we turned into the Jewish cemetery we were no longer
speaking: we were absorbed into the silence of the snowy air that
could be punctuated but could not be overcome by the din of the traffic around us. In the center of the cemetery we came upon two locusts
standing next to each other like twins, but not identical, for one was
leafless while the other retained much of its color, bright in that pale
daylight, golden and even green in places.

Honey locusts, my father said, and I was shocked, for this was
the same species under which Kew and I had stood more than a year
before when I had remembered Hannah. I said I didn't think they
grew here, only maybe black locusts, but my father said, "No, this is
Gleditsia triacanthos, not *Robinia pseudoacacia*, which isn't native here
either. The bark of the two trees is quite different. Honey locusts are
all around you here, but they're a cultivar that produces no thorns.
It's only the original species, the kind that dropped thorns all over our
yard in Cincinnati, that won't grow here. I believe when the French
first wandered around this country they called the honey locust *épine
du Christ*, the thorn of Christ."

I was looking up at the trees, at the snow and the light falling
through them, and I could hardly believe what my father said. But I
knew that he was right. I knew that for lack of thorns I had failed to
recognize these old companions, and I knew that all I had written in
the old music notebooks, fantasy and memory, present and past, the
real and the more than real, had grown and branched from a simple
mistake, from this tree I had seen and not seen. I smiled and looked at
my father and saw that he was smiling. We were silent, and we looked
up through the honey locusts at the snow falling on the dead congregation of the righteous and on the living trees.

Acknowledgments

My mentors and peers at the MFA Program for Writers at Warren Wilson College witnessed and encouraged the origin of this book: I thank them for creating a rich and dynamic environment in which to study the art of fiction. I owe a particular debt for artistic guidance to Karen Brennan, Megan Staffel, Jeremy Gavron, and Bennett Sims.

To the places that appear in the novel I also owe a debt. The narrator and characters are of course not real, but the places are (as was the weather reported about them), and I recommend every place mentioned in the book as worthy of the reader's interest. Characters and narrators are, as Lawrence Durrell said, a function of landscape, and to that I would add: So is the author.

Above all I thank my wife, the poet Katie Hartsock. Poets are a sometimes wild, often a joyful lot; but novelists brood, especially one engaged in writing a novel of consciousness like *Absolute Music*. Katie persevered through my much brooding. To her—and for her—I offer my most profound praise and gratitude.

This book was set in Plantin, designed by Frank Hinman Pierpont and Fritz Stelzer and published in 1913. It is based on the "Gros Cicero" type created by Robert Granjon in the sixteenth-century which the modern designers found in the Plantin-Moretus Musuem—an institution devoted to the history of printing —in Antwerp, Belgium.

This book was designed by Shannon Carter, Ian Creeger, and Gregory Wolfe, and proofread by Sharon Mollerus. It was published in hardcover, paperback, and electronic formats by Slant Books, Seattle, Washington.

Cover photograph by Jennifer Jankowsky. Used with permission.

CPSIA information can be obtained
at www.ICGtesting.com
Printed in the USA
JSHW021948140922
30518JS00001B/60